The Light Is Ours

ANN HEYSE

THE LIGHT IS OURS

Baileys Harbor, Wisconsin

Sand Beach Press
7672 Stone Ridge Lane
Baileys Harbor, WI 54202

Heyse, Ann
The Light is Ours / Ann Heyse

Cover art and internal sketches by Ryan Miller

ISBN: 978-1-7367902-4-3
LCCN: 2023909529

FIRST PRINTING

Look for the helpers.
You will always find people
who are helping.
—Fred Rogers

To David:
Thank you for our life together.

Eleven lighthouses were constructed on the Door County peninsula from the 1850s to the 1880s. As many as 1,000 ships sailed up and down the Wisconsin coastline of Lake Michigan each month in those years as the Great Lakes surged with commerce and trade.

Roundstone Light is a fictional, twelfth lighthouse built on the Lake Michigan side of the peninsula, north of Cana Island but south of Northport and Death's Door. Shallow Island is also imaginary. All of the characters are fictional. In all other ways, this account endeavors to be historically accurate.

1

ON A COOL night in June, 1871, Captain Arden Anderson fought himself out of a nightmare. Heart racing, he listened to the sounds of the ship as he calmed himself from the dream. The whirr of the hull against the water. The jib and mainsail humming, but a topsail that thwapped erratically in the wind. His two-masted schooner, the *Jenny Marie*, was heading north along the Wisconsin coast of Lake Michigan at full sail. He roused himself, lit a lamp and tried reading but lasted for only a chapter. After several minutes, he set down his book and dressed hastily. He blew out his lamp and walked out of his cabin into a night full of stars.

Arden, young for a captain at age 31, stood for a few minutes looking out at the passing water below and the night sky above. He knew constellations, the movements of planets, the great crevasse of the Milky Way. He walked across the deck of the *Jenny Marie* to his first mate who stood at the ship's wheel, holding their course against the night winds.

Solomon acknowledged him. "Captain," he said, and Arden nodded back.

Solomon looked at the captain's sock feet and smiled. It was rare to see the younger man not formally dressed. Only on the hottest days of summer would Arden leave his jacket hanging in his cabin. He laundered his own shirts and bought new ones before the old ones could fray. Always immaculate. He was clean-shaven, too, unlike most seamen. There had been years of long hair, brown with blonde sun streaks, but never a beard. In calm or rough waters, he was practiced at keeping his hand steady as he pulled a sharp blade down his face.

Solomon surmised the likely reason the captain was awake and out of his cabin. There had been many times over the years he had seen Arden wake himself out of horrible dreams. He had known Arden before the War Between the States and then during it. They spent off-seasons on a farm with apple trees and laughing children; even there the captain's sleep was plagued by dark memories. This was their third season sailing Lake Michigan, but Solomon was the only one on this ship that knew Arden's nightmares stemmed back to his days on another ship, the *Flying Falcon*, a clipper that had sailed the Atlantic years before.

Tonight, as the ship whooshed ahead steadily through waves, Solomon might have brought up the subject had they been alone. But Finn, the deckhand on duty, was sitting on a tarp near the bow and within earshot, so Solomon said nothing that might hint at the captain's secret. There would be no talk of the matter tonight. Solomon knew from experience there would likely be no talk of it at all.

Arden evaded all questions about his earlier years, about what had happened when he was barely fifteen, when he'd unknowingly signed on to a slave ship. He'd shown up pre-dawn as requested to a ship he thought was hauling cotton or tobacco, ready to take on a man's job. The *Flying Falcon* sailed out immediately with men barking orders to stow his duffle and start pulling lines. They were not pleasant men. Five miles out of the harbor, it was clear he was part of something horrific. Slaves were beneath him, under the deck where he walked. They were in chains, and no one but Arden seemed to mind.

His days and his weeks were full of meanness and cruelty. Violence and threats. Laughter at all the wrong things. Arden being watched every minute. He stayed longer than he should have, but shorter than most. Short enough to be horrified. Long enough to never forgive himself.

One summer morning aboard the *Flying Falcon,* he was made to throw a dead boy about his own age overboard. Dead, but eyes open. In a dream years later, Arden thinks the boy is watching him. "I am afraid of the water," he tells Arden. "Can you at least close my eyes?"

The dreams came without predictability. Even now, with a ship of his own and the summer season ahead, a nightmare might come out of nowhere. As it had done tonight. He had wakened to the sounds he could not forget: moans, shackles clanging, and women weeping. Even smells from that ship came back. Fetid sweat mixed with shit and fear.

Now, close to midnight, Arden and Solomon stood together looking out at the dim line of land and the night sky above. The loose sail had only grown worse, so Solomon sent Finn aloft to tighten the line. At this late hour, the rest of the crew was below deck, asleep after loading cargo in the Chicago harbor all day. Arden had made the decision to sail through the summer night. Weather was always a risk, but the skies had seemed calm. Now, hours later and at least 60 miles north of the city, the *Jenny Marie* was making good speed. In deep water and several miles out from the rocky Wisconsin shore, there were few dangers to fear.

"Wind Point Light will be our next marking?"

"Yes," Solomon replied. "I expect to see its beacon in a few hours. I assume you want me to lower sails, wait until daylight to go into harbor?"

"Can you keep us out far enough to drift safely while we wait?"

"Aye, Captain."

"Then wake me at first light." He looked back at his first mate as he headed back to his cabin, and added, "Thank you."

This time, Arden slept without dreams. Sails hummed in the wind as Solomon held a northerly course. At about three in the morning, Wind Point Light came into view and Solomon once again called on Finn. They lit more lanterns, and between them, the two men lowered enough sails to slow the ship's progress north. When light started to gather in the east, Solomon instructed Finn to knock on the captain's door.

~

Summer light came in June, but not summer heat. The freezing temperatures and dark winters of the Great Lakes meant that cold water and cold winds lingered. It was not unheard of to see ice chunks floating in May on the northernmost runs of Lake Michigan, and June was only slightly better. Arden pulled on an extra sweater before greeting Finn and going below to see about coffee. The cook had just begun to make breakfast and a few of the men were stirring. He did not begrudge the crew staying under blankets, avoiding the cold. Soon enough they would be called to work.

Coffee in hand, Arden was soon conferring with Solomon about the best course into port. He rarely disagreed with his first mate's judgment, and before long, the sails were adjusted. The entire crew had tasks as Arden steered their way into the busy harbor.

Shipping had been in full swing for several weeks, and this morning the docks of Milwaukee were bustling. Most ships had harbored overnight and waited until daylight to sail. As the *Jenny Marie* tacked in, she passed many other ships on their way out. Departures meant ample slips were available for the *Jenny Marie* to find mooring. It did not take long to throw lines, tie up, and register their arrival with the harbor master.

2

MOST OF THE day was spent unloading the cargo. The *Jenny Marie*'s entire delivery this morning was a shipment of wheels for a wagon supplier in Milwaukee. Each iron wheel was heavy and had to be lifted from the ship's hold and wheeled onto a boardwalk where his crew dodged the other merchants and crews handling crates and barrels, duffles, and lumber. It was a long process and a strain on the backs of his men.

Evan Donahue, the wheelwright and owner of the wagon shop, came to Arden with his payment as the last wheel left the ship. The sun was shining, and the temperature had warmed. The two men stood together at the water's edge as they watched Arden's crew finish the task. A gregarious person, Donahue seemed in no hurry to rush away from the pier. His talk was friendly. Wagons, according to Donahue, were now a necessary commodity. "All across Wisconsin," he said, "foot paths and trails are widening into horse tracks, and horse tracks are widening into roads. Settlers are buying land. Pioneers are coming from faraway places to farm. Merchants are setting up shop in expanding towns.

"And they all need wagons," he told Arden. "Wagons will soon replace ships. Nobody in a wagon goes into the water and down under in an October gale. And think about winter! You captains can't go anywhere in winter, but cold doesn't stop a horse and a wagon!" Arden smiled and nodded, acknowledging Donahue's point. But as he turned to look at the busy harbor, Arden was not worried about his own future. He knew ships. He did not doubt that they would be needed for a long time.

However, Arden *did* need regular customers. His was a ship for hire, delivering cargo for anyone looking for transport. Arden had spent the previous two years on the Michigan side of the lake and would now have to earn a reputation on these western routes. Thanks to money left him by his father, he owned the *Jenny Marie*, but expenses were high. He was optimistic, though, as the season had already been lucrative. In the six weeks since they started, he and his crew had made several runs hauling cargo in both directions.

Donahue was right about the state's interior; inland towns *were* growing, but so were the towns along the shoreline. The construction of new lighthouses was making the shipping routes less dangerous. Additionally, there was money to be made in wood. Door County, in particular, was cutting down its trees. Lumber camps had hired men to work in miserably cold conditions throughout the winter not only to fell the trees but to haul the logs across the frozen ground and stack them in piles along the shoreline. Stacks and stacks of wood were waiting at every dock, and the *Jenny Marie* was the kind of ship that could haul them back to the waiting builders of Milwaukee and Chicago. Arden had been told he would have no problem finding buyers for wood.

Now, in Milwaukee with wagon wheels delivered, there would be an overnight mooring fee to spend the night at the slip, but Arden decided to let his men have an evening off the boat. He gave instructions that the crew should be back by midnight. The *Jenny Marie* would sail north in the morning. His cook had been gathering food supplies and was glad to hear that he too would have a night off. As was his practice, Solomon spent most of the day in port out of sight, helping below deck, not walking the piers or spending extra time in town. He was a large man, slightly intimidating to those who did not know his quiet temperament. With his black skin, it was better to not go far from the boat. Arden checked lines and moorings, gathered up some of the final litter from the ship's hold, and was just ready to stroll away from the docks and find a restaurant for an evening meal when he was approached by a man with questions.

The man was middle-aged and well-dressed. The first thing Arden noticed was how he attempted to avoid the plentiful and unavoidable gull droppings on the docks. Fishing boats tied up at these same piers, and gulls swooped around those boats every hour of the day. The man seemed ill-at-ease, but as he came close to the *Jenny Marie,* he approached Arden and called out to him from the pier.

"Are you taking cargo? Can I hire your boat? The harbor master told me you might be available."

"Possibly," Arden answered, stepping off the ship onto the ramp. He introduced himself and reached out his arm to shake the man's hand. "What are your needs? What is your cargo?"

"Name is Ethan Boggs," the man replied, but he did not take Arden's outstretched hand. "I am the representative of a wealthy client. He has offices in Chicago, but I am here in Milwaukee procuring certain supplies and a crew of workmen for a construction project on an island north of the Door County peninsula. We need to transport building supplies north, along with myself and five men. After the delivery of those supplies, I would expect to stay on as a passenger on the return voyage south."

"Those are a lot of logistics to discuss, sir. And in general, I am not in the habit of transporting people. I have only one steerage cabin and my ship is better suited for cargo. But we are heading to Door County anyway to pick up lumber, so I am willing to talk."

Over dinner, the two men discussed arrangements. The cargo would consist primarily of building materials. They would haul wheelbarrows, saws, trowels to mix concrete, shovels to dig. A cook-stove was needed, along with pots and pans, linens, and foodstuffs like flour and potatoes. An earlier crew was already on the island and had built a workmen's bunkhouse and a summer kitchen. The additional crew of five men included a surveyor, draftsman, and three masons who would begin work on a large residence. The men understood that their living conditions on the island would be primitive and rough, so they would not expect good steerage cabins on the ship. They could sleep wherever the captain could find them room.

Boggs paid for their meal at the restaurant. The pay Boggs offered Arden for the transport of cargo was enticing. It would take one day, according to Boggs, to load the ship. He had purchased the supplies; now it was only a matter of arranging for supplies to be delivered from local shops to the docks, and for the loading. His crew would help. Arden and Boggs concurred that they would need a minimum of three days to sail to the island and a day to unload before the *Jenny Marie* could sail south again. Boggs produced a detailed map of Shallow Island. This, along with satisfactory answers to Arden's questions regarding access to the island by boat, assured Arden that the trip was possible. And, Boggs implied there would be more trips to Shallow Island, not just this year but next year as well. "The project," he said, "will be massive. Lavish. My client is an extremely wealthy man."

Throughout dinner, Boggs was all business. He asked nothing personal about the captain and divulged no information about himself. Arden was polite to the waiter; Boggs wasn't. They each ordered one glass of scotch, but Boggs took his handkerchief out of his pocket to wipe the glass clean before drinking. Arden noticed one other detail: he sniffed his food before eating.

If all went as planned, Arden reasoned, the venture seemed like a good risk. If the weather cooperated, he could deliver his cargo to Shallow Island then pick up cordwood from a dock in Door County on the way back south.

The only ambivalence Arden felt at the end of the night was about Boggs himself. He was not the kind of man that would like the open sea or do well in unpredictable weather. Ships were not clean, and they smelled. Arden was direct. "I will gladly deliver you and your supplies and work crew to Shallow Island," Arden told him, "but I prefer that you find steerage back to Milwaukee from Washington Island on a different ship than the *Jenny Marie*." They would be slowed, he reminded Boggs, by stopping for wood on the return voyage at one of the docks north of Sturgeon Bay.

Boggs was emphatic in his refusal. He said he'd prefer as few changes as possible in a voyage that was likely to be uncomfortable and difficult as it was. He would prefer to grow accustomed to one ship rather than two. When Boggs wrote the contract, he included his own name as a passenger both to the island as well as the return to Milwaukee on the *Jenny Marie*. After hesitating, Arden agreed. By the time their dinner was finished, they had signed their names. Loading would start in the morning, 9 a.m. Sail would be the following day, Thursday, June 10, 1871 at dawn.

3

SHE HAD FILLED the water pail too full. As Meggie lugged it up the winding metal stairs, cold water sloshed onto her feet. She cursed quietly, then began to lift the pail one step at a time. Step. Lift. Step. Lift. The thump of her feet and the clank of the pail on the metal steps became a rhythmic pattern. The sounds echoed inside the tall tower as she climbed the 79 steps that took her to the top of Roundstone Light.

Counting the steps was one of the first things she and her brothers had done when they moved with their family to the lighthouse five years before. Now her youngest sibling Gillian did the same when she practiced her counting or delivered a snack for their father as he sat for hours on the landing just below the Light. Thirty-four steps up to the first window that looked out to the north. Thirty more steps to the small desk where their father kept the log of weather and winds, the number of ships that passed in a day, and the record of anything unusual or noteworthy throughout the days of the shipping season.

A final fifteen stairs grew progressively more narrow and steep as they spiraled round to the top of the tower. At the top was a small space barely big enough for two people in addition to the impressive Fresnel Lens that took up most of the room. The lens was as tall as Meggie and weighed over one thousand pounds. It had taken a team of experts three weeks to assemble it five years earlier when the lighthouse opened.

Glints of morning sunlight caught the complicated arrangement of glasses and mirrors as Meggie put down her bag of rags and supplies on the floor of the lantern room. The lens was impressive even in its current state of dull and gray—a result of burning oil all night which had muddied the many pieces and deposited on them a smoky film. Before beginning her chore, she stepped to every window and looked out in each direction. From the ground to the top of the light tower was 120 feet, and the tower, as well as the lightkeeper's house, sat atop a high limestone bluff. *It's almost dizzying,* she thought. *Some people would be scared of this height.* Lake Michigan was blue and sparkling, and the sun shone warm into the lantern room. After her winter, this early June morning was a reminder of all that was good in this northern Door County, Wisconsin wilderness. *At least my socks will dry today if I hang them in the sun. Finally, a day without gloom.*

Far out on the lake, two ships were at sail. Both came from the south. The first, with all sails unfurled, would not likely be turning into Roundstone Harbor. Her father had taught her to look for the signs. It would sail north without stopping. A schooner came not far behind it, closer to shore. Not at full sail. Moving more slowly. Her crew would just now be seeing the lighthouse tower and the keeper's house adjoining it. Shallow rock ledges just a few feet underneath the surface of the lake made the entrance into port tricky, so the beacon light at night and the tall tower on clear days were helpful landmarks to warn ships of the danger and to aid them as they navigated their way into the channel and the deep harbor. Once ships passed them at the north side of the harbor, captains tacked south and west to arrive at the small village of Roundstone Harbor where docks and piers waited for them to unload and reload their cargo.

After she had come back last month after nearly four years away, Meggie offered to help her father with the daily chore of washing the light. There were many tasks as a lighthouse keeper, but washing was one of the most necessary and repetitive ones. Every night the same oil that kept the wick burning and the flame alive also produced soot. The burning oil spread a film on every piece of glass that made up the Fresnel Lens. With that magical combination of smaller lenses, the tiny flame that her father lit each night was refracted and reflected so that their beacon could be seen twenty-four miles out on the water.

It would take more than one pail of water before her job was done, and the water was already cooling when she dipped in her hands to wet the rags and wring out the water. She had forty pieces of glass to disassemble, to handle carefully, wash, dry, and put back in place. It wasn't a quick process, but she was glad for the chore.

This task gave her a place to withdraw to, an excuse when visitors came. The last thing she wanted to do was answer questions from townspeople who came "to visit" but brought with them pity in their eyes. This place with its beauty might heal her if people and their "sympathy" would not remind her that she did not belong here, back at the Light. When she had left four years earlier, she was in love and was weeks away from marrying. Meggie thought then that she was walking into everything. She had been wrong. She had come back a widow, and instead of everything, she had nothing. So much of nothing.

She listened to the wash of the waves rearranging the rocks far below her on the beach below the Light, pulled the rags from the bag that she had hauled on her shoulder, and carefully took down the first piece of glass.

4

A FEW DAYS later, in early afternoon, Kate McGinn walked along the rocky beach back to her home at Roundstone Light. Her feet were cold, and she had to pick her way slowly over the rocks. It was an overcast sky, and the cold Lake Michigan winds blew in her face. While in town, Kate had stopped at the grocery and purchased more items than she probably should have. Her bags were now heavy and cumbersome. Her mood matched the gray of the sky.

Kate was of average build, but in this northern Wisconsin wilderness that attracted people of Scandinavian descent, she was the shortest of her friends. And the best dressed. Her sister Emily, in particular, was quick to pass along to Kate the dresses that she no longer wanted, after Kate had mentioned in a letter there were no dressmakers in Roundstone Harbor. Most of Emily's cast-off dresses were too elegant for this pioneer, fishing village where practicality was much more important than fashion, so her sister was not doing her the favor that she intended. Kate folded away the ones made of satin and velvet but was able to wear a few of the plainer ones. Along with everyone else in this climate, she needed clothes that were warm. In her case, she also needed clothes that were easily washed of the blood or pus or phlegm that splattered her clothes when she was caring for patients.

As she walked, her thoughts turned back to the blacksmith's son, only three years old, who had a worrisome fever. This was the third morning in a row she had checked on him. It was likely infection from the gash he sustained two weeks earlier when playing in his father's workshop. Kate had treated that, too, washed it well and given repeated instructions for changes of the dressing. Kate now worried that his symptoms indicated tetanus as he was running a fever, a sure sign after an injury like his. Today, she thought she had heard a slight slur of his words, but with a child so young, it was hard to tell. Disturbingly, he had no appetite. If it *was* tetanus, there would be little she would be able to do other than help his parents care for him and wait with them. And watch. Survival statistics were grim, but not every case was fatal. The child might recover. It was too early to know.

Spring was nearly ended and summer was on its way. *I have no business complaining,* Kate thought, chiding herself her foul mood. Every year since they had moved first to Wisconsin and now farther north to Door County, she fought the same fight with herself to stay cheerful in spring. It was no surprise to her that winter was cold. But it lasted too long. In her childhood, flowers bloomed by Easter and color had returned in full blaze by mid-April. Not so at Roundstone Light. There were no flowers in March, and none to look forward to in April either.

By the first week of May, the snow finally melted. Her children found ramps that had pushed themselves out of the forest floor. Kate sent them out with small shovels and spades, and though the garlicky smell was strong, it was nice to have a change to the potato soup that they had eaten so often throughout the winter. And then finally, a few weeks after the ramps emerged through the ground, wildflowers appeared among the patches of snow that hung on in the shade. Trillium first, then forget-me-nots and lilies-of-the-valley with a sweet fragrance in the woods. Finally, buds came out on trees and burst into all shades and hues of green, everything verdant and full of life. Immediately though, spring was over and it was summer.

As the wife of a lighthouse keeper, she could not linger in those lavish gifts of spring. Right alongside the joy of that green came the simultaneous flurry of readying the Light. As much as they thought they had prepared and were ready for the first lighting, there was always too much to do. The supply boat came as soon as the ice in the harbor was out; all those supplies for the season needed to be organized and stored. The lighthouse board provided paint each year with the expectation that rooms should be painted. There was spring cleaning. The damp that was pervasive at the Light had to be mitigated. Boards had rotted, moss had gathered on stones, and mildew had found its way into linens and on the backs of doors.

Then it was gardening. As soon as they could dig without finding frozen ground, all hands turned to preparing the soil, then to planting. Whatever they would grow for themselves needed to carry them through for another year. Her husband Jack, lighthouse keeper of Roundstone Light, had purchased an excess of seeds in Green Bay. They had plans for raspberries bushes and a few more apple trees. Kate would grow herbs along with their vegetables. They were still learning which plants would grow in the rocky soil that surrounded their home at the Light.

Having Meggie home would be a help, Kate acknowledged. Kate reminded herself that she needed to be cheerful for her daughter's sake, home after a tragedy. *And really*, Kate, told herself, *what do I have to complain about? It is not* my *child with tetanus. I have a house that is grand and a husband that is good. And it is almost summer, and there are flowers in bloom.*

She put down her bags again to readjust her cloak and scarf. The afternoon had brought in fog, and she was full of damp. Her hair would be soaked by the time she finished walking the nearly two-mile stretch of beach and climbed the stairs to her home at the Light. Kate picked up her pace and trudged ahead.

5

IT WAS JACK'S practice to sleep for a few hours in the middle of the day after being awake to tend the Light in the night. He slept in snatches at night, often only a few hours in total. Jack was extraordinarily conscientious about the lantern and could not sleep entirely at ease through the night after it was lit. He would never forgive himself if it were to go out, even for a short time.

Now it was early afternoon, and he poured himself a cup of coffee. Jack drank quickly, then wiped his beard with his handkerchief, a habit his wife had encouraged early in their marriage. He put on his jacket and boots and walked out the door and across the lighthouse yard to the top of the bluff. From his high vantage point on the bluff where the Light and keeper's house sat, Jack saw his wife Kate walking toward him, just a speck in the distance. He started down the high staircase of steps that took him to the beach below.

Once down, he could not walk as quickly as he would have liked toward Kate. The rocks were uneven, and the irregular gait jarred his back. Nevertheless, after a few minutes, they met. He hugged her and took up the bags she had set on the ground when she greeted him.

"You've got a lot in these packages! I will likely go into town later. You could have left them for me, Kate."

"I know that, Jack. Thank you. I didn't think at the time that they would grow so heavy."

He smiled at her. "Usually you know everything, my Kate," he kidded. "And usually, you have everything figured out ahead of time!" He changed subjects. "How's the Henderson boy?"

"I'm afraid it's not good, Jack. It's likely tetanus."

They were both silent as they made their way along the beach to the steps. Gulls flew over their heads. The water was at their right, waves splashing, and the treeline was to their left. In some sections of the shoreline, the stones were smaller, on their way to becoming sand. Having been shifted and rubbed against each other by eons of wave action, the stones were smooth. Many were round or oval, and it was from these that the town had been named, along with the lighthouse where Jack was keeper.

"Have you spent much time with Meggie today?"

"Just a bit. She finished washing the lens while I was napping, and she was reading, just now, when I left her. She seems content enough today."

Kate nodded and their conversation turned to their afternoon chores. With the damp, it would not be a good day to air things out as they had hoped. Jack would focus on rearranging and cleaning the oil shed. He wanted to build a new set of shelves. Kate also wanted shelves built in the basement to store the vegetables they would preserve later in the summer. As soon as there was a calm day, Jack planned to push their boat to the shore, row across the harbor to buy lumber, then transport it back to the Light across the water. It was the easiest way to get big items to the Light, but could only be done safely when the weather was right.

The couple was used to doing their work separately, used to spending their days at work on their own chores. Jack's duties kept him awake in the night, and Kate did not expect his help or attention during the day. They both assigned tasks to their children and supervised them. Summer was different than winter when the couple had long hours in each other's presence, days at a time. There was plenty of time for talk then.

Kate had bought meat for a stew and wanted to begin preparing it right away. When they reached the landing at the top of the stairs, Kate took back the packages Jack carried and went into the house while Jack turned toward the oil house.

~

Meggie looked up from the book she was reading as her mother came in and offered to put on the kettle for tea. She helped Kate unload the food and put it away.

"After tea, I'll get started on dinner," Kate told her. "How are you today?"

"The pain in my stomach is better. Almost gone, I think."

"I'm not sure you should be hauling the water up the light-tower, Meg. Shall we ask Philip to do it before he leaves in the morning for school?"

"No, I like the water heated some, so I'd just as soon do it myself. I think I can manage. I don't think I'm overdoing it. Truly the pain is almost gone, and I can't bear to just sit and do nothing! It has been just over three months since my surgery."

"Yes, I suppose you are right. Still, I think that lifting isn't good for your internal scars, or for your external ones either. At least I'm not worried anymore about infection from your surgery. If that were to have happened, it would have happened by now."

"I guess I should be glad of that. I'm supposed to look for things to be glad of."

"Infections *are* always a worry. It's one reason that doctors say to rest after surgery." She looked at her daughter. "And how do you feel otherwise? What about your sorrow?"

"What would you like me to say? That I am *fine*? I don't know that I will *ever* be *fine*."

Kate didn't answer immediately. She took down two tea cups from a shelf and put loose tea leaves in a small metal infuser. "Well, someday you might be, Meggie. *Fine,* I mean. *Ever* is a long time."

"I don't know what you want from me. That I am giddy and carefree like I was when I left home? That I undo the last four years and go back to being a child?"

Kate opened her mouth and then shut it again. After a moment of searching for a careful reply, she said only, "I only want you to be less sad, Meggie. It is what any mother wants for her children, grown or not."

Meggie's tone became less accusatory. "I'm sorry. It's just that I can't imagine not being sad. I know men die. I know husbands die. I know there are plenty of widows and that other women have loved their husbands and lost them. I just didn't expect that I would be one of them."

Kate put her hand on her daughter's shoulder. "We are all broken-hearted about what happened to you. All I can say is that I think someday it will hurt less. And you *might* find love again. It *is* possible."

Kate could tell immediately she had said the wrong thing to her daughter.

"*That* was not helpful," Meggie said coldly, anger rising. Kate could feel her daughter's shoulders tense. The words she had thought were comfort to her daughter were apparently not.

"Do you not understand me at all? That I had a life that was happy far away from here that you know nothing about? I loved a man and he loved me, and now I never *want* to find love again."

Meggie took up her book from the table and left the room. Kate sighed and rubbed the rim of her teacup. She drank until the cup was empty, then stood up, put on an apron, and began to cut the small chunk of meat she had purchased earlier into bite-sized pieces. Her younger three children would be home from school soon.

Upstairs, Meggie was still seething from her mother's words. She sat in her room on the second floor of the house, a space her father, Jack, had partitioned off for her in the bedroom she now shared with her young sister, Gillian. When she had come home a month ago, he had enclosed a small section of the room so that Meggie had her own lamp, sitting chair, and writing desk. That, in addition to a bed, made her room small but comfortable.

Meggie sat for a few minutes at the desk and then took pen and ink and her diary from the inside of the desk.

June 1, 1871.

I will never marry. I do not want a second husband that I would always compare with my first. And, unlike these men with their lusts in the wilderness, I am practical now about what a second marriage would be. The men here have many desires and few choices, so they might say they do not care that I am damaged. But give them a few years and they would hate me. Who wants a woman that cannot lift a child, laughing, onto his lap? Who would not begin to begrudge the woman who cannot bear him a son to chop wood or help put the hay in the barn? Who would not resent, over time, a barren wife who could not bear him a daughter to collect eggs, to adore him? After a time, a man would grow disappointed.

I do not want to marry. What are my choices here, anyway, where every man is a lumberman, sailor, or farmer? They all need women who want to clear land, knit socks, slaughter chickens to make them a stew. They want to grow families so they can grow their farms. Every man here who says he could love me is wrong. Childless, barren? Even though I do not look at them, still, apparently, they are looking at me. I have seen it already—once at church and many times on the docks. They show interest in me on their faces when they think I am desirable. Then someone tells them the news in whispers, a side conversation: She is a widow. She cannot bear children. *Their thirst for me is snuffed out like a candle. Their fleeting interest in me was nothing but an open door slammed shut.*

My mother thinks she is bringing me comfort by saying that I could find love again. But I have no interest in another man. I am a widow and will always be childless. But I will not be pathetic. I am here only to heal while my body rearranges itself from the scars of childbirth and the surgery that came after. I am here only to heal while my grief subsides.

Then I will go away alone and not look back.

~

Hours later, after supper had been eaten and the children were all in bed, Kate climbed the tower stairs to sit with Jack. He would have given her the lantern room's only chair to sit on, but she had brought up a blanket to fold and put on the top stair. She sat with her knees pulled up tight and her back leaning against the short wall of the small room.

"I can't seem to say anything right, Jack."

"I'm sure you meant well, Kate."

"I did. I meant only to encourage her. But she took it all wrong. Implied that I treat her like a child."

"It's understandable. Meggie is trying to find her way. None of us thought she would be back here with us. Maybe her anger at you is only part of her grieving."

"I know that she isn't meaning to hurt me with her words. I'm just trying to figure out how not to hurt her with mine."

Jack came over to her and took her hand to help her up. He wrapped his wife in his arms and held her close.

"There was so much pain today," his wife continued after a while. "I left little Thomas lying feverish and the worry of his parents so strong it felt like fire in the trees out of control and uncontainable. Then I walked right into more pain sitting in my own kitchen. Meggie's pain is deep, and I can't help her swim in it."

"Our daughter will be fine, Kate. I am sure of it."

"I'm not, Jack. I wish I could be as sure as you. I worry about her moods. I worry about her sorrow. And I worry about *my* moods that are every bit as fickle as Meggie's, perhaps even more so."

"I am no stranger to your moods, Kate. It seems to me you regain your smile when the winter ends."

Kate nodded.

"I also know you aren't a woman who wallows in misery. You solve problems, Kate. You will come to peace with Meggie."

The fog of the afternoon had lifted well before sunset. Now winds were pushing clouds to the west. As they looked out over the water, an occasional break in the clouds revealed an almost full moon. Kate stayed a while longer, then left when she started shivering from cold. Jack listened to the sound of her steps echoing as she walked down the curving, metal steps of the light tower. He heard the door to their home open and then close shut.

6

RAIN STARTED AS dinner ended. The family had watched high banks of clouds come in from the west, and as the children were heading to bed, both lightning and thunder were fierce. Gillian, five years old and the McGinn's youngest child, had been asleep an hour or so. Kate was saying good night to her sons, Philip, who was twelve and Peter, aged seven, when she heard rapping at the front door. It took a moment to register that the sound was not thunder until she heard Meggie's voice talking to someone in the kitchen.

Jack was already up in the light tower. Kate hurried to the kitchen to find Spencer Armont there, dripping with rain.

"It's our Laura," he told them, his voice thick with accent. "She can't breathe." He imitated gasps of breath to emphasize his point and to make sure he was understood. "And," he pointed to his face and his skin, "blue."

"I'll change into something warmer. Mr. Armont," Kate told him quickly.

She turned to her daughter. "Would you get my bag, Meggie?"

When she returned in warmer clothes after just a few moments, Kate continued speaking to Meggie. "I may need to spend the night in town. I'll be either at the Armont's or with my friend Mary. Will you tell your father? Will you help get the children ready for school in the morning? Fix them breakfast? Make sure they have lunches packed? That Gillian dresses warmly enough and that Peter remembers his mittens and hat? And Philip is supposed to return a book to Mr. Stangl. And he comes home hungry, so make sure he has a lot in his lunch."

To all this Meggie nodded and helped speed them out the door. Within just a few minutes Kate was out into the night with a man who spoke little and needed to hurry. Despite the rain, Meggie held the door open for a few minutes and watched them go. Armont held his lantern high, first swinging it in front of him to see the path and then behind him so Kate could follow. Meggie watched until the swinging light was just a dot in the night and she herself was wet and cold.

The Armonts had not made a good first impression in the village. Barely a week after their arrival, Spencer had broken the nose of a man in the lumber yard on the outskirts of town. Kate had been summoned. Armont had been let go from that job for the incident and now worked as a stone cutter in the new quarry. Even there he had developed a reputation for his anger. Fran, his wife, was a small woman in contrast to Spencer's burliness. Kate had met her twice at events in the town. She struggled with English, and she had not spoken more than a few words at either meeting. Worse, she did not look up into the eyes of the women who tried to converse with her, a sign, Kate assumed, of her unease about life in this new place. Her reticence might be caused only by her lack of fluent English, but Kate wondered about the woman's life at home with a man who broke noses.

Still, Armont was courteous to her on this hurried walk. In one spot the path was slippery from exposed rocks that were slick with rain. He stopped, held the lantern, made sure she had good footing. In other places where the cedar roots protruded, he again slowed his pace and held the lantern high so that Kate could find her way. He carried her bag in one hand and the lantern in the other so Kate could, for the most part, keep her shawl tight around her.

The tall trees on their two-mile hike protected them somewhat from the rain and buffered them from the harshest winds. They did not talk as they made their way quickly toward town, and Kate thought about what she might find when she arrived.

Kate had not expected to practice medicine or to be "doctor" when they arrived at Roundstone Light, but that *is* what she had become over the past five years. Only two months after their arrival five years before, she happened to be at the dock with Jack on a late winter morning. They arrived as a crowd was gathering around the harbormaster's son who had fallen through ice floes on the lake, gone under, and been pulled from the cold water unconscious. In that public space at the dock, with many eyes watching, Kate sprung instinctively to action. She felt a slight pulse, so she began resuscitation, first pumping his chest to dislodge water. Within seconds he was gasping for breath but breathing again. She tore the wet clothes off of his near-lifeless body and called for warm, dry coats and wraps to counteract the hypothermia that might have otherwise killed him.

By the time his mother had been found and brought down to the dock, she was able to hold a fully revived son. Jack explained that Kate had some medical training, and almost instantaneously the townspeople had complete confidence in Kate's medical skills. Since then, there had been numerous broken bones to reset. There were discreet questions at church about "women's matters." She was asked outside the grocery about kidney stones, about cures for gout, about their children's fevers. She correctly diagnosed a tumor, and though she sent the woman on to a surgeon in Green Bay, the husband reported to the town that the doctor had praised Kate's discernment. Now, it was Kate that they called when people needed medical help.

Emmaline Jackson was a good midwife, and Kate was glad she was not called to handle those cases. Kate had watched one woman die in childbirth years before, and she never again wanted to watch a mother leave behind a young husband and tiny infant who would never know its mother's love. Emmaline had arrived in the town about the same time as Kate had, and the two women were friends. Emmaline loved to deliver babies and had been particularly busy in the last two years since the town was growing with settlers who were building their families along with their houses and taverns and shops. Five new babies had been born in the last year, three of them baptized in their church just last month. Kate was happy to rejoice from afar at the birth of babies. She was happier to set bones, to diagnose infections.

Here in this new land where survival was tenuous, the fragility of their bodies was only one of all kinds of risk for new settlers. Would their land bear crops? Would the winter blizzards starve them? Would the pittance they were paid for their labor be enough to buy a horse, a wagon to clear their land? Would the land they wanted to build on be snatched up by another? It was all gamble. And everyone knew that not all gamblers win.

Life was fragile in this northern wilderness. Kate had grown up in privilege, in a city where winters were cold but blizzards did not blind for days at a time. Established cities meant the possibility of warmer homes, better nutrition, and other people that could be hired to do hard labor. With all those things came better health. Though Kate had seen plenty of poverty and squalor in the tenements not far from where she had grown up, there were also churches and charities and missions that offered help.

Here in the northern woods, no one expected anyone else to help them survive. Here, fishermen were lost at sea in their boats. Loggers lost limbs and sometimes their lives when trees fell in the wrong direction or when axes slipped. On farms, accidents happened. The cold took a toll on bodies. If there were wounds, it was hard to keep them clean in a cold cabin with no hot water. Infections were common. Disease was all too often untreatable.

On top of that, people in this wilderness often came to Kate too late. They waited. They ignored a pain or excused away a sense that something was wrong. They were busy. They had no extra money. They did not have the luxury to care for themselves. Some were stoical, believing their broken bodies were not worth saving. Others said what happened, for good or for bad, was God's will and not to be tinkered with.

She reminded herself that her father, a doctor, had not saved everyone either.

"Healthy people don't call for a doctor," her father had told her once, when there had been a particularly long stretch of deaths in his practice. "We do what we can. That is all."

She wished she had inherited his objectivity. In those rooms where she was asked to go when things were dire, to those rooms where children were feverish or a husband was barely breathing from the loss of too much blood, she could almost see invisible figures in the room. They sat as spectators, waiting: would death or life take the body? Kate sat in the middle with her patient, with her rags and her compresses and her stethoscope, watching, too.

Dr. O'Connell had been dead for twelve years, and many times in those years since her father's death she had wished she could ask him questions, especially now that they lived at the Light. She read journals and books, but she wanted to ask him about medicines and treatments. She wished they could talk about diet and nutrition, about diseased blood, about insanity and alcohol and frostbite. If deformities were linked to incest. If dirty drinking water caused dysentery and jaundice. What would he recommend for a child who limped or stuttered?

Kate pushed these questions out of her head and followed the swinging lantern in front of her. The rain pelted them as they came out from the shelter of the trees. It was a welcome sight to see lights of the village in the distance. The path widened, and Spencer Armont and she were able to walk more quickly. Spencer was almost running as they turned west onto a muddy track. Past a few houses, then a few houses more, and then he was stomping to brush off the excess dirt on his shoes. He pushed hard on the door and led Kate into the small, one-room cabin where his wife and small daughters were waiting.

7

KATE TOOK STOCK. The cabin had little furniture except for a bed, two chairs at a table, and a rocking chair where Fran sat. Her face was tear-stained and white, and she barely looked up when they entered. The baby, Laura, was still and was lying on a blanket on the bed next to where her mother sat. A second daughter was asleep on a blanket nearer the hearth, but the room was cool. The fire in the stove had not been attended to and was nearly out.

Throwing off her wet shawl and scarf, Kate crossed the room to examine Laura. The baby looked lifeless, but Kate felt a weak pulse.

"Quickly! "Kate instructed softly but firmly. "We must get her up." She thumped on the child's back, dislodging phlegm. The baby's eyes fluttered open, barely.

Fran was quickly at her side, reeling off words in a language that Kate could not understand.

"She says she thought Laura was gone." Spencer translated. In her relief and desperation, Fran grabbed the baby back from Kate, crying and moaning as she held her, smoothing her hair.

"No, she is still alive. But she's in trouble, Mr. Armont. Please, we need a strong fire. We need hot water. We need rags." Unsure of how much he understood, she pointed at the stove and the kettle.

Like her father had done, Kate took care to show calm. Wits in an emergency were preferable to speed. There were steps to be taken, and panicked decision-making was not constructive. The first thing they needed was hot water. The child needed hot compresses, but these would take time. Until then, Laura's best chance of life was in her mother's arms. She was living, but her breathing was shallow. There was little they could do now except wait for the fire to get hot enough to heat water.

As soon as she could, Kate soaked rags in water almost too hot to touch and applied them to Laura's chest. She rubbed eucalyptus. Menthol. The phlegm needed loosening, and her lungs needed to be cleared. All through the night, they kept the fire hot. Kate and Fran took turns applying hot rags to Laura's chest, and slowly, by dawn, Kate sensed improvement, a slight ease in the child's breathing.

After several hours, Spencer lay down on the pallet and dozed, but neither Fran nor Kate slept. Fran spoke in whispers while Armont slept, but Kate could not decipher her words. After several tries to communicate, both women took to hand gestures and silence. More than once through the night, Kate thought: *she is only a child herself.*

In the dark of the night with only the fire burning and the lamp at the table, Kate had looked more closely at her surroundings. There was one cup and saucer displayed on a shelf. Kate guessed Breton or Basque. A book that Kate assumed was a Bible. A quilt for the bed and a second one for the pallet on the floor for Hilde, the sister who had thankfully stayed asleep through the clatter of the night. The Armonts had more possessions than some who had come with only the shirts they wore.

Still, it was dirty. Kate did not see a tub for bathing, although she knew that many villagers kept their tubs outside. Hilde's hair was unbrushed and matted, and Fran's was greasy. She would try to remember to bring soap and encourage the family to wash. She could see there was not a lot of food in the house, but was thankful for the tea that was plentiful. The two women had drunk several cups through the night. The privy outside in the back was acceptable.

At about 11 in the morning, Laura's color was better. And although it worried Fran, the child was now crying which was far better than the silence of the previous night. When Laura began to nurse, Kate felt that the worst had passed.

With assurances that she would return in a few hours, Kate opened the door and walked into the heart of the village. Her friends Mary and Henry Miller owned one of the biggest houses in the village, and Kate knew she would be welcome to sleep for a few hours in their extra bedroom.

~

While she slept, Jack walked into the village to check on Kate and to get news of the Armont child. Kate was sleeping, and instead of waking her, he left word with Mary.

When she woke in the late afternoon, her friend Mary passed on his message. "He wanted you to know that he and Meggie are managing just fine, Kate. And that if you need to stay another night here, you should do that. Selfishly, I'd love for you to stay! Henry will be gone to a meeting this evening, and I'd like nothing better than a long chat with you!"

Kate smiled at her friend. "Thank you, Mary. I'll check on the Armonts and hopefully be back in a few hours. Don't do anything special for supper, please."

Kate and Mary were friends because they were of like minds. Both women followed politics. Long an advocate of a woman's right to vote, Mary had participated in formative meetings of women's suffrage organizations and had attended the 1869 convention in Milwaukee where Susan B. Anthony and Elizabeth Cady Stanton spoke. Both women had read every word of the state constitution drafts and had followed the controversies around Negro suffrage. They were proud that Wisconsin had been one of the first states to give Black men the right to vote in 1866 and had applauded the passage of the 15th Amendment the previous year. Now, they were interested in talk of women's suffrage. In their conversations, Kate and Mary railed against the laws that prohibited women from owning property. The laws were unjust that prohibited a mother's custody of her own children if a husband divorced her. In Wisconsin, a woman could not own her own business, something that rankled Mary who had brought money to the marriage and had a better business sense than her husband. It was Mary's decisions and involvement with hiring and financing that had grown their quarry business, not Henry's.

The Millers had a porch with a view of the lake. When Kate returned, the two women sat out in leisure enjoying the long light of the early July evening.

"There is talk of a state medical board forming," Kate told her friend. "It's not a bad thing overall. It will give licenses to doctors, make sure people are qualified. Doctors will have to pass exams, show proof of education."

"Kate, this is big news. It will affect you, won't it?"

"Yes, of course. But I have never claimed to be a doctor. And if a certified doctor comes to the peninsula, I would defer to him. But yes, it may change whether I can continue to help people in our town."

"What a man's world this is! If you could do it all over again, and you were born a man, would you have liked to go to medical school? Be a certified doctor?"

"Of course! I have always loved the way bodies work. Just like my father did. I suspect that our son Frank does as well. When Frank writes of his science courses in the university, I am almost jealous of the things he is learning. I wish I could hear everything he hears in his classes."

"Why was your father so willing to let you learn, to teach you? He surely knew it was not a job that a woman would be allowed to do."

"I have asked myself that many times. It is another question I wish I'd asked him when he was alive. I've come to realize that he was not a man that cared much for convention. Many of his doctor friends did not treat indigent immigrants, but *he* did. He touched the skin of black men whether they were slave or freedmen. I was young, but I remember a controversy between him and his peers at the Baltimore hospital. His hospital board questioned him about his involvement with charities for slaves who had reached freedom through clandestine connections. They thought it was improper to treat runaway slaves. Or maybe just to treat any black man at all. But he held his ground. He said he would treat whomever he liked. They objected, insisted he disassociate from their hospital. But he did not stop. He did not give in to their demands, and in the end, they let him stay because they needed him."

"Kate! He sounds like a man I would like. I wish I had known him. And it explains why you think the way you do. What of your mother? You have told me only a little about her."

"Well, she was a rebel against convention in her own way, too, I suppose. She traveled, left us with servants and governesses and my grandmother for a time so she could attend abolitionist meetings. She traveled with famous speakers as they went around the country. She was never a speaker, but I think now that it was she who provided most of the funds, so they were probably happy to have her along on their circuits."

"Another independent woman. I would have liked her, too!"

"It's funny. I can be proud of her now, but as a younger girl, I resented her. She left us for months at a time. I was angry. Maybe my father sensed that and it was another reason he took me along with him on his calls."

"Often?"

"Yes, almost daily. I'd finish my studies with our teachers in the morning, and in the afternoon, I would go where he went. By the time I was eighteen, I went with him nearly every day to the homes of the richest people in Baltimore, as well as the tenements and slums."

"It's startling that he took you along. What did you do? Why do you think he let you accompany him?"

"Maybe he wanted me as nurse. Maybe he thought my presence would soften the angry fathers who did not want him there at all, who were only worried about how much it would cost them. Or maybe he wanted me there to hold the mothers that needed holding when they collapsed, started weeping." She was silent for a moment, then continued.

"Or maybe he knew that I was good at it. And that I was fascinated by it all. My older sisters read novels, but I devoured his medical books. I studied the pictures of anatomy and learned the names of the arteries. He didn't care that it was a man's profession. When I was with him, he showed me how to splint a finger, give a shot, relocate a shoulder. With a patient's permission, he guided my hands to feel an enlarged spleen or to listen for an unnatural heartbeat. He explained to me the reasons he chose each prescription or what he suspected for diagnosis or cause."

"What happened when you left Baltimore? Did you continue?"

"No. It was over. *Not a woman's place*, of course. Besides, I was building a new life with Jack. We moved around for the first few years, so it wasn't easy to find ways to be involved. I helped as a nurse in an indigent clinic for a while, but then I got pregnant with Meggie. After that I was home, raising small children. During the war, I am sure I could have worked in a war hospital as a nurse with every man wounded and crying with pain. Tetanus in the arms and legs because of a hasty amputation on a battlefield two hundred miles and ten days away. Typhoid rampant. Men who had gone into war thinking it sounded like glory. I wanted no part of that. Besides, the children were small, and Jack was gone so much with the war. So I was busy at home.

But can I tell you a secret?"

"Of course, anything," her friend smiled.

"Jack and I had a doctor friend in our church. Every Sunday he passed along to me the medical journals he subscribed to. It was my guilty pleasure. Our pastor said we should spend the Sabbath afternoon with our Bibles, but I spent the afternoon poring over those journals instead."

Mary laughed, and their talk turned to news of the town. There was a search for a pastor. The school was bursting with enrollment. A new carpenter had announced he was hiring a crew to build houses. The women talked until mosquitoes bit at their ankles and the night filled with stars.

8

BOGGS KEPT MOSTLY to his cabin while the *Jenny Marie* was at sea. Before they left port, Boggs had insisted on prying open each box and inspecting the contents before his workmen were allowed to store them in the hold. He watched everyone, missed no details. On the first morning at sail, Arden expected Boggs to watch at the rail as the *Jenny Marie* left port. There was a lot to watch: seamen high on yardarms, all extra hands pulling line, shouts as boats came in too fast or too close, gulls swirling. Instead, as they steered out into the lake, Boggs indicated that he would be in his cabin. Before he went below, he stopped halfway across the deck to address Arden.

"I assume you and I will take our meals separately from the hired men and your crew?" It was more a statement than a question, and it had come when Arden was distracted. One of the lines to the main jib was not smooth, and neither he or Solomon were happy with the way the canvas caught the wind. Arden watched as Solomon relayed instructions to a crewman who was aloft in the rigging.

He nodded, "If that's what you prefer," he told Boggs. He knew it was common practice to host passengers at the captain's table, and the ship had come with silverware, goblets, and plates for that purpose. In the three years he had owned the ship, Boggs was Arden's first formal, paying passenger, so it had not been Arden's habit to dine separately from his crew. He had not given it much of a thought on this journey, except to give earlier instructions to the cook to purchase and prepare food for their additional passengers.

The second night at dinner was no more pleasant for Arden than the first. Boggs was not a conversationalist. He took no interest in history or in science. He was not a reader. If he had a family, he did not speak of them. There were few topics to discuss. The only words he used were to complain about the noise of the crew or the unacceptable taste of his food. The weather on their second day had been dismal, first fog and then damp and rain, so Boggs had spent only short spans of time on deck. He did not interact with others and remained aloof. He came out to eat lunch. Now here he was back for dinner, formally dressed, a fact that raised snickers from the men in his employ who had little to do except play cards in the galley.

Arden and Boggs sat down together. The captain poured wine and then thanked his cook for the plates that were served them moments later. Boggs did not acknowledge the cook. Arden watched as Boggs sniffed the items on his plate and proceeded to fastidiously cut his food into tiny pieces. Boggs commented that the parsnips in the stew were overdone. Arden did not reply.

When Arden talked of the weather, Boggs' response was only: "The weather is miserable."

After that, they ate in silence. Boggs continued examining each bite of food before putting it in his mouth.

Unexpectedly, Boggs spoke. "I see that you are familiar with your crew," he stated in a tone of voice that could only be taken as a criticism.

Arden looked up. He was quiet for a moment before answering. "I assume you are referring to the fact that I talk with my men?"

Boggs nodded.

"You disagree with my belief that my men are worth talking to? You don't think so?"

"You are naïve, Captain."

Arden tried not to read a note of condescension in his words. Boggs continued quietly, "Men scheme. They will take your place if you do not keep them in theirs. Men work for one reason alone: money. I pay my men, so they look to me. But the second I become their friend, they will get ideas that they are like me and you. Obviously, they are not."

"You and I disagree on this matter, Mr. Boggs." Arden ate a few more bites of his stew and took a sip of wine before continuing. "If I treat a man as a man, as a person with inherent dignity, he will be loyal. I can trust that a man will return respect for the respect that I give him. I have come to do this with my men."

"Hah!" Boggs practically spit. "Such thinking is what took us to war. It is ludicrous to say we are all the same. There are classes for a reason. Society functions when people know their places and remain in them. Trust? Loyalty? I say again, you are naïve to think it is not every man for himself."

"So you are against the American ideal? The idea that all men have a right to rise to a better station in life? I contend that just because a man has ambition does not mean he will turn against an employer who has treated him well."

"You are a young man, Mr. Anderson. I will attribute your idealistic views to that. When you are older, you will certainly come to see that people are not to be trusted. Especially the ones who are beneath us in circumstance."

Boggs took a sip of wine before continuing. "You talk of equality. But I think I have caught you in an inconsistency. Where does that put the slave you call Solomon that you keep on this ship?"

Arden, stood up, angrily, almost tipping the chair. He rarely raised his voice, but in this case it was loud. "Solomon DuPree is *not* a slave, Mr. Boggs. He is my very competent first mate. You insult me and him by thinking that he is otherwise. Solomon is a freedman, through papers, through the law, and as of eight years ago, by the law of this land."

"Emancipation!" Boggs said the word with disgust. "What that bastard Lincoln did was wrong, freeing all them. Now they wander the country trying to take over what is rightfully ours."

It was quiet in the galley. The men on the other side of a partition in the tight quarters below deck had heard the captain and Boggs raise their voices. They had stopped their own chatter and were waiting for the next words of their bosses.

For a last time that evening, Arden, still standing, addressed Boggs. His voice was calm and controlled, hiding his seething anger. "We are at opposite sides, it appears, on these topics, Mr. Boggs, and will discuss them no further. We should arrive at the island tomorrow, if all goes well with the winds. For the rest of this sail, you may continue to eat at this table, but I will not join you. The same will be true on the return. From here on out, it will be best if our interactions are few."

Boggs was wise enough not to answer. Arden took his plate into the galley, nodded to his men, who slowly returned to their own conversations. Then he climbed up the steps and went to the ship's rail. There were still hours of daylight, and a light rain was still falling. The *Jenny Marie* had slowed since earlier that day, but they were still moving north. Arden started to relay to Solomon their conversation, but then stopped himself. Solomon would find out soon enough about Boggs' words. There was no need for Arden to tell him. As soon as the men finished their dinner, one or two at a time came up from below to tell their own versions of what they had heard.

~

"It is nothing new," Solomon said to him, an hour or so later, after the word had spread to the crew on deck. Arden stood at the rail outside his cabin. Though he, as Boggs pointed out, talked to his men, they did not initiate conversation with him. The exception was Solomon, who had given the wheel to the crewman on watch, and walked to the place where Arden stood. Both looked out at the water.

"That's quite true, Solomon. You are right, of course. It surprises me, though, that nothing has changed. After Lincoln? After a war? And here in the north where the residents fought for your rights?"

"It appears that not *all* of them fought for my rights," Solomon said sardonically.

Arden turned to him. "You are always less angry than I am."

"I have long years of practice," Solomon replied.

Arden nodded at his friend, and was quiet in thought.

Solomon continued, "There were plenty of times I was angry enough. But there was never any winning in it."

The rain had stopped. As night came on, the *Jenny Marie* headed into clearer skies. Color from the west extended north, and a cloud bank to their starboard side turned pink.

Arden and Solomon walked back to the helm, and Arden took the wheel. "How about *King Lear*?" he asked Solomon. "The part where he is an angry king?"

Solomon paused for a moment to bring the right passage to his mind. He settled in on a bench. He began reciting the words of the play. Word for word. Flawlessly.

The year before, one of his crew that was able to read followed along in Arden's book of Shakespeare's plays as Solomon recited word-for-word from *The Tempest.* By the end of the season together, it was like a game for all of the crew to gather and listen and watch the finger follow along. Last year Solomon had memorized *Julius Caesar* with the help of the same crewman. Solomon read on his own and memorized bit by bit, scene by scene. Gavin tested him the next day, correcting a misspoken word or reminding of the line that came next until Solomon had put it to memory, along with the seven other plays he already knew. His talent to remember the lines was impressive, and though Solomon never meant it as performance, it had become good entertainment to the crew to hear him speak the lines. In the plays he knew the best, (and *Lear* was one of them,) he changed voices to distinguish the characters. For other plays, he just stared ahead at the horizon as if reading an invisible book in his mind.

Tonight, first three, then nearly all of the crew, along with Bogg's men, sat on the deck and watched him. A few had pipes or rolled cigarettes, which Arden allowed in the evenings for those not on watch. The men listened as the sky turned pale and the first stars came out. *Lear* and his daughters, *Lear* and his fool, *Lear* in the storm. For over an hour, Solomon recited the play he had memorized years before and still remembered.

9

THERE WERE NO more notable occurrences between Boggs and Arden. The *Jenny Marie* sailed north through the night past the entrance to Roundstone Harbor and past the Light that was a welcome signal as they sailed up the coast. By about two in the morning, they were just south of the tip of the Door Peninsula and could see the Pilot Island Light when Arden ordered the sails to be lowered. They anchored off shore from the small settlement of Newport as Arden had no intention of going near Death's Door passage at night. Too many ships had been lost there, too many crews perished and cargo ruined or gone. Thankfully, moonlight helped them see to lower the sails. Though the crew lit lanterns to see as they pulled on the lines, their job was made easier by the extra light of the nearly full moon.

It was Arden's intention to pull anchor and raise sail after sunrise. From the maps and from what Boggs had told him, it was necessary to access Shallow Island from the west. He had a choice, either to sail through Death's Door passage, then turn north until the island came into view, or travel straight north up into the deep lake, go past the island, then turn west and south again to access the west side, where Boggs had assured him a dock had been built for their arrival. The longer way meant they could avoid the dangerous channel between the tip of Door County and the islands north of it where the waters from Green Bay and the waters of Lake Michigan were constantly battling. Those churning waves and colliding currents were as dangerous as the shallow reefs that dabbed the channel, and it was no wonder that Death's Door was a recipe for shipwrecks. Still, if he avoided Death's Door, there could be difficult maneuvering to bring the *Jenny Marie* in to Shallow Island.

He would evaluate the winds again right before sunrise. Unlike the oceans where he had sailed as a young man and the Gulf of Mexico where he had sailed in the War Between the States, Lake Michigan's winds could change from hour to hour. On this lake he had experienced three seasons in a single day.

Until dawn, then, he assigned only two men to keep watch and told the rest of them to get a few hours' sleep. Rather than sleep below deck in the extra hammocks that had been hung for them, most of Boggs' men spread bedrolls and blankets on the deck and slept under the summer night stars. It would be their last night of leisure before they began work on Shallow Island for three months at least. Boggs had not enamored his way into any of their liking, and there was a sense of trepidation among Boggs' men as they wondered what their summer would hold.

Arden was glad they were close to their destination. Just a few hours sail, one route or the other, and they would be on the island by early afternoon. It would take a few hours after that to unload, then they'd be on their way back south again. Boggs would be unpleasant, but Arden had lived through unpleasantries much worse.

~

Shallow Island was not large. Part of the archipelago of islands that extended north from Door County up to the Garden peninsula of Michigan, it was barely a mile across and only two miles long. Still, it had a beauty that Arden could admire, and he could understand why a person with means might choose this location to build a house that was grand. Nothing he had seen in Lake Michigan could compare to the mansions of Rhode Island that he had sailed past as a child. But having seen them, he knew there was a certain kind of man who wanted a mansion by the sea. Unlike the others on board who ogled as the house came into view, Arden was impressed but not startled.

Arden had chosen the longer way of steering up past the island and then a turn west and then south again. There was indeed a long dock as Boggs promised, and the *Jenny Marie* came in smoothly. The water inside the bay was calm and clear, so that the bottom seemed close. Arden feared for a moment that the boat would hit bottom, but thankfully, she did not. The pier was situated in a good place, set to accommodate ships such as his. They tied up quickly, and soon every man on the ship was in action.

A man named Tim Fowler greeted them. He shook the hands of his new laborers and pointed up to the bunkhouse that was back from the beach at the edge of the tree line. "Take your things there and meet the cook. He will show you your places. Then come back and help us unload. We will get you situated and ready to work when all the supplies have been carried and stored in the sheds."

Boggs had hung back. Fowler saw him and frowned.

"I'm surprised to see you, Mr. Boggs. I didn't think you liked sailing."

"I don't, Mr. Fowler. But I am willing to do as Mr. Lewis requests."

"Will you be staying then?"

"No, I am only to check on the progress. After the unloading is done, I will expect to meet with you and get a report on the construction. Our boss is eager to know if the project is on schedule."

"We both know the man's schedule is malarkey." Fowler said. "All the money in the world can't stop rain from making mud. Supplies don't come on time. We work as fast as we can. There is progress, you'll see. But as you know, he has made changes to his initial plans, and those have slowed us down."

"You can complain all you want, Mr. Fowler. I will write down what you tell me and relay your news to our employer."

"Do what you need to do." Fowler sighed. "But I hope you brought all the supplies we requested and more. And I hope you brought food. Our men are hungry, and they are tired of fish for every meal. They are thirsty, and we are all ready for beer."

He turned to his laborers that had gathered at the dock, ready to begin unloading. "There'll be beer for each of you when the unloading is done!" This news made them quick to form a line from the ship's hold to the deck, then to the gangplank, then to the pier.

Once a sizeable number of crates was sitting on the pier, planks were put down over the rocks on the beach with hope that their wagon could ferry the supplies from the ship to the building site. The site was up a steep bank, mostly dune from sand deposited eons ago. But after a half hour of effort and frustration trying to push the wagon on uneven ground and through sandy soil, they abandoned their plan and decided instead that the men would carry the heavy boxes using their brute strength.

Boggs stood with a log book and meticulously checked off each crate as it was brought up from the ship's hold. He had numbered each box and checked off a list in an elaborate record-keeping system that made sense only to him. Arden overheard one of his sailors quietly ask Solomon if Boggs had checked the boxes going in and there had been no stops since leaving, why he needed to check them again going off. Solomon shrugged and told him that *the man apparently finds it hard to believe men can be trusted.*

The heaviest item was the last, a cast iron stove that would go to the kitchen in the bunk house. The five new laborers that had come on the *Jenny Marie* brought the number of the island's work crew to sixteen men. Two cooks were needed and two stoves, not only to prepare food but to give heat when the work continued into the fall. It took four men to lift the heavy stove out of the hold, to inch it down the gangway, and to heave it slowly up the path and across the yard to its place inside the long wooden structure set back in a line of trees.

Outside the bunk house that adjoined the kitchen were tables and benches, and Boggs had reluctantly given permission for one of the newly-arrived barrels of beer to be tapped as a reward for completing the task of unloading. The sailors were invited to join them. Out of the wind the sun was warm, so there were men sitting and lying about the yard as all work had stopped for the day.

Even Solomon had left the ship and joined them in the warm afternoon sun. Reluctant at first, he was relieved to sense no animosity at his presence. In fact, it was the opposite. Shortly upon Solomon's arrival, a gregarious man named Rivers identified himself as a veteran in the Union Army. Several of the men already at work on the island, he said, had served in the Civil War.

"Nearly 200,000 Black men served the Union," Rivers announced to the group that was sitting in the sun drinking. "In my unit, those men worked harder than we did. And for less pay. A buddy of mine owes his life to the Negro medics." He turned to Solomon. "Our captain was not allowed to give people like you guns, but you helped us win the war." He nodded at Solomon, moved closer to the man beside him to make more room, and motioned Solomon to join him at the table. "Did you fight with us?"

"Navy, sir," answered Solomon. "On a ship to deliver supplies for our side."

Clearly, Rivers had some kind of sway over the other men, and there was no resistance to Solomon's joining them. Arden had witnessed the exchange and wondered if Boggs had been there what his reaction would have been.

Over their beer, there was friendly conversation between the new arrivals and the men who had been at work on the island already. The men on the island were eager for news from the world and the nation. The newly arrived laborers had questions about the project. "Are the work hours strict? Do we take Sundays off?" All who were seeing the site for the first time were curious about the size of the building and what the owner planned for the future on Shallow Island.

Boggs and Fowler would likely need time to discuss details of the project. Boggs had papers and a pen. And lists. The men at the tables and in the yard watched as the two men walked around the property. They had drawings to consult. Boggs pulled out a table from a shed and wrote notes. Despite his earlier criticism of their boss, Fowler was knowledgeable of the project. There were answers for each of Boggs' questions. Together they examined corners and walls, pointed at the spaces where windows would go.

Though the unloading was complete, it became obvious to Arden that they would not be leaving immediately. After giving his assent while they waited, many of the *Jenny Marie* crew followed others down a path to look at a spring of fresh water on the east side of the island. At a far side of the yard, the cooks had planted a garden and there was discussion and advice from one of the new masons who had grown up on an Ohio farm. Gulls flew overhead in a blue sky. For once, Arden was not in a hurry to get back on his ship.

10

BOGGS CAUSED NO problems on the return trip to Milwaukee. He stayed mostly in his cabin. The conditions for sail were good as they traveled south. Arden knew there was wood stacked high at Jacksonport waiting at more than one pier, so that was their aim for the night. The *Jenny Marie* made it through Death's Door and all the way to the logging village in one long day. There was a hotel in the town; Boggs announced he would take his dinner there and pay for a night off the ship.

"We will begin loading early in the morning, and it should take only a few hours," Arden told him. "Please be here at the dock by 10."

When it came to matters of business, Boggs was polite. "Of course, Captain. I will be here. Now, I hope I can find something better to eat than the unsatisfactory fare on your ship."

No one was sad to see him leave the ship, walk up the pier, and turn left to the hotel that stood out from the other buildings in town with a recent coat of white paint.

The cook, Oscar, had heard the conversation. Arden gave a shrug and told him, "Give it no mind, Ossy. I don't know if *any* food could make that man happy."

In town, Ossy came across a local farmer who was selling fresh strawberries. Hours later, he was preparing shortcake for dessert. He did not keep it a secret that he was glad that Boggs had missed out on the treat.

~

The docks were mostly full when they arrived in Milwaukee two days later. Arden had hoped for one of the closer docks, but he and Solomon maneuvered the *Jenny Marie* skillfully into a slip on one of the newer, southern docks. Boggs left quickly, informing Arden he would return with his payment later that day.

Arden paid the slip fee and talked to the harbor master. Each pier had separate instructions for unloading. Arden also needed names of any customers who would be interested in buying his wood. It didn't take long for Arden to meet a client who wanted to make those arrangements, as wood was in high demand. By late afternoon, Arden had not only sold this load but also signed a contract with a construction company to bring twelve more hauls of lumber back to Milwaukee. It was good news. As the crew worked to unload the last of the wood onto wagons, he told each of his men there would be a small bonus added to their pay. There had been tension between two of his crew just that morning, a dispute over a small thing that Arden sensed was about something bigger. A bonus was a good distraction.

The afternoon was warm. Ships came and went all around them. Shouts about lines and sails could be heard. Gulls squawked. Most activity at their dock stopped as a magnificent big ship came into the harbor and sailed past them. Crews and captains, dock hands, and passengers conversed about the huge brig and its several square-rigged sails. Four sailors stood aloft on the yardarms, two on each side of the center mast. There were guesses about the cargo and admiration for the ship's impressive size.

The crew of the *Jenny Marie* sweat as the men passed piece after piece of the wood stacks down a line and onto wagons. Arden's news of a bonus made his men eager to complete their job quickly. When they finished, they jumped with whoops and splashes into the water, then dried off lazily in the sun while they waited to be paid.

Half an hour later, Boggs returned with his payment for Arden. He arrived just moments after Arden had signed his contract for the twelve additional hauls of lumber.

"I had expected you to carry more supplies to Shallow Island for me," he said, displeasure in his voice.

"As I recall, you told me when we signed our contract last week that it was a possibility. You did not offer anything more concrete."

"You might have done me the courtesy of waiting for my return. I needed to know that you were reliable. I needed to know that your ship could manage the access to the pier at Shallow Island. I have brought you a contract to deliver more supplies for us."

"I am afraid you are moments too late, Mr. Boggs."

"Whatever it is, I will pay more."

"I will not go back on a contract I have signed with another," Arden insisted.

"I will pay you half again more than I paid you for your initial haul for us."

Arden felt irritation rising. If Boggs was willing to pay that much for a second haul, he certainly could have paid that same amount for the first.

"Here is what I will do, Mr. Boggs," Arden answered. "It is June. I will haul twelve loads for my new client. I suspect that will take me into August. When those hauls are complete, I will contact you to see if you have need of the *Jenny Marie* in the late summer and fall."

"Damn it all, Captain Anderson. This means I will have to sail again. My employer was clear, I must accompany each hauler on their first trip. I could have been done with this lake once and for all if you would only agree to take the work."

For a moment Arden was tempted. To take supplies at a high price to Shallow Island without Mr. Boggs would have been a nice way to spend the summer days of July and August and September. But he was a man of his word and would not go back on a contract.

"I'm afraid that is the way it must be, Mr. Boggs. I cannot help you until August. I will contact you then."

"I will be in Chicago, Mr. Anderson. Thank God I can take a train from here to there and get off a ship. In your hands, along with your payment, is a business card with the address of my company in Chicago." Boggs turned around and walked angrily down the dock. He did not acknowledge the crew that was watching the exchange, the men whose life he had depended upon for the previous seven days. He did not say goodbye to the captain. Arden watched him go, then went immediately to his cabin to count the money from Boggs. Moments later he was doling to each man his pay plus the bonus he had promised.

The *Jenny Marie* was suited for hauls of lumber, and June and July turned to August. Weather was always the factor that made hauls easy or difficult. Only a few storms in July hindered them from making good progress with cargo as they made runs up and down the lake, almost all to Jacksonport and back. After many hauls to the small village about half way up the Door County peninsula, the *Jenny Marie* and her crew were recognized at those docks. Solomon was no longer a novelty, and he went along with the crew to the grocery and the tavern on the nights they lingered for a few hours or stayed overnight in a slip.

There were men in Jacksonport who had fought in the war. For two of them in particular, their enlistment had been completely on moral grounds. "A slave is a *man* and not a beast," they had proclaimed, and in an odd sort of way, Solomon's presence in their town made them proud. When, years before, the debates in the town had been divisive, both pastors in the town had taken the side of abolition. "To read the same Bible as we do and still enslave a man? Such thinking is abhorrent to God," they said from the pulpit. That liberal thinking seemed to have carried over to the bars and the groceries as Solomon and the men of the *Jenny Marie* went about town. If there were men or women who felt otherwise, those residents kept their feelings to themselves.

And as only one person, Solomon was no threat. The town might not have accepted his skin color so readily if he had moved there with others, in a large group of settlers. He was one sailor who came in and out of their town for only hours at a time.

In reality, he was not much more than a curiosity to those who encountered him. Men at the docks talked *about* him but rarely talked *to* him. When Solomon was out of earshot, people in the village asked his crew questions: "What kind of slave had he been? Had he been a slave at all? He was educated, it was clear. Hadn't it been illegal to teach a slave to read? There can't be many first mates who are Negro. Does he have an accent from the South? Had he been brutally treated like those people who suffered on horrible plantations? Do you think he has scars on his back? Was he lashed?"

Solomon in fact *did* have scars from a lashing. But the men on the *Jenny Marie* were loyal. They did not disrespect him by fueling rumors of stories that were Solomon's alone to tell.

~

There were questions about Arden Anderson as well. "What made him want to hire a black man as first mate? Why isn't he married? Is it true that he owns the *Jenny Marie?* He must surely have come from money. What is his past?" And because Arden was silent about his own past, the crew had few answers. In their conversations at mealtime, Arden asked about his men, but they did not feel free to ask questions in return. He was their captain after all. And Arden never talked about himself. Places he had been, yes. But not his own stories.

"I know he was in the Navy in the War. Do you know what he did?" Finn asked Solomon as they were coiling lines together after leaving a dock.

"First Master and then Lieutenant. He sailed up and down from Baltimore to wherever they needed him to go. Sometimes way around Florida and west to the Gulf of Mexico, even as far as Baton Rouge and New Orleans."

"For the whole war?"

"Yessir. The whole time. Without any breaks," Solomon answered. "Most men were on for a year or two at a time. But not Captain Anderson," he explained. "Our captain just kept going. Except for a sister, he didn't have much of a family, although he left for a week when his uncle died. Some of those runs were dangerous, too. He delivered supplies under cannon fire more than once. And without those supplies of ammunition that we brought to the Union troops who were fighting in the south, who knows, the Confederates might have won."

"*We*, Mr. Solomon? *You* were there with him?"

"Yes, for the last year or so. I was in the Navy, too. The captain arranged it so that I was on the same ship with him. They had me as cook's boy. Peeling potatoes." He said this with a hint of a smile. "Ironic, huh? I could have built those boats we sailed. I could have climbed every mast and furled canvas better than those crews ever did. But they had me cutting carrots. I just watched as they raised sail and took them down again. Half the time they couldn't get the wind right. I served them their suppers and kept my mouth shut about lines and winds and currents and tides."

Finn started to say more, but Arden joined them as Solomon continued.

"Supplies on the way down," Solomon finished. "And then, on our way back north, we carried the wounded."

Arden added, "Those are days I am happy to forget. There was moaning all day and all night. The smell of blood and rotting limbs. Men with dysentery that could not hold their shit, so bunks had to be washed down every day."

Solomon nodded. "They had me doing *that*, too," he said. The two men caught each other's eyes and when the captain got up, it was clear the conversation was over.

The summer sails were lucrative for Arden. Besides the hauls with wood from Jacksonport to Milwaukee, he was always able to find people begging him to make deliveries to ports in Door County. The *Jenny Marie* delivered to both Baileys Harbor and Roundstone Harbor. Each of those stops lengthened their trips to Jacksonport by only a few hours. Typically, they dropped off their cargo in the northern ports and were docked in Jacksonport with daylight to spare.

The channel into Baileys Harbor now had a range light system that made sailing into the harbor possible even at night, and they did that twice in July. When the two lights were lined up, one over the other, it meant the ship was in line for safe passage into the harbor. A second blacksmith was setting up shop and the *Jenny Marie* delivered his anvil, his tools, some ingots of steel.

Roundstone Harbor had a beautiful lighthouse that sat on a high bluff. It had been built with white limestone blocks and was set in a clearing of trees on the bluff, so even in daylight it was a recognizable landmark. The Fresnel lens shone out 24 miles according to the maps, although Arden had never been out that far to test it.

As his contract for cordwood came to an end, Arden asked himself what obligation he had to keep his verbal promise to contact Ethan Boggs once the last delivery of wood to Milwaukee had been completed. Was it necessary, really, to sail down to Chicago to find the office of a rich man only to pursue the possibility of hauls way up the shoreline to Shallow Island?

In the end, it was partly decided for him. On the last drop-off of wood, Donahue, of the Donahue Wagon Company found Arden at the Milwaukee docks.

"Captain Anderson! How fortuitous. I am here to find a hauler to take two wagons down to Chicago. Would you do it?"

"Possibly," Arden answered.

"Can you believe that my wagons are now going south? There are plenty of wagon companies in Chicago, but I have two customers there that want mine! I have told them there will be freight costs, of course, but they are willing to pay. So I am in need of you! What do you say?"

The two men discussed a price and shook hands. Finding business was not Arden's favorite thing to do, and here it was, once again, falling into his lap. But it meant, too, that he had no reason to avoid Chicago. Instead, after he delivered Tom Donahue's wagons, he would have an unfriendly meeting to look forward to with Ethan Boggs.

11

MEGGIE WAS SETTLING in to the routine of chores at the Light. The pain from her surgery and internal scars had subsided. As to the loss of George, she cried less often. She had hoped that the beauty that was all around at the Light would be solace, and it was. Herons. Ospreys. Thimbleberries. Rides with her younger two brothers in the rowboat across the calm bay, and picnics at the water's edge. Water warm enough for swimming. The chatter of Gillian, her young sister. Reading a book in the sun on a chair at the beach. Sunsets that could make a person cry from their beauty.

Her parents had stopped asking the tedious, repetitive questions about how she felt, what she was thinking, how she was. They must have discussed it because their questions had stopped suddenly. Or maybe they sensed she was settling in to her grief. To the fact she would live with unanswerable questions. A few days before, when Gillian had asked her a question about George, Meggie had answered. To the point. Without tears.

Things had changed in the village since she had left four years before to marry her husband. There was now a church that the McGinns attended in town. There were boarding houses and a grocery store. There were also young women that had come to the village, unlike the first settlers who were predominantly single men. A few wives had come "sight unseen" to the wilderness, to men that decided to stay once they had been paid out by the logging camps. In addition to the loggers and fishermen, couples were also coming, some with children. It was a far more active place than the one she had left a few years before.

Meggie had begun to think of two women in particular as friends. Kira was Norwegian and had come with a group from that country just after Meggie had left. Kira knit beautiful mittens, and Meggie had first met her when she had gone to her house to purchase a pair. Though her accent was strong, Kira was a talkative person.

"Please come often," Kira told her. "Good for my English. Good for.. how do you say it..for the lonely?"

"Loneliness," Meggie had replied with a smile and a nod of sympathy. The home was warm. There were wildflowers in vases, and yarns of every color were displayed neatly on a shelf. Those colors brought a simple beauty to the room.

"I *will* come back," Meggie had told her, and she had. Partly inspired by Kira, Meggie had taken on a difficult knitting project and had needed Kira's help, which she gladly gave. Now the two women met almost weekly. More than once they sat outside the small house under a lean-to built by Kira's husband for shade while they knit and chatted in the blue-skied summer afternoons. Kira talked about leaving Norway, about the things she missed from home. About her father dying in front of her when she was only sixteen. Kira was the first person in Roundstone Harbor that she told about George. How much she missed him. How he had been handsome. How, according to the people that told her, the fire that burned him made his face unrecognizable in the coffin.

When she met Charlotte at church, Meggie liked her immediately. She was cheerful and friendly, but opinionated, too, and not afraid to express her opinions. In Sunday school, she asked questions, spoke up, disagreed in a way that was never disrespectful or argumentative. She and Meggie talked of books they read. Charlotte had a particular interest in glass, and wanted details about the Fresnel Lens at the Light. Only a few weeks after they met, Meggie had invited her to the Light to see how the intricate pattern of the beacon worked. Charlotte and Jack spent over an hour discussing the mechanics of refraction and mirrors, lens and prisms. While they chatted, Meggie lost interest, but she could not help but admire a woman who pursued with such passion an interest in the workings of a machine.

Unlike some of the newcomers to town who came with almost nothing, Charlotte and her husband had brought enough money to build a house. In early spring, right before Meggie had come home, Charlotte and William had arrived on a ship that carried their crate full of furniture and home goods, and, impressively to the townspeople, a wagon. It was brought on the same ship, in pieces. Their house, clearly the most elegant in town, was finished in a few months. Meggie and Charlotte were the same age, and Charlotte had invited Meggie to help decorate the house and unpack the linens and organize her kitchen. Meggie had been happy to help and welcomed having a friend to spend time with.

One afternoon while the two women sat comfortably by a window, William brought in a heavy box that had arrived on a boat.

"Oh William! Is it what I am hoping it is? My sewing machine?" She turned to Meggie, excitedly. "I intend to start making dresses. Three have been ordered already, by women who say they will wait for my business to begin. And now it's here!" William pried open the box and helped her lift it to a table. "And every penny I make will be mine," Charlotte said in the presence of her husband. "You agreed to that didn't you, William?"

William was young and clearly enamored of his wife. He was also in the enviable position of having enough money from his growing quarry business so that he did not need more income. "Anything you say, my dear Charlotte," he said to her with affection. He kissed the top of her head. "Just don't get so busy sewing that you forget to put a meal on the table for me and our new baby."

The mood in the room changed suddenly.

Her friend looked at her husband, then Meggie. "I'm sorry, Meggie. I didn't know when I could tell you."

She turned again to her husband, "Oh, William, I wish you hadn't said anything."

William realized his mistake, and turned to Meggie. "How very insensitive of me, Margaret. I apologize."

Meggie's words came out in anger. "Does everyone in this village do nothing but talk about me? Does everyone know my business?" She felt tears well up in her eyes. "Does everyone in this village *pity* me?"

Will found a handkerchief and handed it to her, but he remained silent.

"Yes, Meggie," Charlotte said with certainty. "I won't lie to you. Everyone in this village *does* know what happened to you, that you had a child and you lost him. But I wouldn't call it pity. And to be truthful, I also don't know how to talk to you about it, or about.. my baby in front of you, either. I am sorry."

Meggie got up to leave.

"Charlotte, of course you should talk about your baby! This is good news. To both of you, congratulations!" She paused and took a deep breath. "I am a widow, and you, Charlotte, are not. I have had a deep sorrow, and I am glad you have not. Some days for no explicable reason, I am sadder than others, but today is not one of those days. Today, I am very happy for your news. Nevertheless, I think, it is time for me to be going."

Will stood awkwardly, and Charlotte gave her friend a hug.

Meggie's Diary: August 3, 1871

It seems people are trying to protect me. Am I so fragile, so breakable? I cannot marry, but does that mean I am weak, that I am nothing?

I have become resigned, in these months, to my position. I can think now of myself as a widow and claim what I am. I am not unhappy. In fact, it may be that being unmarried will make me independent, not tied to these giddy feelings with which girls in the village are consumed as they contemplate falling in love. In their letters, my cousins dither about the handsome men they think they love when they write to me from their cities in the East. They go so far as to ask me questions about being in bed with a man because I have done it. Do they forget that I was happy, that I loved him, that remembering is not something I want to do?

I will not, however, be pathetic and have people tiptoe around me afraid to speak.

My marriage was short. I was the giddy one then, thinking myself so mature setting up house and being so practical about clothes and curtains. And the laughter as we prepared for a baby, and then the irony—that he died in childbirth instead of me. Or so it all seemed in the blur and the horror of those few days. A long labor. A child that lived long enough to nurse twice. Me in a fever and doctors returning not to birth a baby but to dig and scour and pronounce my womb ruined. Was it a doctor who told me, or was it his sister or his mother who whispered to me about a fire, explaining why George was not there to hold me or to see his newborn son? They cried more than I did. Were they crying for me or for George or because our baby was to have a coffin next to his father whose arms never held him? And I, too sick to attend, could not see either one's face when the coffins were closed forever from my eyes. When they let me go there after three weeks, to the cemetery not far from the water, flower blossoms like snow covered the ground near their gravestones.

Charlotte is pregnant. What will I feel when I hold her new baby? Will I ache for my own? For my little Jamie that was in my arms for only a wisp of a moment? I did not have him long enough to know him. He was there and then he was gone.

12

IT WAS FALL with glorious colors in the trees. Meggie and her three younger siblings had to stop swimming as brisk days followed cold nights, and the lake grew cold. Her sister and brothers were gone now during the day, back at school. Each had chores as soon as they came home. Philip's main job was chopping wood. Their lighthouse living quarters had been designed with several fireplaces, and those fireplaces had to be fed day and night. Stacks and stacks of wood had to be ready to last them through winter. In late afternoon each day of the week, the *chop, chop, split* of Philip's axe echoed repeatedly across the yard of the lighthouse and even inside the thick walls of the house.

Peter's job was to haul oil up the stairs to the lantern room, or to the room just below it. He was still small, only seven, so Jack divided his son's hauls into smaller containers. This meant Peter could handle the weight, but he needed to make many trips up the stairs. Peter did it without complaining, especially if his father was in the tower. After Peter's last haul for the day, Jack and he made a habit of scanning the lake in all directions. If they spotted a ship, Jack allowed Peter to use the new scope delivered earlier in the year by the Lighthouse Board to focus in on it. Jack knew many of the individual ships by their shapes, having watched the same ones come and go up the coast all summer. Peter liked the challenge of identifying them. It felt like a game he played with his father.

Gillian's task was to help with dinner. She seemed to have added an obligation on herself as well: to report to her sister and mother in extended detail everything that happened at school that day. Meggie and her mother more than once had to ask her to cut short her chatter.

Shorter days and longer nights meant the Light had to burn for longer periods of time. Jack spent more hours in the tower, less time in the yard, less time in town. The glass was dirtier each morning. Meggie needed more rags and more water than when she had begun this chore during the longer days of spring.

The garden had flourished over the summer, and they had put up beans and tomatoes. Herbs hung in bundles in the kitchen to dry: rosemary, thyme, sage, basil, dill. Carrots and potatoes and turnips and squash were on shelves in the root cellar. Thimbleberries had been made into jam. They had eaten cherries but had not found a way to preserve them.

Meggie walked into the village two or three afternoons each week through the end of October, and then less and less often as the weather grew colder. Sailors and everyone up and down the shorelines of Lake Michigan knew that fall storms were the most brutal and dangerous. The docks were less busy. Now, only four or five boats stopped each day.

The lights had helped make sailing safer, and ship builders had been experimenting with designs that tried to adapt to the waves and winds of the Great Lakes which were different from the waters of the Atlantic. But nothing could help ships in storms with fourteen foot waves or winds of 40-plus knots. Again this year, there were shipwrecks. North of them, not far from Death's Door, a ship went down in a storm. Apparently, there were no survivors. A second ship sunk in the heart of Death's Door, this one occurring in conditions that weren't even severe. Waves had been high, though, and winds just wrong for the barge. The crew had a lifeboat and all but one got safely aboard, then rowed into Detroit Harbor, cold but alive.

Then a ship went down close to Roundstone Harbor. High waves had driven a schooner to rocks just two miles south of the village. Thankfully, every one of the crew made it to shore. News of the shipwreck came to Jack by messenger in the early morning. When the five sailors came riding into town on Leif Larsen's wagon a few hours later, several townspeople gathered to meet them.

Jack, who was a deacon at the church, agreed with the town pastor, Rev. Stivers, that the men be allowed to shelter in the church building for the week. Also, Jack and the harbor master wanted news of the ship. Jack needed to record the time and location of the disaster for Lighthouse Board records, and the harbor master wanted news, too. Harbormasters up and down the coast were the unofficial journalists of shipping news on the lake. Sailors came to the docks with their news: which boats were good under sail, which had good captains, which boats paid the highest wages or had the best food. From the harbormaster they learned equally helpful information about anything noteworthy that happened on ships. News of a shipwreck spread quickly.

Jack and the reverend were waiting in front of their small church when Leif pulled up in his wagon with the men in the back.

Reverend Stivers greeted the men, "We are glad you are safe. Thank God that He spared your lives." The men nodded their thanks as they jumped off the wagon. One of them tried to say something, but could not reply without coughing.

"I think my wife should have a look at you," Jack told him. "She might be able to help with that cough."

"And we are trying to gather clothes for you." Reverend Stivers added. "And some blankets. The women are cooking food. We hear that you lost everything."

"Yes, sir. Thank you. I am Captain Johnson. I knew there were reefs in the area and tried to steer us away. But the wind was too strong. We could not go against it. We felt her drag and then hit the reef. She cracked, first in one place then another. We thought at first we could stay there on the reef and wait it out, but with each wave, more of our ship was breaking apart. I gave the command to leave. Even our Jimmy, who could not swim, made it to shore. I was with him and helped him hold on to a floating timber. The water was only deep over our heads for a few feet, then sand, and we could practically walk into shore after that. We sat on the beach, cold and wet for a time and watched the ship break to pieces."

The men from the village asked more questions, trying to learn an exact location of the wreck. Leif knew the location best as it was within a half mile of his inland farm, and gave his best estimate.

"It is all under water," Captain Johnson said. "There was no use to stay there and watch after seeing it sink. And we needed to get shelter. Thankfully we saw a light in the distance. We stayed together as the rain pelted. The forest was thick going, but thank God for the light in their cabin."

"The Larsens?"

"Yes, he and his wife. They let us crowd into their house and sit by their fire. We stayed in their house through the night, naked under blankets while we tried to at least dry our clothes. And now here we are."

"We are sorry for your disaster, Captain." Reverend Stivers told him. "But we are glad for your lives."

"I have a further question, gentlemen," the captain said. "Our boat went down not too far off shore. Some of our cargo might wash up. I hated to leave the site. Will there be scavengers or salvagers that will take it all before we can rescue it?"

"Perhaps, but not likely. You could hire a boat at the docks to row you down to inspect it on the next calm day. But I wouldn't go out on the water 'til the Lake settles down. There will be dangerous rollers for another day or two after last night's storm. No one will be scavenging for anything, at least not for a few days. You should rest here for a day or two."

"I am not sure I can hire anything, sir. Every penny I had was on that ship. I was in debt before and now I will be more so. But I thank you for your kindness to me. And to the men. And sir," he added, turning to Jack, "I heard you say your wife is a medical person? Can she look, too, at our Rex? I think his arm is broken. We were all battered and churned in the waves."

"Of course, Captain. My wife is quite experienced with broken bones."

"I think you will find our village a good place," Rev. Stivers told the group of men as they walked into the church. "It is grim news for all of us to hear of the wreck. There are wives and mothers here who go to sleep every night fearing the same fate that you just suffered. Almost everyone in this town is in some way tied by their livelihood to this water. We appreciate the lake, but we fear it. You will find that the people here will help you however they can."

"And jobs?" one of the men asked. "Can I find work here, and a place to stay? Are men hiring?"

"Yes," both men nodded. "Yes, certainly." Rev. Stivers took the men into the building, and Jack went off to find Kate where he had left her inside the grocery just down the street from the church.

A few weeks after the wreck, the lights all over the lake were shut down. The pace of life slowed for the McGinns. Lots of reading. Games at the table. Meggie had more time to write and to think about what was ahead.

Meggie's Diary: December 10, 1871

I do not need a husband, I think, to be happy. If I move away from here, there are things I can do. Yes, I will miss the arms of a husband to wrap me as George used to do. He would sing a sweet song and sway me some mornings when we were getting dressed, standing behind me with his arms all around me, say he was sorry to leave me for the day, say he was tempted to not let me go. I will miss that.

I will miss, too, the presence of a man sitting next to me reading, like Father and Mother do in the winter. The Light has been off now for one week, and they sit together with their books, not talking, for hours some afternoons.

They have told me I can stay as long as I want. But I have set for myself a limit of no more than a few months. Next September, I think, at the end of summer. By then I will make plans for what to do, where to go.

13

ALL THOSE YEARS ago, when Arden disentangled himself from the horrors of transporting human cargo, he was only six months past his fifteenth birthday. He spent the next five years fleeing his shame on ships that took him to Lisbon, Morocco and Rome. To the Azores, to Nice, and to Sicily. To the Caribbean and back, then to Europe, as far away as the Aegean and Greece.

There were months of wind in the sail and hours in ports. They traded nothing illicit. Spices and teas, linens, crates full of oranges. For a while, horses. Inks and dyes. Perfumes. Gemstones. Gold bracelets and earrings hammered by the best jewelers in Venice. Glassware and kaleidoscopes. Figs.

In Cartegna, he had fallen in love. One simple errand in port had led him from one contact to another. And then to a clock merchant's daughter with soft skin and soft hair and eyes the color of the olives that lined the terraces on her family's hills. Days later, he watched his ship sail out of port from the family terrace surrounded by lemon trees while her father talked to him of astronomy and her sister practiced the piano. Her favorite place in the city was the library. There, and the bench where they sat together that looked over the sea. Her laugh was like music. She did not say anything at all when he told her about his old secret, about the slaves that were shoved below deck. She was quiet and her eyes filled with tears. He loved her that she did not try to find words.

But strings were attached. The tailors brought in for him were happy to measure and sew clothes for the weekly dinners. The villa to the west of her family's larger one would be available for him and for her (once he proposed.) They'd expect he would want to redo the accompanying gardens. But there was always the question that lurked behind all of it: why? Arden had contacts in the harbor, his father had a business in America with wine, he could write and speak well to their guests. He had manners, and their daughter was smitten. Still, Arden was suspicious of how easily they let him into their home, to their family, to their daughter. He did not fault her, but she came with too much. If she had wanted to leave, he might have taken her with him when he knew that staying was not something he wanted to do.

Half a year after arriving, Arden was down again to the ports. He found a ship that would sail out in the evening. He was gentleman enough to say goodbye. He did not need to say it in words as she read it on his face. He had liked the gardeners, the cooks, and the family. He had loved her.

For another year he went in and out of the islands in the Caribbean Sea. Sugar cane, mostly. Havana, Port au Prince, Dominico. He was first mate, handling ship funds, giving orders, earning money enough to buy a meal in port. Earning respect. He began dressing well. Each time they came into Trinidad, he went back to one particular woman. He did not tell his secret to her, not even when she shook him awake and held him in the night when his nightmares came.

~

After five years of travel to faraway places, he thought less often about the slaves he had helped to transport and the cruelty he had witnessed. He thought more about the sights he had seen and the work he had done. He divulged nothing to anyone about his past. *Better,* he thought, *not to reveal it, not to remember it.* Which was fine until an unexpected nightmare disturbed his resolve and he knew that none of his guilt was assuaged.

He was twenty years old when he knocked on his father's door, when he stood on the porch of his childhood home wondering if his father would answer. He was a prodigal, certainly. In addition, he brought Solomon with him, a man with black skin who lay in a wagon outside in the drive, bleeding and barely alive.

If Richard Anderson had not been ill, would he have welcomed his son as warmly? There was surprise at first, then tears in his eyes, then unabashed weeping. Arms opened wide to hug his son. In Arden's entire childhood, his father had only been cold and unaffectionate. The most Arden had hoped for when he arrived home to this porch was a place to sleep for a few nights. To be welcomed as a son with no questions asked was a mercy.

While his son had been away at sea, Richard Anderson had suffered a stroke. Now, he slurred words. This made him reticent to say much of anything at all. That was another mercy. Arden's childhood had been full of paragraphs of expectation: what a boy should or should not do, what behaviors of Arden's were unacceptable, and why Arden and his sister Sally were not developing adequately with their studies, with their comport, with their character.

His mother had been as warm as his father had been cold. She defended her children, gave as many words of encouragement and praise as their father gave criticism. She sang songs in the morning and lullabyes at night. She invited friends with children the same age as Arden to come to the house when his father was gone. Those were days of picnics in the yard, tree swings, and laughter. But when his father was at home, the mood was somber. Severe.

Sally, his sister, was older by four years. She was eighteen when she married. Their mother had been sick at the wedding but had tried not to show it. Sally left with her husband John to begin a new life in Ohio. Arden carried the small daguerreotype portrait of his mother with him on the ships that he had sailed, the only thing he had taken with him from home. His mother in a rose-pink dress, slender and smiling at her daughter's joy. Smiling as she ignored the fact that her husband thought John not a good choice of a son-in-law. Smiling, though cancer was raging through her body and she grieved leaving her husband and son.

When she died in that spring, Arden was 14. His father said only that he must take pain like a man. Soon after, his father left, too. "Business in Europe," was all he had said to Arden when, six weeks after they buried his mother, he left Arden alone in the house with two elderly servants. A tutor came four days a week to teach lessons in Chemistry and Mathematics and Greek, as if Arden had any reason at all to want to learn.

So, at barely fifteen, Arden left home to make his way on his own. He sent letters enough so his father had known he was not dead but alive in other parts of the world. Five years later, in February, 1860, Arden was back again, there at his father's door.

Within minutes Arden's father summoned help to move Solomon in from the wagon. He arranged for the bed to be made in the front bedroom and a fire to be lit. He sent for a doctor to treat the man that his son had brought with him. He insisted that Arden eat while they waited for the doctor to come. Arden slept in the same bed that he had left five years before. Little had changed in his room.

It was an all-male household to which they'd arrived. They were father and son, two servants, one medical caretaker, and Solomon. His father no longer went out. The servants knew the older man's routine so there was little need to talk, and the house felt eerily quiet and still. Arden had remembered his father more formidable and the house more intimidating. Now both the house and his father were stale.

Owen Burlington had been hired for care-taking duties after Richard's stroke, so his medical knowledge was invaluable in aiding with Solomon's recovery. With his care, the infected wounds began to heal. He had been too weak to eat, but now Solomon was hungry again. After a few days, Arden, Solomon, and Richard developed a habit of sitting together in the parlor.

It was Solomon who started conversations. Though Arden's actions to purchase Solomon had been kind, they had also been rash. When he had gone unexpectedly to a clandestine auction, Arden purchased Solomon with no forethought at all. A man with a whip had begun to thrash Solomon, and Arden purchased him in order to save Solomon from further cruelty. Four days later, he showed up at his father's house with a stranger, a man that was bleeding from severe wounds on his black skin.

It turned out fortuitously. Solomon knew Shakespeare. He knew history and philosophy and geology. His first owner, Jean Dupree, had an extensive library that Solomon had been encouraged to use. Dupree built ships and sailed them, and Solomon had stayed on with Dupree even after he was given his freedom. Solomon was nearly thirty when Dupree died, but he had money of his own, Shakespeare in his mind, and skill with small sailing vessels. He was a man rising. Freedom had not lasted, though; he was one of many freedmen who were kidnapped and taken back to the south for labor. And cruelty.

Solomon had a sardonic humor that Richard enjoyed. Despite his limitations with speech, Richard followed the conversations that filled the spring-time evenings. He nodded or shook his head, added a word here or there. Solomon and Arden were patient when he tried to string together words in a sentence. He could write phrases on a slate, write sentences on paper if they gave him plenty of time. These slow ways of communication did not stop Solomon from asking questions, and Arden learned more of his father in those days with the three of them together than he had known in all of the years of his childhood. Richard put answers on a slate: the names of his sisters, the number of horses his family had owned on a farm, the place he had met Arden's mother.

~

Since his stroke the year before, the small business that Richard owned was stagnating. He had loyal clients and employees that kept things operating, but there were decisions to be made. "Could you go in?" he asked Arden. "To the office? Learn the business?"

"I'm not ready to commit," Arden told him. "I am only twenty years old. I'm not sure what I want to do next. I am weary of those years-long trips at sea on a ship, but neither do I think I want to be in one place. And I never intended to stay here. Besides, I know nothing of business!"

Go to the office. Talk to them. See. Then decide, his father had written. There were associates managing his warehouse. The wines that he ordered from France and the whiskeys from Scotland had ready customers in America. Richard said, "They will need leadership soon. It could be yours."

Arden was less worried about his father's business in those first weeks home than he was about Solomon. Owning slaves was legal in Maryland in 1860, and with fugitive slave laws, Arden did not trust that Solomon was safe. Baltimore had always had a large population of freed blacks, but people were suspicious of black men with wounds and broken bones. There were bounty hunters looking for fugitives. And there were men hired to take freedmen—even freedmen with papers—and make them slaves again. Arden had released any ownership of Solomon almost immediately after their arrival. Although Solomon was once again free, Baltimore was not a safe place for him to stay.

Arden sent letters to his sister Sally in Ohio and was waiting to hear. After a few weeks Solomon was able to stand and walk with the help of crutches. If Solomon could travel, Arden hoped he could take him to his sister. Or, if Sally and John denied him and could not take Solomon in, Arden determined he would go north with Solomon. "After that, maybe," he told his father." After that, I am willing to see if your business is something I could do. "His father nodded, lifted a hand in agreement to say *thank you, I am content with your answer.*

In those five years away, Arden had missed his mother, but never his father. He had remembered him only as domineering and critical. Had he ever imagined his father like this, a man so unlike the one he remembered? A man who could not speak or walk from dining room to porch unassisted, but could show love with a gesture? Who looked at his son and teared up in gratitude because he had come home?

Each day as Arden sat with the two men in the parlor of the house where he had lived as a child, Solomon healed and Richard declined. His father was both less of a man and more of one.

In those weeks together, the relationship between father and son was not the only surprise. What was the word for what Solomon was becoming to him? If it weren't for the color of skin, the word would be *friend.*

When the letter came days later that Sally would take him, they had only to decide the best means of transport. That, and whether there would be money enough to pay for more doctors should Solomon need them at Sally and John's. "I will pay back what I can when I am able," Solomon told them. "Will there be a way I can work in Ohio?"

Arden asked his father if he would consider a small loan.

In the morning an envelope was at Arden's place at the table with a sizeable amount of money. The scrawled message must have taken his father a long time to write:

> *This is the first thing you asked of me, so I give it gladly. It did not matter to me what it was. Still, I am glad you asked for help for another and not help for yourself. Your mother would be proud.*
>
> *Buy land for Solomon. Make sure there is money for shelter for him, for food, for a wagon, for books.*

A second letter was addressed to Solomon.

> *You must not pay me back. You have returned my son to me. It is enough.*

14

ARDEN DID NOT stay long with his sister when he went to deliver Solomon. A black man could travel across state lines only if a white man would vouch for him. Even then it was risky, but their trip first by carriage and then by a wagon was without incident. Arden did not do much more than see Solomon delivered to the farm, eat a few meals, and talk in formalities with Sally and John.

It was the first Sally had seen her brother in five years. He had been at sea, sailing all over the world in merchant ships. He had sent them the occasional letter. A few presents for Christmas. Postmarks from Marseilles, Lisbon, Sardinia. Suddenly, Arden was in the states again and had sent a flurry of letters and even a telegram asking if they would take in a freedman. No details except that the man was injured and weak. When they had said *yes,* days later Arden and Solomon had arrived, and then Arden was gone again in two days.

He made promises to his sister that he would return and that he would write often now that he was only states away. The siblings were not together long enough in those two days to reacquaint. The focus was on Solomon, on meeting the children, on moving the furniture around to make room. Two days was not long enough to begin to bridge the five years they had been apart.

Arden had neither the time nor the inclination to tell his sister about his experiences since she had left home to start her own life with a husband and he had left home, alone. She had planted an orchard and nurtured her children in a valley that was sunny and green. He had struggled to hold his footing on ships in raging seas and winds and waves. He had been battered by weather and men that were mean.

Sally was like her mother in temperament, cheery and kind. "You are less talkative than I remember you, Arden."

"Hmm," he nodded.

"Were they good years away or bad years?"

"Some of both, I suppose."

"Well, you are certainly grown. Not the young teen that you were when I left home. Self-assured, now. Independent, I'd say. But not as light-hearted."

Arden was not inclined to say more, and Sally did not push him. She could not put her finger on his brooding. Was it loneliness? Shame? Anger? Or was it normal to be disengaged and distant after all that time away from people with only water all around?

His short stay was also logistical: there wasn't room for two additional men in the house. Sally and John had moved the two children into their room and given Solomon the room where their children normally slept. Arden slept on quilts on the floor in the parlor. Besides, he had given a promise to his father that he would return quickly. He had promised to talk to the older man's business associates and learn more about the company dealings. *There is a place for you in the company if you want it*, his father had written.

~

But he did not want it. He returned from Ohio and spent several weeks in his father's office. There were letters and meetings and hours of scanning through columns of numbers in books. A person needed to be hired for the warehouse. There were documents to be translated. There were inventory records that should be compared. It was a small company with only five employees. From what he could tell, they were competent people, and they were patient with Arden when they explained the tasks that needed to be done. He understood that it often took more of their time to explain than to manage the chores themselves.

There was little he liked about his home town. After years on a ship, he was not at ease with the clamor and noise on the streets. Beyond that, the politics of America annoyed him: its divisiveness over slavery and its hypocrisy about inalienable rights that were granted to only white men. Greed, rather than progress, prevailed. Factories and businesses prospered while the tenements of Baltimore filled to the brim. He was not ready to imagine himself as a man who required ledgers, a desk, particular clothes, and an air of sophistication.

At home, his father talked less, slept more.

Arden met with the company's lawyer. "What would happen if my father's company no longer existed?"

"There would be other companies that would be happy to take over the work."

"And the employees that work for my father?"

"They could likely as not get jobs just as good somewhere else."

"And the warehouse? The office? The inventory?" Arden had asked.

"You'd get money from the sale of the warehouse and the bottles inside it. There are some large bills to be paid, but with the sale, you'd be ahead. The office is rented year by year. When the lease is up, you'd walk away unfettered."

For another ten days, Arden went to the office and warehouse, conflicted. He told no one of his conversation with the lawyer. But ten days was the extent of his wondering. One late afternoon he was sent a message from Owen saying he should come home. *Your father has suffered a second stroke.*

After that, his father lingered for another two weeks. His speech was gone and he was bedridden. Arden went to the office in the mornings then spent afternoons reading books to his father. He learned to interpret the small gestures of his father's eyes when Arden asked simple questions: *should he stop reading or continue? Should he let the light in or close the curtain? Would he like a drink of water?*

How could the wasting away of his father's body be accompanied by the gain of something that had never been there between them? There was less of his father, but there was more of him, too.

Early one morning Owen woke Arden to urge him to come to his father's room. Twenty minutes later Richard was gone.

~

There was no need for a large funeral. He wrote Sally and told her the burial would be small, and that she, with small children at home, must feel no compunction to attend.

He began the slow process of shutting down his father's business, discarding the contents of the house, and finding new positions for the servants. It was gloomy: the reading of his father's letters and business dealings, the emptying of drawers—including contents with a few items left of his mother's—and the persistent understanding of how alone he was. A letter came from Sally that cheered him.

Dear Arden,

We agreed to take Solomon because it was the right thing to do. John and I had talked all along should we be part of the underground railroad if we lived in a state with slaves. But I have to admit, it was one thing to do all that talking and another to have a sick, broken-boned man appear out of nowhere, along with my brother who had grown himself up since I saw him. You came on those horses and I thought, Lord, give me strength, two babies and now a man with black skin and crutches.

But it has been nothing like that. Two days after you left, Abby climbed right into his lap. Now, Solomon tells her stories and sings her songs. He plays little games with her and she is content if he is nearby. Three nights ago Solomon put Simeon to sleep by saying his Shakespeare, then Solomon thanked me for giving him a chance to remember the words instead of me thanking him for giving me a night off from putting our baby to bed. Somehow, even with his crutches, he helped John with the pruning of the apple trees and I heard them laughing out among the rows. Before now, John hasn't laughed much in these years on the farm.

When he needs to sit down, Solomon sits at the table and cuts potatoes or carrots. He cards my wool. He helps me make jam. And do you know that he has the most beautiful handwriting? Not this one, of course, but I dictated to him a letter to a friend and he wrote it so I could keep knitting. And he is quick to hold the baby when I have chores to do.

He wants to leave us as soon as he can find work, says we have done too much. But we are in no hurry. The children have grown fond of him and would miss him if he were to go. As would we. The money that you put in the bank here for land, we are wondering… We are wondering about selling him ten of our acres? It might help us to buy some machinery for our trees, and we have more land than we need. The land that we'd sell him would be good land, suitable for orchards. We could be neighbors and that would be good for all of us.

Arden wrote back immediately and agreed to the sale. He stayed in Baltimore another four months. The employees of the company were let go with a severance. The company assets were sold and debts were paid. The house, too, was sold, and Arden sorted and sold or gave things away. His father had not been a social man, but word spread through town of his death and of Arden's presence as an eligible bachelor. Women who had known his mother made his acquaintance, especially women with daughters. They were helpful with the distribution of the contents of the house, and he was willing to attend dinners in their homes, but after years on a ship with wide open skies, he found the dinner parties confining. Although he found more than one young woman attractive, he struggled to find anything of substance he could say when he was expected to make conversation.

The house sold quickly, and there was no reason for him to stay in the city any longer. He packed a crate full of items for Sally. There was money enough for Sally and John to add on to their house. And more besides that. He put his half in the bank. He left Baltimore in June of 1861 and traveled to Ohio, where he spent the summer and fall with them all in their green valley full of apple trees. Solomon had not only healed; he was becoming strong. The sale of the land to Solomon was finalized, and together they all planted trees on his land and worked on building a cabin. Arden spent time with the children; now he was Uncle to Abby and Sim.

Until the building projects were finished—the addition to John and Sally's house and the new cabin for Solomon—Arden slept in a tent that he had brought with him along with a cot and a mattress. *More comfortable, by far, than the bunk on a ship*, he told them. It was summer, and he was fine in the yard. There had been money enough to hire a carpenter right away. By the time it was autumn, he and the children had new rooms in the house and Solomon would move soon to his own home nearby.

But Arden did not stay many nights in the new addition. The confederacy had seceded and the Union was recruiting men to fight. Sailors were needed. The Union Navy had ships, so he joined. His enlistment was easy, and by December, Arden was hoisting sail again and eating fish every night of the week.

He was on ships for five years while people took sides in the war. Young men on both sides had grown angry enough to shoot guns through trees, into fog-filled meadows, and over farm fields because they were told other men were their enemies. Men on each side wanted their own version of America so badly they would die for it. And women on every acre of land in both the North and the South grieved for husbands and brothers and fathers and sons.

He spent most of his twenties at war. The Navy was not that much different than merchant ships, some captains skilled and some not. A lot of time waiting for orders. When they came into ports, there was talk of battles and skirmishes, politics, and burial grounds. Whenever they landed, there were newspapers to read with reports of defeats and of victories, of which side was ahead. Of assassination. Of surrenders. But mostly Arden raised sail, stayed alert on his watch, played cards down below when the winds were too cold or the seas were too rough to stay up on deck. There were moments of danger when the supply runs they made coincided with battles. There was stink when they began carrying wounded men back home.

In the letters that Arden and he wrote to each other, Solomon said watching apple trees grow was not a good way to help other men become free. He was ready, he said, to leave Ohio, to join up. He had planted trees on his land, and for a time he had thought about staying. There had been Alice, a woman who had come north with so many others. A woman who had scars both inside and out but sang deep and clear and true like a flowing river. She was enough to make Solomon think twice about leaving. But she did not stay, so neither did he.

For fourteen months, Arden and Solomon sailed up and down the Atlantic coast, taking ammunition and food and blankets and gunpowder to men who said men with black skin were worth dying for. The last year of the war was the hardest. Brutal battles and so many wounded men. Countless men lay on deck or in quarters or the ship's hold, men with gangrene in their feet or arms that were bloody stumps. Men that had nothing left in their faces where eyes had once been. Men who'd had no idea that war did not mean some kind of glory. Men who'd had no idea that coming home with only one eye or no hand to hold a plow was the kind of sacrifice they had been asked to make.

~

After the war was over and they were finally sent home in 1866, Arden and Solomon went back to Ohio. They stayed through a summer and a fall and a winter. All around them was grieving for men lost at war. Everyone in the valley was tired of talk of politics and battles; they were happy to send children to school and to build coops for their chickens. It was respite to watch apples grow and to pick them. They worked hard at the cider presses. They pruned trees. The trees that Sally and John had planted four years before when Solomon had first arrived to stay with them were maturing.

But after a second year in Ohio, in 1868, both Arden and Solomon began to feel restless. Solomon had deeded the land back to Sally and John before joining Arden in the Navy. There were not enough blacks in the valley for Solomon to feel welcome, for him to think of that land as his home. They all knew without saying he was too out of place to stay there forever. It had been a good dream they had had, for him to own his own orchard, to farm next to them, to live as equals and friends. But it was a dream like the mists that settle on apple blossoms in the morning and are gone in the harsh afternoon sun.

"I prefer ships and the water to trees and the dirt," he told them. "Though, please, never think I'm not grateful." So just after winter, the two men left. Arden had been ready for months. The Great Lakes were opening up. Trade was bustling. With the money his father had left him added to savings of his own, Arden could buy a ship. Solomon and he spent time in docks searching; they talked to shipbuilders; they shopped in marinas and shipyards. They found the *Jenny Marie,* and she had been a good choice. Their crew, with a few exceptions, had been competent and good companions while they sailed for two seasons on the Michigan side of the lake.

15

ARDEN'S LAST HAULS to Shallow Island in the fall of 1871 had gone smoothly. Boggs, for all of his unpleasantries, paid promptly and well. In their final trip of the season, they removed six men from the island, men who were ready to get out of the October weather. It was getting too cold to mix concrete and mortar, so the construction on the building project was shutting down for the season.

When the passengers were delivered and the signal lights throughout Lake Michigan were turning off for the year, Arden still did not release his crew. The ship needed to be readied for winter. For two years he had stored the boat in Chicago, but he had come to trust the Milwaukee dockmen and their harbor master who told him the Milwaukee River was a good place for his ship to winter. It was brutal work for them through December. Sleet and cold and the wind off the lake made their days miserable. They lodged in a rooming house near the river with other men who were also working on ships. Solomon needed to lodge farther away, in a part of the city where blacks offered housing to other blacks. He had not been welcome in the same space as the rest of the crew. Arden did not like the living quarters, but it would be temporary. The lodgers were coarse men who drank too much. Arden allowed drink on his ship and among his men, but never in excess.

Sails came down off their rigging. Arden had hoped to put the sails away dry, but there were more days of icy rain than there were of sun, so at last they folded them damp and hoped they would not mold over the winter. It took two and sometimes four men to fold and cover them, to haul them below. Every part of the rigging that could come off did. The lifeboat was covered. The latches were oiled. Ropes were stuffed into gaps and caulked. The *Jenny Marie* was lined right next to ships like her. By December there were lines of ships up and down the banks stripped naked and bare. Like trees without leaves, the boats looked skeletal, stern. By Christmas, everything, whether man-made or natural, waited stoically for winter.

Oscar, Finn, and Lam had jobs in Milwaukee waiting for them once they finished with the *Jenny Marie*. The men would be ice-cutters through winter. The ice blocks they would cut from the frozen lakes in Wisconsin would be stored in warehouses in hay and sawdust and would last well through the following fall. Each man promised Arden they would go to no other ship than his when he needed them again in the spring. The final two seamen had already told him they wouldn't rejoin the next year. "I have no regrets, and I'm grateful to you, Captain. But I want land, and I hear they are selling it cheap in the Dakotas," Allen had told him. Gregory had a mother he needed to see in Michigan. He doubted that he would come back.

~

Solomon and Arden had plans, as usual, to go to Ohio for the winter. It was the closest thing the two men had to a home, and

Sally and John appreciated the winter help. In the past three years since Arden owned the *Jenny Marie*, Solomon and Arden had come in the winter to help them add on to their barns, prune trees in their orchards, repair broken machinery, and do whatever else needed doing on the farm.

When Arden was satisfied that he had done everything he could to the ship, they said good-bye to the *Jenny Marie,* sitting idle and bare-boned in Milwaukee. The two men traveled to Ohio in December, two weeks before Christmas. When Arden and Solomon walked in on a blustery day, Sally was all smiles.

"You have made it! We are so ready for you!" She hugged her brother first and then Solomon. "The children are so excited they can hardly stand it! When is Uncle Arden coming? When is Grandpa Sol coming? They ask the same question ten times a day!"

John came from the barn and greeted the men warmly. Sally had soup ready for supper, and the men ate it eagerly, hungry after their train ride and the six mile walk from the station.

Abby was twelve and Sim was now ten. Arden met them on the path as they came home from school, and the children were all chatter and excitement until dinner. They wanted a snowball fight with Arden in the yard. They begged both men to come to the stable to see the family's horse. Abby showed them her drawing, Simeon wanted to play jacks.

"These children are still exhausting, Sally!" Arden laughed, when she announced it was bedtime.

"And you both must be tired. We will have many days to talk."

January and then February came and went. Solomon and Arden were happy to help with chores during the day, to play with the children during the evening, and to talk in the living room around the fire at night.

There was snow, but there were days of balmy sunshine, too. Days where they raked under the trees or trimmed branches. John was glad for their help this year building a small tool shed.

At day's end, Solomon worked on memorizing *Henry IV*. Sally and he talked about Dickens. They all read and discussed the articles that they read from *Harper's Bazaar*.

One evening, John was out at a church meeting, and the children were asleep. Solomon and Sally and Arden sat together in comfortable chairs, reading. Sally put down her book. "I never heard the whole story, you know, about the day you two met."

"It is not a good story," Arden said.

"That is not true, Arden." Solomon said quietly. "It is a very good story." The two men were silent. She waited for one of them to proceed.

"Do you know where I was, Sally? The summer that I was fifteen?"

"You told me you were on a ship, Arden. That you were part of a crew."

"I was, Sally. I was." He took a deep breath, as if it hurt him to continue. "You were here already with John. Just married. I was alone that whole year while Father was away in Europe, and I don't think he cared whether either one of us was alive or dead."

"I think now he was grieving our mother."

"Yes, that is likely true. But he paid no attention to me. After our mother died, he went on a trip to England. He left me alone with the servants and Mr. Bradley who came every day to teach me. I had no one to talk to, no friends. I was there outside of town with nothing to do. I noticed an ad in a newspaper for ship's crew. Leaving Baltimore. You know that I'd spent time on our uncle's ships for three summers before, so I thought I would be an adult. I would take my life into my own hands. I found the office the next day and signed on. I left a note the same day for our father and another one for my teacher saying I would be back in the fall."

"And you sent me a letter, too, saying the same. I remember."

"I was so proud of myself. I took the small amount of allowance money that father had left me to pay for a horse to take me to the dock. I had been instructed to arrive early, before dawn, and I did."

As a habit Arden did not drink alcohol in the evening, but he got up, went to a cupboard and poured himself a glass of sherry. He offered the same to his sister and Solomon, but they shook their heads. They waited for him to continue.

"As soon as I arrived, we set sail. The crew had been waiting for me. The first mate, a man named McRee, yelled at me to stow my duffle and go help with the lines. Within minutes we were out of the harbor and sailing right into the sunrise. There was the usual excitement of raising the sail, of feeling the wind catch, of the captain steering the wheel and heading into open sea. I was busy with lines and had hardly more than a few moments to get my bearings on the ship, to see who else was on crew. It had happened so suddenly. We were immediately at sail."

Sally started to ask him a question, but Arden shook his head. "We were well out of the harbor, maybe five miles out from land when the door to what I assumed was the hold opened, and a man climbed out. He was carrying a gun."

"Speak now all you want! Speak! I say, like animals, speak!" I did not understand what he meant. He snarled his words, half like a joke and half like a command. He motioned to one of the crew. "Go down now and ungag them." A youngish man, not much older than I, went down the same ladder, and in minutes I heard both men and women yelling and cursing and moaning."

"I knew it almost immediately, though I could hardly believe it was true." Again, Arden's voice got quiet. He practically whispered the next words.

"*Slaves*, Sally. *Slaves*. Mostly kidnapped freedmen. I was crew on a ship that was carrying *slaves*."

"Oh, Arden. You never told us."

"How could I tell you? To this day I find it reprehensible. To this day I hate what I did."

"It sounds as if you were trapped—every bit as kidnapped as the men below."

"No, Sally. You cannot call *me* kidnapped. *I* was not in chains. *I* was not the one gagged in the harbor. Lyons had kept them quiet through the night in the harbor by drugging them, then holding a gun to their heads if they started to stir.

"The owners of the ship, our bosses, had a scheme. It was well established from years of this wickedness. They paid money to kidnappers and traffickers to find men and women. They kept these people chained in a barn on the outskirts of Baltimore. When they captured and gathered enough—about thirty—they drugged them and gagged them and carried them like bundles onto the ship in the black of night just before they sailed out. If anyone woke up in the night, Lyons was there with a gun to keep them silent. And then we sailed off, just a few hours later, in the morning.

"I threw up. I vomited all morning. I considered jumping overboard and swimming to land. I vowed I would jump off at whatever port we came into and report them to the constables."

All three were silent. Finally, Sally spoke.

"How horrible, Arden. I wish you had told me before," his sister said softly. "You were a child. You cannot hold yourself responsible."

"You are wrong, Sally. I *am* very much responsible." He took a sip of his sherry. "Because I did *not* get off at the first port. I did not report them to a constable. No. I stayed aboard for six more runs, or was it seven? They told me I needed to stay, so I did."

Arden sat like a man who was beaten or flogged. He had finished. Sally and Solomon watched him, moved by his pain. The older man stood up and went to Arden. With gentleness, he put his hands on Arden's head for a moment, as if blessing him.

"Hell is empty, and all the devils are here."

"Which play?" Sally asked quietly.

"The Tempest. Act 3, I believe." He continued speaking with Sally. "Arden has not gotten to the *good* part of this story, to the part where he is *good*. But perhaps this is enough of the story for tonight."

When Arden stood up, Sally hugged him for a long time; her face was streaked with tears. "You were young, Arden. So young." She pulled back from the hug and looked at him straight in the eyes. "I am so sorry for you, my little brother. And now I am glad you have told me."

She checked the wick in the lamp at the window so it would burn bright until John came in. First Solomon and then Arden went to the outhouse and then to the beds in their rooms.

16

EVEN BEFORE SHE remembered it was Christmas, in the early stage of awakening, Kate heard the silence. It took her a moment to realize what was different. It was the lack of waves. Waves were the constant backdrop of their life at the Light. Even on early mornings when the lake was like glass before the morning breezes came in, there was a *lap*, a gentle *swush*. Theirs was a rocky beach, so normally the water rolled small stones up with a *gurgle* and *splash*, back with a *gurgle* and *splash*. In storms, waves pounded and crashed. In gales that blew up high breakers, the family needed to raise their own voices to talk over the roar. In all seasons but winter, the constant motion of water meant perpetual noise.

The quiet made her come suddenly awake. She roused herself from bed and looked out the window; the sun was only now rising as the barest light filled the east. Jack's place beside her was empty and cold; he often rose quietly to start the morning before her. After years of his erratic risings in the summer nights to tend the Light throughout the dark, it was not unusual for her to have missed his leaving her this morning. She dressed hastily and went into the kitchen where a fire had been lit in the kitchen stove. Jack's drained coffee cup sat on the table. She looked at the empty coat peg and the empty spot by the door where his boots were kept. Kate threw on her cape and gloves and walked quickly to the overlook to scan the view to see if she could locate Jack. She glanced at the spot where they kept the scope and took it with her to cross the yard to the overlook at the top of the bluff.

Before Kate even reached the clearing and the viewing spot, the reason for the silence was immediately apparent. Huge sheets of ice had drifted in from far out in the middle of the water. No waves could find their way to the shore. Instead, the waves of the huge lake were muffled, held captive and silent underneath huge horizontal walls of ice.

Where yesterday anyone could have walked on the sandy shore, today an additional twenty feet of temporary, white shoreline extended out in the water. The sheets of ice were thick, and already she saw children, just specks in the distance way across the harbor, playing on the icy strand. She also saw a new ship in the harbor. It was still, so it must be at anchor. It would have been at risk from the weight of the ice floes had it been caught at the pier, so it was wise to be tied up away from the shore. There would likely be discussions in the village as to how well the pier itself would fare against the assault of the ice.

Although ships were rare in winter, they were occasional, so she quickly surmised that Jack's early morning absence was related to the ship at harbor. It was possible that the captain had been chased into harbor by the ice, or perhaps he was delivering more metal to the blacksmith who was waiting, she knew, for a delivery. Now, with the ice, it would have to wait in the harbor to unload. Either the ice would break up as it sometimes did at this time of year, or they would do the unloading in a dinghy by taking small batches one at a time to shore.

It was cold, but the lack of wind meant that it was not uncomfortable for Kate to take in the view that lay before her. As the sun made its way higher in the morning sky, rays of light caught the snow and ice that surrounded her, and everywhere that she looked was a glistening wonderland. Below her and way across the bay, she could make out a figure leaving the dock and coming her direction. She was fairly certain it was Jack, hurrying home. It would be at least a half hour's walk before he arrived. She could tell he was walking quickly. She knew he would be anxious to return before the children woke up on Christmas morning.

Christmas, she thought to herself. *Merry Christmas, Kate*, she said to herself cynically. She did not share Jack's love or his enthusiasm for this day. She tried to be cheerful for the children's sake, and it was true that their excitement helped. But for Kate, it was this season when she missed the elegance of the big East Coast cities she had left behind when she moved here with Jack. She found herself jealous of her sisters and the parties they would have attended for weeks; the special foods, the fine presents they would open, the gifts from the shops in Europe or straight from the new factories that could supply them with practically anything they desired. Their son Frank had arrived a few days ago, home from his studies at college. He had brought packages and letters from her sisters. Their newsy reports only contributed to Kate's envy.

Unlike her, Jack had not known lavish Christmases, and he, like the children, was content with the small, out-of-the ordinary surprises that made the day worth anticipating. Jack liked the simple pleasures of the children's toys, the silly games, and the meager gifts they gave each other. Both she and Jack were active in Advent activities at Church. This year especially, she had found herself feeling superior in that setting, too. There were no elegant candles, no embroidered altar cloths, no beautiful music to make

Christmas special. Jack, on the other hand, had grown particularly pious this Christmas. He said that Jesus being born into poverty was a lesson to them that "fancy" wasn't necessary. "And can you imagine what the shepherds were thinking out there in the field?" He was gushy with sentiment.

The religion here is fine, she thought, *but that is the most I could call it. How can a person's faith grow in a tiny, cold, rough-hewn building with a pastor who is well-meaning, but mispronounces basic words when he reads? Who, when I asked him, said he does not like to read at all'?* She put such thoughts out of her head. She watched Jack coming close. He would be happy today, and his mood would be contagious. She was glad he would give that to the children.

Kate stood for a few more moments and watched the gulls rise in the morning sun, their wings reflecting golden light. The view in front of her *was* stunning. White snow dusted the evergreen branches of the trees above her. There was no breeze, no wind, not the slightest movement of air. Already the dim dawn had turned into bright morning; now the sky was blue and cloudless, the white snow glimmered, and the ice glinted as the bright sun fired the crystals into a thousand sparks.

As she watched Jack's progress toward her, she realized she could hear faint shouts of the children in the village playing on the ice. Someone else in the village was chopping wood. Then, a door slammed. In their five years at the Light, Kate had never before heard sounds from the village, and if anyone had asked, she would have thought it impossible that sounds could carry so far. The silence was remarkable.

As she turned back to the house, Kate grabbed some logs from the outside wood pile to throw in the stove. She went inside to stir up the fire and put on a kettle to have a cup of tea ready for Jack when he came in. She tried to work quietly in the kitchen, starting a few preparations for their big dinner later in the day. Amazingly, the children still slept, but Jack had barely walked in the door when Peter and Gillian scrambled over each other in their excitement to get down the stairs and into the kitchen.

"Merry Christmas," Jack yelled, and with one boot on and one boot off, swept them up together in a bear hug.

"Can we wake up Meggie and Philip and Frank? Please? Isn't it time to open presents?"

"You know the rule, children. Everyone must be here together, before we go into the other room and start with gifts," Jack said these words sternly with a hidden smile. "So, yes, go wake up your sister and brothers! Tell them to hurry."

Philip came down the stairs almost immediately. He sat down and stuffed some bread in his mouth as soon as he said "Merry Christmas." His father and mother laughed at him, and he smiled back, quietly. Frank poured himself coffee. Within a few minutes, Meggie was struggling in, dragged by her younger siblings, a big smile on her face.

"You're a beautiful Christmas package, Meggie," Jack said as he gave her a Christmas hug. Her disheveled, blonde-streaked hair hung in curls. She held hands and twirled in a circle with her little sister across the small kitchen floor.

The next few hours were noisy and clamored. Frank shouted as loudly as the younger children, and he wrestled on the floor with Philip and Peter. He insisted to Kate there would be no harm done by throwing the new ball back and forth across the room. Jack put Gillian on his knee and spoke very seriously to her new doll just as though she were a new member of the family. For Kate, there were three new books and a sweater knit by Meggie.

"How did you keep this a secret, Meggie? When I was last teaching you, you hated to knit, and you weren't very good at it!

Now look at this lovely stitching! It's all perfect and evenly lined up, just like you've been knitting forever."

"It's hard to have secrets from you, Mother, but I have a few," Meggie smiled. The rest of the family received new scarves knit by Meggie. Only Jack had known. It was he who had bought the yarn for Meggie last time he provisioned in Green Bay. Kate got up and headed for the kitchen. "I guess it's a day for secrets," Jack said, and the children giggled.

~

They'd agreed to eat only a large breakfast, not have lunch, and save room for a big evening dinner. Late in the morning, Kate was at work in the kitchen while the children and Jack played a new game in front of the fire. She had just begun to knead some bread when Jack opened the door to the kitchen.

"I've not got good news," Jack said quietly. "I've been waiting for a good time to tell you, but I think it might as well be now." Kate looked at her husband, searching his face for clues to what he was saying.

"The ship in the harbor has a sick man on it, Kate, and I've promised the captain our help." He paused. "I know it's not the way you want to spend Christmas, Kate, but I think you've got to go."

Kate sighed. She couldn't talk right away. She paid attention to the dough in front of her, thankful she had something to beat and pound at that particular moment. *This is perfect,* Kate thought sarcastically. *On my Christmas, I get to go to a cold, disease-infested ship to treat some drunken, smelly sailor. Back in Baltimore, my sisters are eating their Christmas feasts in warm, elegant dining rooms.* She did not voice any of her thoughts aloud.

Jack knew her well enough to wait for her to speak. Finally, she looked Jack in the eye. "Well, what's the problem, and why do they need me?"

"They've got a passenger on ship, and he's too weak and ill to even move. Perhaps infection, perhaps disease, they aren't sure. I spoke to the captain this morning, and they're quite certain that he needs medical attention. You know as well as I do that you're the only person in this town who can help." He paused. "It's Christmas, Kate. Wouldn't our Christ be glad that we're helping out on His day?"

"Don't be putting that religious talk on me, Deacon Jack." She said this with a bit of anger at her husband. "Of course, I will go, Jack, Christmas day or not. And you don't need to pressure me by adding this church talk."

"You're right, Kate. I'm sorry." He paused. "It's just that I am really hoping you'll go."

"All you needed, then, Jack, is to ask me. Give me some time to adjust to the idea. Yes, I am reluctant. But truly, I was only pausing to think about this bread rising, and about our dinner, is all." She took a deep breath. "When is the captain expecting us? Can we go soon, so we're home for dinner before dark?"

"My Kate," Jack said, as he gave her a big hug. "I love you for coming here with me to this wild, lonesome place, and I love you for your beautiful dark hair and your blue eyes, and I love you for your kindness."

Jack looked at her again, as if reading her mood. This time he looked even more bashful. "There's one last thing, Kate. Do you think you could spare some of your sweet holiday breads and some of your candies for the captain and his men? Of course, it's alright if you haven't enough to share, but I think you'd give the men on that boat some Christmas cheer if you had any to spare."

"Well, it means less for our dinner tonight, but I've got a few loaves and a few sweets I can wrap."

"Children," he walked into the other room, "we're going off to the *Osprey*, the ship in the harbor. Who wants to come?"

In under a half hour, all the children were wrapped in their warmest clothes and were waiting for Kate. She thought maybe Meggie or Frank would have stayed back, but they seemed willing and ready to come, so she kept quiet. Jack carried her medical bag, and the older children carried the food, so Kate's hands were free to hold Gillian's little mittened hand down the long steps to the beach.

17

ON THEIR WALK to the village, Frank and Peter challenged the rest of the family in a snow ball fight. The oldest and youngest sons ran far ahead and tried to pummel the others as they walked along the beach to the village. The siblings pummeled back, and in this way the whole family made slow but happy progress into town. Icicles dripped and glinted in the sun as they walked sometimes on the sand, sometimes on the ice banks.

As they drew close to town, Kate looked at the rows of houses that lined the main street. It was only two years ago that a second street had appeared with new houses. Smoke rose straight up from house after house. She knew, having been inside several of them to treat small ailments or injury, that today was a rare day of rest for most of her neighbors.

Compared to the majority of people in the village, their life as lighthouse keepers was comfortable. Although it involved plenty of hard work and included occasional danger, a well-built house was provided, as was a steady salary, and often, healthy portions of provisions. It was not so for many people in the village. Most stayed, but some left after a season or two, driven out by the hard work and the cold and the impossible odds of the first few years of settling in this rugged place.

The captain of *The Osprey* came walking up from the dock to meet the family. He must have been watching for their coming, as he met them at quite a distance. A dinghy from the ship was now tied up at the pier, and boards had been laid over the ice in a makeshift plank to give them access over the ice to the smaller boat.

Jack quickly introduced Kate to Captain Belder. The children followed behind them as they headed to where the dingy was tied.

"Children! You don't all need to come!" Kate was surprised that her whole family was following.

Jack interrupted. "It's fine, Kate. The captain told me he has children at home the same age as our Philip and Peter. He's missing them today, so we will all chat while you're busy."

"I should think the children would be happier in the village," Kate answered. "Besides, it will be cold on the ship!"

"It's alright," both Frank and Meggie said at the same time. "Besides, it's Christmas! We should be together as a family."

The other children hurried ahead and climbed into the small boat. Kate started to object again, but by then, the captain had already untied the small boat and was ready to row them the short distance to the spot where *The Osprey* was anchored. Crew from that ship waited, ready to help lift them with strong arms up onto the ship's deck.

The distance was short to where the ship was anchored out beyond the ice. While they waited for each of their children to be helped onto the ship, Kate turned to the captain. "What's his name?"

"Ma'am?"

"The sick man, what's his name, Captain? And please, how long as he been sick? What can you tell me of his problem?"

"Why Stein- Steinman, ma-am," he stumbled over his words. "You'll just have to see for yourself, please. I really can't say much of what's wrong with him."

She started to ask more, but Jack nudged her. A slight shake of his head was his way, she knew, of asking her not to say more. Captain Belder led her away from the sleeping quarters and toward the hold. Although Kate was no sailor, she had been in enough ships to know the standard layout of sailing vessels.

"Captain, surely, you don't put a sick man here in the hold? I'm disturbed, sir, that you wouldn't give him a better place in his misery."

Again, the captain appeared to stumble over his words. Jack gave another look as if to tell her to hold her tongue, but Kate persisted. She waited for his answer as he started down a ladder into the front of the ship's hold.

"When he got sick, ma'am, we isolated him from the other men. You'll see it's alright in just a minute. He's right over there by that light we've got set up for you."

The captain went first, then Jack followed. When Kate finished her climb down the few steps of the ladder, she waited for her eyes to adjust to the darkness. She looked over into a corner, lit with a few candles. She saw no bed, no person. Instead, the captain pointed to a very large box.

"Captain, I'm afraid I don't understand!" Kate was not usually given to anger, but she felt it rising up. Before she could speak further, Jack was at her side. He had taken her hand and was leading her nearer the light and the huge wooden carton. The children came quickly behind her, and as they approached the big box, Jack and the children yelled, "Surprise! Merry Christmas!"

It took Kate a moment to absorb what was happening. As if in slow motion, she saw Jack and the children's faces: happy, bright, eager, excited, and all of them gathered around the big box in front of her. The box was open only on one side and inside was a large, beautiful piano. It was constructed of mahogany wood with intricately carved legs and inlaid ivory cutwork over the keys.

"It's all yours, Kate. We had it shipped to Chicago, and my friend, Captain Belder, arranged to have it loaded onto his ship and bring it here to you. He is delivering canvas for the sailmaker as well. It was God's doing that they arrived last night, just as the ice came in. It's God's doing that it came in on Christmas, don't you think? Merry Christmas, my love."

"But the sick man?'

Jack, the captain and the children laughed. "There is no sick man, Kate! How else could I have persuaded you to come to town on Christmas Day? I knew my only chance was to appeal to your kindness."

"I'm afraid I'm not a good liar, Ma'am," said Captain Belder. "It was not easy for me to think what to say to your questions! But this makes me happy, to bring you this present. I am glad I could be part of this gift."

The realization of what was in front of her was only just beginning to sink in. Kate sat down and fingered the keys gently, then sounded a chord. The captain had thought not only to bring a light for her, but a pot of hot coals sat near her feet to warm her. Meggie and Frank were still smiling as they watched her. The younger children were huddled close to Jack, wide eyed.

Captain Belder spoke again, "It will take a while—maybe even days—before we are able to move this box into town, Ma'am. It would be best if the ice floes go out and we can pull up to the pier to unload. But for today, we'd all appreciate it you'd play for us right here and now. You can play as long as you'd like."

Kate turned to the captain. "I have sorely misjudged you, sir. I am grateful for your help. I never dreamed of such a gift." She turned to Jack. "How did you d-"

Jack cut her off in mid-sentence. "Questions later, Kate. We want to hear you play."

Kate sat down and fingered the keys. "It's been a long time," she said. "I don't know how much I'll remember." She started with a few lonely notes with her right hand, then chords with the left, then melodies which came spilling out of fingers in a way mysterious even to her. "All those years of practice as a child have paid off, it seems."

Her children and Jack sat near her for three quarters of an hour. She played a hymn for Meggie and a Scottish tune for Jack and two short etudes by Mozart. She played a song her father had loved, a chorale by Bach, and a folk song for Peter. The acoustics were quite good in the hold of the ship; the lovely, resonant chords bounced warmly against the thick wooden walls. She looked at Jack. She looked at the happy faces of her children.

"I don't know what to say, Jack. I never in a thousand years thought I'd have a piano here, and yet you've brought me one."

"It's a beautiful sound to hear, Kate. Why don't you play a bit more while I take the children over to the Johansons? We'll leave you here by yourself for a while. You stay and keep playing. Come join us at their house when you're done, or else we'll come back for you in an hour or so."

"You couldn't have done anything better for me, Jack. I love this piano, and I love you." He smiled at her, gave her a quick kiss on the cheek, and then Jack left with the children.

When Kate was left alone, her songs strayed from the music she had learned and perfected and memorized in her years of study with classical teachers. Instead, she played her own improvisations, music that she made up as she went, songs that she played by ear. Although she was accomplished at reading music and knew her classics well, it had always been when she put aside the sheets of music and played without inhibition that listeners took notice. When she had first met Jack and she played for him, he told her that the piano had never much appealed to him until he had heard her play.

As she played in the dimly-lit cargo hold, her music made her reflective. She was chagrinned at her selfishness earlier that day. She thought of the loneliness that often beset her in this place. And Meggie. How could she let go of the worry she had for her daughter? Music was a language she missed speaking. She did not know, until she had it again, how empty she had been without it. *I think this is the way that I pray,* Kate thought.

Over an hour later, Kate came back to Christmas. With strong chords she started with *The First Noel,* followed by *Hark the Herald Angels Sing,* and *O, Holy Night.* She played every carol she remembered. With *O Come All Ye Faithful,* she played her last notes of the day and sighed deeply.

She had been inside the dark hold for almost three hours; the coals at her feet were out, and her fingers were stiff and cold. Kate closed the piano gingerly, tenderly, and climbed up the ladder onto the deck of the ship. When her eyes adjusted to the brightness, another surprise awaited her.

Totally unbeknownst to her, a crowd had gathered on the shore right in front of the ship. The entire village was there, and as she climbed the ladder to the ship's deck, a quiet applause began. Gradually, the whole town was clapping. Men, women and children were on their feet, some even cheering. Surprised, she smiled, gave a slight wave, then scanned for Jack in the crowd. In a few minutes she was back to shore in the dinghy, and a few people who knew her best stayed a moment to speak to her. Most of the others yelled out "thank you" as they gathered up their blankets and their families and walked back to their homes. Jack and the children soon surrounded her, and within a few minutes, there were only a few clumps of people who remained. Two men shoveled snow on a fire that had been burning in their midst. It had kept the crowd warm as they had gathered to listen to Kate's concert.

The afternoon light was waning. It would be dark in an hour, Jack reminded her, so they started home. On the way, he and the children gave her details of the remarkable afternoon.

"I hadn't given even a thought that people could hear me!" said Kate. "I thought maybe the sailors, but certainly no one else."

"Sound traveled far today. Everyone commented on it. This quiet day meant your music drifted up and down the streets, up to the top of the bluff and as far away as the Riding Dawn Stable," Jack told her. "Jensen told me that as soon as he heard the music ever so faintly, he quickly put his wife and children on the horses, and they galloped in to be close."

"Others did the same, Ma. Because it was so still, the music carried everywhere, and people came here to be close enough to hear every note."

"When we left you, Ma, they were already beginning to gather. They were coming with blankets to sit on and more to be wrapped in. After a short time, Mr. Warren built a fire to keep us all warm, so everybody just sat and listened. Nobody talked. Nobody wanted to miss a single note of the beautiful music."

"I saw grown men and women brought to tears, Kate." Jack added. "Got me emotional, too, just watching them get all misty eyed, and happy, and wistful. They had the looks on their faces like they were in a faraway place, back to their pasts, somewhere other than here and this hard-scrabble life they lead."

"Not everyone was crying, Pa!" Peter piped in. "Most people looked happy to me! Mr. Jensen, he was dancing! He gave his baby to Mrs. Olanski to hold, and he danced with his wife whenever you played something fast. And the carols, Ma! You really didn't hear us singing the Christmas carols?"

Kate shook her head no.

"Yes, that was the best part," Philip said. "Everybody sang, excepting Margaret Brewster and Emmett Higgins, but they never do what they're supposed to."

"It was like angels singing, Kate. The whole town sang *Hark the Herald Angels Sing,* even Mr. Whitfield. He stood off by himself, and he still scowled, like he does about everything, but even still, he was singing Christmas carols."

They walked home as quickly as they could, stepping mostly in the tracks they had made earlier that day in the snow.

"It's a very good present you gave this village today, Kate." Jack said as they walked together, Kate's arm in his.

"Thanks to you, Jack!" Kate smiled at him affectionately. Gulls flew over their heads, and as the sun began setting, they all felt the temperature dropping.

"Well, I admit, I was pretty sure *you'd* be happy, Katie, but I hadn't planned on the village enjoying the concert. That was God's doing. Call it the-gift-of-the silent-day or the-gift-of-the-ice-floes, but I will call it a gift right from the hand of God. I watched their faces as they listened, Kate. They were like thirsty people drinking water."

Meggie laughed and rolled her eyes. She came closer to Kate and put her mittened hand in her mother's. "You are being a bit melodramatic," she said to her father. "But it *was* great, Ma." She continued, "I've heard you sing plenty, Ma. I've heard pianos in Toledo and in Chicago. I even remember the organ in Baltimore when you took us there when I was still little. But I'd forgotten how pretty *your* music is, Ma. I realized today that there are people here, especially some of the children, who have never heard beautiful music in their lives. We have a few fiddles, and Mr. Jansen's flute, and of course there's hymn singing on Sunday, but Ma, I know this is the prettiest music some of these people have ever heard. Father, you did a really good thing, bringing this piano here to Mother."

They were quiet the rest of the way home. The cold made them walk quickly, and the boys let it be known they were hungry. Right before they reached the bottom of their long steps up to the top of the bluff, Jack sent the younger boys on ahead. "Philip and Peter, run ahead of us and get that fire in the stove blazing. We'll all be ready for some warmth!"

Kate gave the girls directions about preparations for dinner as they walked the steps to the top of the bluff, then trudged the last steps on the path that led to their home at the Light. Jack lagged behind for a moment while Kate and the girls talked.

He looked back across the harbor and at the ship, and at the lights beginning to come on in the many windows in the town. He was a man who, at times like this, was full of emotion. His eyes filled with tears as he breathed a prayer of gratitude. Then, he turned around and walked quickly back to the house, grabbed a few more big logs for the fire, and stomped his boots on the stones outside. He would be happy for the warmth of his family inside. He could hear their laughter even through the thick walls.

"Merry Christmas!" he called out, and he pulled the door shut on the darkening night.

18

THE MCGINNS WOKE up to light snowfall. The younger children had been back at school for a few weeks since Christmas. They had gone off early as usual, but at ten in the morning, a blizzard was on them. Jack went into town, took them out of school and walked them home. In that short span, maybe only an hour and a half, at least three inches of snow had fallen. More fell throughout the afternoon.

Kate worked with the children on their studies in the afternoon, and by 4:00, when the boys wanted to go outside and build a snowman, there were ten inches of snow on the ground. Jack announced it would be good if everyone went out—perhaps an entire snowman family was needed. Gillian was delighted and asked if her father could help with hers.

Jack strung a line from the oil house to the edge of the house and hung lanterns. The snow waned, and the winds that had swirled the snow earlier were gone. By evening, there was a crystal clear sky and even a reddish sunset in the west as the light faded. Stars began to appear.

They ate soup for dinner, and bread that Meggie and Kate had made earlier. The exercise had done them all good, and they were chatty around the table.

"I am thinking of leaving after next summer," Meggie announced.

"Meggie? Can I go with you? Where are you going? Can I help you pack your clothes when you go?" Gillian was immediately full of questions.

"What do you think you will do?" her father asked.

"I am thinking of starting a business in Toledo."

"I assume you understand that it is not easy for women on their own in business," her father offered slowly, taking care not to respond quickly. "I am not saying that it is right, but many people think that business is for men, and that…"

"And that a woman belongs in the home." Meggie finished his sentence. "Of course, I know that. But in Toledo, there were widows who ran boarding houses. I bought dresses from a woman who owned her own dressmaking company and hired five women employees to sew for her. And there was a third—I don't know if she was a widow or if she was single and never married, but everyone I met in Toledo bought their hats from that woman milliner. So it's possible."

"Of course it's possible, but in the future." her mother joined in. "The women's suffrage movement is growing. I think we will have the vote in not too many years. And with that will come more opportunity for women. I think our time will come, but it is not quite our time yet."

"Why Toledo?" her brother asked.

"I liked it there with George. I made friends. His mother and sister are there. His sister's husband is a banker, and would help me, I think. He has helped me already with the money George left me."

Jack was quiet. "I think it is risky, Meg. And I hate that you would go so far away from us here. Couldn't you stay here and find something to do? This town is growing, too. If it's business you want, the needs for shops and stores will only grow here on the peninsula."

"And is it so necessary to leave *us*? Why do you prefer your in-laws over us?" Kate asked.

Meggie answered her quickly. "This is not about your feelings."

"She is right, Kate." Jack said. They exchanged a look between them. Kate got up from the table and started cleaning the supper dishes.

"Meggie," he addressed his daughter, "you are welcome to be here as long as you would like. But you are an adult. We do not expect you to be with us forever. We will help you as much as we can. I don't think it's a good idea, but that doesn't mean I would stop you. And, this is still months away. There is a lot of time to think, to make decisions and plans."

Kate said nothing else for the rest of the meal. Thankfully, Gillian had asked how to spell the word *milliner.* Meggie agreed that they could make hats out of newspapers after dinner.

When the children were all in bed, Kate came in to Meggie's room. Meggie was at her desk writing, so Kate sat in her chair.

"I am sorry, Meggie. That was selfish of me."

"Sometimes I feel like you are perfect. But then you say things that make me wonder whether you understand me at all."

"Meggie, I am too quick to react. My first thoughts, and words, I'm afraid, are negative before they are kind. But here is the truth: I worry about you. You were happy with George and we were happy for you. You left for Toledo, and that was fine because you were married. We thought he was young, but we knew you would figure out life together. Losing George was not fair, and I suppose I am angry. But to go off by yourself? How can *that* be wise?"

"Ma, you of all people should understand that a woman can be independent! Look at you, out and about by yourself, doctoring every person in this town! You don't seem to need a man to show you what to do or tell you how to do it!"

"That's true, Meggie. But if I weren't married, I doubt the town would feel the same about me. Other women in other places who do what I do are viewed with suspicion. In some places they might even be called witches." She continued, "I agree that these limits they put on us are nonsense. It was not so many years ago that women kept farms alive as their men went off to die in the War Between the States. And who but women kept men breathing in all those battlefield hospitals? *Nurses*, they say, with a voice that belittles their contributions. I know those nurses were as much doctor as the men with that title. The doctors were spread as thin as a mist. *Women* were the ones who doctored the men dying of wounds or typhus or dehydration or sepsis from their amputations. *They* did the work, Meggie. But was that ever acknowledged? It was only the men that were ever talked about. Too many people think it is men that must run things. I am afraid there are people who will stand in the way of you starting your own business. They will not let you succeed."

"Well, Father is right. There is time. I am not sure what I will do, yet. But I cannot stay here in this town, at this Light. I have a life to live elsewhere, and it can't be with you and Father and my siblings. It is not that I want to leave you; it is that I must have my own life."

Kate went close to her daughter and hugged her. "I don't like it, Meggie. But I accept that you want something different than this. I will try not to be hurt when you are ready to leave us again. I should say, actually, that such thoughts on your part mean you are healing. After George. And I'm thankful for that."

Kate went downstairs to the living room. Meggie took up a book to read and sat in the chair that was still warm from her mother's presence. After a few chapters of reading, she transferred her light back to her desk and wrote in her diary.

Meggie's Diary *January 28, 1872*

There are many ways to live without a husband. I dream other dreams than my friends, other dreams than the girls who want only marriage, girls like I was five years ago. I will not be inside a home hiding in sorrow. I will go outside of my home, doing what most women can do but don't. A publisher? A woman who employs sailmakers for the ships that sail past this Light all summer? A store owner that sells perfumes and linens imported from France? I have watched what men do and cannot see why a woman can't do the same.

Unlike my mother, I do not like bodies, the way they get sick and the way they heal. I have looked at my mother's books, the ones that give every muscle a name, the ones that show veins and arteries and the chambers of the heart and the exact location of a kidney just under the diaphragm. When she is called to the people who need her in the village, she does not complain. I think she is fascinated by the way a bone can break and heal, how a simple medicine can help with pain. But I am not enamored of bodies. What do I love? Maybe books. Possibly flowers or vases or clocks. The color that fills the shelves in Kira's home when I walk in, and everything arranged to be pretty. I think I would like to sell pretty things in a store.

My parents will not stifle a venture of mine to leave here, to use the money I was left by my George. I will do something other than marry, something better than marrying.

19

DURING THE EVENING conversations in the sitting room at the farm in Ohio, they had not returned to the subject of Arden's past. Sally knew enough to give her brother time since their earlier conversation. Their daughter Abby was sick with a cold so there were distractions. The three men spent their days together in chores, and the shed they were working on was nearing completion. They had just over a month before they'd go back to the *Jenny Marie.*

One afternoon, when rain began falling, they came in for a cup of tea.

"I am thinking back of your first months with us, Solomon," Sally said as the men settled in at the table. "Do you ever wish you still lived here instead of going off to the war? Do you think that it might have worked to stay here in this valley? To have been our neighbor for the rest of your life?" Sally asked him.

"The apples were good, and I liked to work with the trees. But I couldn't have stayed," he answered. "The two of you were the only ones who sincerely welcomed me. To everyone else I was an oddity at best, and a threat at worst." He was referring to what everyone in the room knew, that the color of his skin was unwelcome in their valley.

"There were a few others, I recall, who didn't treat you poorly." John added.

"Yes. You are right. A very few."

"I think things are changing," Sally said. "There is a town only forty miles from here with all black residents. Word is they are doing well, selling products, building houses and stores."

"Yes, people seem to let us have our own towns as long as we don't live next door. I could have gone to a town like that, I suppose, after giving up here. I'm sure I would have done fine. As long as we stay off to ourselves, segregated, white people think they have nothing to fear. But they don't seem to want us walking their streets or sending our children to their schools or using their libraries or serving on the town boards. So, no. I don't think I could have stayed here, even if I had wanted to."

"You have a good point," John agreed. "Our town is still fighting about how to educate black children. And it's pretty obvious that people like their white churches and their black churches staying just as they are."

"I will always be grateful for what your family did for me," Solomon told them. "All of you—your father and Arden and you and John—all of you gave to me more than I deserved. But do I regret leaving this place where I was the only black man? No, I have no regrets. Three-plus years was a good time to try. But no. When Arden sent word of the offer of the ship and the Union Navy, I was happy to return to the water."

"This is a good place to come back to in the months we can't sail, Sally," Arden jumped in. "I'm glad you welcome us back here year after year. But I think Solomon and I are the same—we miss the water when we're away from it."

"It is true," Solomon nodded. "To unpathed waters, undreamed shores."

Is that a quote from *The Tempest*?" Sally asked.

No, *The Winter's Tale.*

"Say it again?" John asked.

"To unpathed waters, undreamed shores.' It's the only line in that entire play I remember."

"Well, *that's* a first," Arden quipped. All of them smiled. Their tea break was over. The rain had stopped and they went back to work.

It was the 4st of March, three days before they planned to leave Ohio and go back to Milwaukee. The lights all over the Great Lakes would come on in early May, and Arden and Solomon calculated they'd need several weeks to get the *Jenny Marie* ready to sail.

"Will you tell me the rest of the story?" Sally asked after a big dinner. The children had gone off to bed. The day had been balmy, with sunshine and a hint of spring in the air. They had tapped the maple trees in their woods, and Sally boiled down enough sap to make a maple cake. Everyone had full stomachs, and the night had a feel of contentment.

Arden did not have to ask which story she referred to. He began. "When I *did* leave the Flying Falcon, I left without pay. McRee hammered it home when I thought about leaving, and he used it to get me to stay: *You signed on, boy. There will be no money until fall.*"

"I had only a few dollars to my name—the ones that I had carried with me and hadn't spent. It was enough to buy me a room in a hotel in Richmond—the place we were docked, but it was a place where I knew no one. We had other cargo to unload and, in a moment when they were not watching me carefully, I left the ship. I registered in a hotel under a name that was not mine, and I spent two nights in that room without leaving. Really, I hid there, without food. I am ashamed to say that I peed out a back window." All of them laughed.

"The hotel was in view of the dock, and I stood out of sight by the window and watched. I watched as they waited for me. I watched as McRee paced on the ship, looking angry. Finally, the ship sailed out of the harbor. I went down for some dinner and had twenty two cents left after I paid for my food. I had worked for two months and had no money to my name."

"Why didn't you come home then, Arden?" Sally asked.

"I was ashamed. I was also humiliated. I had been duped, and I felt if I told Father, he would like me even less. I was determined to earn money, and this time be wiser. I went back to the docks and asked around. *A big ship is coming in any day,* I was told. *If they want crew, you should sign on.* The harbor master took pity, let me sleep in a corner, and the next day the *Golden Star* sailed in. She was magnificent."

"That is the one where you sailed the world?" John asked him.

"Yes, for the next three and a half years. Bahamas, Dominico, Cuba, all the Caribbean Isles. Ecuador. Portugal and in to the Mediterranean. Capri and Cyprus. Spain and Morocco. And a ship with sails that sped us faster than light. I stayed for a while in Spain then signed on with another ship for just over a year.

"But five years was enough. When I landed back in Richmond, I had money enough to come home. I spent several days in the city. I bought clothes and shoes. I went to a lecture and a concert. There was a library, and I stayed there for two entire days, reading newspapers of things I had missed.

"One afternoon, I overhead news of an auction, a sale. There was excitement, and also whispers. I could sense by the way men were talking that it was furtive, clandestine. They mentioned property, and I thought they might be selling land. I had new clothes. I had been to a barber. Maybe these men thought I was the type of man with money. For whatever reason, they invited me.

"It was horrid. A slave auction. Slavery was still legal, although it was becoming less acceptable. They brought in men and women, a few children as well. People heckled, made fun, as if they'd attended for entertainment alone. The auctioneer was the same type of a man as McRee, cruel to his core, and inhuman. He'd say "*Turn to your left*, or *bend over*. If he or she didn't do as he asked, he whipped them."

He continued. "I had been away on a ship. I had been to glorious places. I'd wandered streets with cathedrals and eaten dinner in towns with white-washed walls. I'd seen castles with fountains and towers with roofs that shimmered like gold in the sun. In some of those places, people of all colors walked together on the streets. Slavery had been outlawed for decades in Europe, and people with black skin all over Europe walked the streets free. I had hoped, when I came back, that slavery was on its way out, that people here had changed when I was away."

Solomon picked up the narrative. "I was one of those ones being auctioned in that line. I had seen such things before, but I was older this time, less inclined to acquiesce." He shook his head, remembering. "Hmm." he sighed. "That man and his cruelty. Pulling down the blouses off of the women. Poking us like we were animals, making us look like we were not human."

"Solomon started reciting his Shakespeare," Arden continued. "But *that* made the whipman angry. He told him to be quiet. Solomon did not stop, so the man whipped him."

"I *did* keep on going, didn't I?" Solomon turned to Arden, remembering.

"You recited. He whipped you. You recited; he whipped you again. He yelled at you to stop. You did not. I think you spoke louder as you went along. He whipped you again. It was quite remarkable that you spoke as long as you did."

"It was quite remarkable that I remembered the lines, considering how much that whip hurt."

"At one point you fell down. You kept speaking! You got up again, and he just whipped you more."

"What were others doing? The ones that were watching?" Sally asked.

Arden paused. "When I was on the *Falcon*, McRee told me that I needed to think of those people below deck as livestock, a species beneath us in intelligence. I don't know if he believed that or if he said that in order to justify what he did. I tend to think he believed it. And I think the same about the men and women who were watching at the auction."

"In my experience," Solomon added, "there are very few white people that think of me as equal to themselves."

"To answer your question, though, Sally," Arden addressed her, "at first there was jeering. They were on the side of the auctioneer. But after a while, the crowd grew quieter. Who could not see what Solomon showed them? With every word that he quoted, we could see that he was more than we would ever be. The man that whipped him was in appearance a big man with a big whip, but in reality, he was a *small* man. Angry and mean. A quite *small man.*" He smiled at Solomon. "If ever there was a man with dignity, it was Solomon and his Shakespeare."

"I'm afraid I had quite a lot of blood, too."

"Yes, Solomon, you are right. A lot of blood." He turned to the others. "I bought him. I practically threw the money at them while they took him out of the shackles. I hired a carriage. It was not easy to find a doctor that would treat him, but after a few tries we did." He spoke to Solomon. "I was afraid you would die that night for lack of blood."

"It is a long way from Richmond to Baltimore, Arden." His sister wondered. "How long did it take you?"

"One carriage after another. All night and a day and then another three nights. We found Quakers outside Washington that helped us, and we slept for a night in comfortable beds. And then more carriages. Twice we were stopped and I told them you were my slave. Which I guess at the time was true. One of the first things I did when we got to Father's house was make sure you were free."

"And then it was only weeks after that that we met you," Sally said to Solomon. "Your infections were not good when you arrived."

"And the children were babies, then, weren't they? And now they are grown." Solomon reflected.

Sally addressed her brother, "It was a good thing that you did, my little brother."

"It was not good enough, Sally. Nothing I've done will ever make it good enough." Sally and Solomon exchanged looks and shook their heads.

"I wish you could believe otherwise," was Sally's response, but she knew she was unlikely to convince him.

Soon after, Solomon launched into a section of *Midsummer Night's Dream*, a scene that had them all laughing from his reciting.

20

WINTER LASTED WELL into March at Roundstone Harbor. The air began feeling different in April, but still there were snows. Jack lit the Light the first week of May, and now ships were coming with more frequency into the harbor. On any early June morning, Meggie and her father would generally have been together when they boarded a ship that tied up at the Roundstone Harbor docks. She didn't need protecting, but Jack knew sailors could be rough and crude, so it was his habit to accompany Meggie onto the pier. Today, however, Jack was particularly concerned about the bolts that were prying loose from the oars on the rescue rowboat, and being always conscientious about having the small craft ready and in good working order, Jack left Meggie at the edge of the dock. Jack walked quickly up the harbor road, onto the village street, and was soon on his way up the hill to the blacksmith's in search of what he needed for the oarlocks.

Meggie was led onto the *Jenny Marie* by one of the ship's men who had been sitting on the dock. He gestured for her to stop and wait on deck while he went in search of the captain. The view from the ship's rail was a fresh perspective of her village, and as she waited, Meggie mused for a few moments on the picturesque houses. Behind her, across the harbor, Roundstone Light stood stately, commanding. Although it was not even ten in the morning, the sun of early summer was shining brightly; the lake was a deep sapphire blue, and the waves were choppy. It would be a warm day—one for opening windows, airing out the house, and working without chill in the garden. She was content to let the sun warm her as she waited unhurriedly at the ship's rail.

When Captain Arden Anderson had been summoned about a message from a village woman, Meggie was not what he was expecting. The captain was usually non-plussed: all business, sparse with his words and not given to long conversation. But the sight of Meggie wearing a blue dress and smiling at the gulls above her, then chatting with the village sailmaker, was enough to make him pause in his steps. He watched her for a moment before she turned and realized his presence.

"Can I help you, Ma'am?"

"Good morning." She, too, hesitated. He was not what she had expected either. "I am here to ask about laundry. If you or your men have clothes that need washing or mending. We don't ask on every ship, just the ones that will be here more than a day or two. My mother has found that sailors often have this need. We both like to sew, and the price is reasonable."

"Thank you. I'll ask the men and bring you what we can. Where can I find you?"

"At the Light." She pointed to the house across the harbor. "It is a ways, though, as you can see. I am happy to wait if you prefer."

"No, it would do me good to be away from the ship for a few hours. What is the best way to get there?"

"There are two ways. You could take the beach, but then you'd need to climb the tall stairs up the bluff. With your sea legs, that might seem like climbing the Himalayas to you. Or, you could take the path through the woods. If you go past that last fishing shanty on the left, you'll see a path start on your right." He came next to her at the rail of the ship as she pointed out the path.

"It's hard to see from here, but once you're there, you can see a clear path that heads our direction. It winds through the woods for a while, and it's a little longer than the beach way, but the grade is gradual."

"And to what would you compare the path, since you are fond of geography?"

"An explorer's trek, perhaps? Like Stanley or Livingstone in Africa?"

Arden smiled. "Forgive me, but you seem very well read for a woman in the northern woods of Wisconsin."

"Then you shouldn't stereotype us all as the same!" She laughed. "But I suppose I was born into reading. My parents insisted that we all read, and I have kept up the practice. They wanted us to have an education equal to the ones they received in the best schools in the East, so we have a large library at home. And the library box that the Lighthouse board brings in our supplies is still my siblings' favorite part of the delivery. Every month or so we get a whole new set of books."

"So your father is Jack McGinn, the lighthouse keeper?"

"He is."

"I met him briefly last year. He has a good reputation among sailors."

"I'm sure he will stop by soon to meet you again. He saw you come in and was worried about the listing of your boat."

"It's not been an easy voyage. I am glad to be off of the lake and here in the harbor. We definitely need some repairs."

"Yes, we've heard that already from the talk in the town. The carpenter, Mr. Foster, in the town is new, so I can't speak about him. But we've got the best sailmaker in the whole peninsula right here in Roundstone Harbor, so you're in good hands in that regard."

The captain had not moved away from her after she had pointed to the trail. Neither had she. Meggie noticed the slight scent of lemon soap on his clothes and the smell of coffee on his breath. He had blonde streaks in his mostly brown hair. Arden liked the way she was unbothered by her unruly hair that had not stayed pinned back but was blowing about her face in the breeze. He liked the sound of her laugh.

"I hope for your sake the repairs won't be difficult."

"It's kind of you to say so." Arden would have continued, but a tallish man whom Meggie guessed to be a passenger came walking briskly to the point where the two were speaking. Dressed in expensive clothing, he looked rudely at Meggie and seemed eager to interrupt.

Immediately the captain's tone changed and he became brusque and businesslike. "Thank you for your offer, Miss," he said to Meggie, addressing her for the last time. "I'll speak to the men, and we'll bring you some things later on."

As Meggie left the ship, she overheard the man talking to the captain angrily. "The carpenter says three to four days! We don't have that much time! Captain, you've got to get us out of here faster than that! I simply can't stay here in this puny excuse for a village."

Meggie walked slowly down the gangway and then navigated her way through the fish nets and lumber on the pier. On the dock, she spoke to the men she knew who were unloading wagons and hauling huge boxes and crates. More and more ships came each day to pick up cargo from the town. The lumber camps outside town supplied wood to Chicago and the southern Midwest. The northern forests were still full, and although the logging teams were moving progressively inland, Roundstone Harbor's deep harbor had easy access for loading the ships. Beyond lumber and quarried stone and fish, there were other outgoing goods such as produce from the farms, or crates full of butter and cheese from the growing number of nearby dairy farms.

Meggie turned back to look again at the *Jenny Marie.* She flushed with the realization that the captain had been watching her for the several minutes since they had parted. The man with whom he had spoken was gone, and he was leaning on the ship's rail, eyes fixed on her. He raised his hand to her in a simple, understated wave.

Self-conscious, she waved back, but turned quickly away. Rather than have him watch her progress along the beach all the way to the Light, she chose the path in the woods and was quickly out of sight.

After Meggie walked out of his view, the captain continued to stand on deck and watch the activities of the men on shore and think about the startling young woman he had just met on the deck of his ship. It was a crystal clear morning; fishing boats were already at full sail, and children played on the beach.

It had been a difficult few days; they had weathered a dangerous storm with high winds and powerful waves that rent his mainsail to a point beyond repair. The storm had continued for hours and they had taken a battering from high waves. One wave came at them at just the wrong angle and its force broke loose some of the heavy steel rods they were transporting. The next few waves turned the loose rods into battering rams and these had gouged two holes in the hull. The holes were not large, but they were worrisome. His men had been able to heave back the rods and put temporary boards over the hole; it was enough to keep them afloat, but the ship was not fit to sail. When they entered Roundstone Harbor last night, they were relieved to find safety and the craftsmen they needed to make repairs.

Who was this woman who had appeared unexpectedly onto the deck of his ship? Most of the young women he had met in the north woods were rough, even crude. They were hardworking but not particularly educated or articulate. And certainly not as attractive. Girls in the East were pretty, but he had found them to be frivolous and snobbish. On that June morning, Arden had plenty of troubles on which he could muse, but it was not predominantly those where his mind lingered as he looked out at the picturesque village and thought of the young woman who had recently walked away.

21

IT WAS LESS than two hours later when Meggie looked up from the garden to see the captain struggling under a large bundle of laundry. She put down the hoe she was using and ran down the path to meet him.

"Sir! Couldn't you have asked any of your men to help?"

"Yes, I could have, but the thought of being alone for a bit was appealing. Besides, I met your father after you left, and he invited me to dinner."

"Wonderful, sir! I'm glad he did. I always wonder if a captain's life is lonely. And my brothers will love hearing your stories. I'm afraid both of them are taken with the idea of a sailor's life, so be ready for questions!" She smiled and reached for one of the duffles full of clothes. He picked up the other two and followed her down the path toward the lighthouse yard.

"I don't even know your name," said Meggie as they walked.

"Arden. It's Arden Anderson. And you're Margaret. Or Meggie, it seems. I asked in the village."

They walked slowly to the grassy green outside the house, where they plopped down the heavy bundles of clothes.

"Would you like something to drink?"

He nodded, so she went inside for a glass.

Kate joined Meggie as she returned to the yard with some water. Meggie introduced them.

"Well, Captain Anderson, thank you for bringing us this work. We watched your ship coming in yesterday. Meggie reports you've made it safely, but that you'll need some repairs. Do you or your men need anything else?"

"Thank you Ma'am, the only thing we need is more time. My cargo is getting cantankerous."

"Excuse me?"

"Along with building supplies, my "cargo" is Mr. Archibald Lewis, and four men that he's hired to work on a house he is building on an island north of here. Some of his supplies were the cause of my ship's damage, but he'll not take the blame, neither financially nor for the time it takes to make the repairs."

"Mr. Lewis who owns factories?"

"Yes. But nothing's gone right since I've signed on with him. He insinuates that I'm doing a bad job with the ship, but the weather's been against us all the way up from Chicago, and I'll not risk men's lives just to get his mansion finished when he wants. He can pay me all the money in the world, but I won't put my men's lives in danger."

"Well, of course, and you are right to feel that way," Kate nodded.

"Forgive my complaining. It's not been an easy trip with my client, is all. He's a difficult man. To tell the truth, coming out here this afternoon, away from the ship, has done wonders for me already."

"Captain, I've heard stories of this Mr. Lewis. I have heard that he's a hard businessman. I expect the problems lie more with him than you. I should think it a compliment he chose you to pilot the ship. Excuse me for asking, but aren't you young to be a captain?"

"Yes, Ma'am, I suppose I am. I am thirty-two, but I've been on ships since I was a child. I had an uncle with a small fleet of ships out of Baltimore. By the time I was fourteen I could just about raise every sail by myself. For years I sailed the Atlantic and the Caribbean and all the way to Europe and the Mediterranean. During the War Between the States, I was in the Union Navy. Two years ago, I began sailing the Great Lakes when I had a chance to purchase the *Jenny Marie*.

"Captain Anderson, did you say you are from Baltimore? I'm from Baltimore myself! Just imagine meeting here, at Roundstone Harbor. Tell me as much as you can!"

For the next several minutes Kate and Arden talked about buildings and companies and street names and people. The three of them chatted as they worked in the yard, separating the laundry into piles. Arden helped Meggie pump water from the well and empty it into a large metal washing tub. Because the day was sunny, they started an outdoor fire to heat water for the rinsing. Kate went back into the house, leaving Arden and Meggie alone with the chore.

"Captain, you needn't stay and help! I'm afraid it's not a glamorous job. You said you're a reader, and there are books inside if you care to relax for a while."

"I'm not minding one bit," Arden replied. "The work distracts me from thinking of my ship. I know our first mate's a good man, and the repairs won't be done today, so it's good to be gone from it. And I'd rather be working than sitting. I'd rather be here than there right now, unless you'd prefer to be alone."

"Of course not, Captain. My brothers and sister will be home from school soon, and it will be nice to have most of this laundry hanging by the time they get here. I appreciate your help, and this day *is* just about perfect, isn't it?"

They talked of Arden's men and his work. Meggie talked of her childhood. She mentioned that she had spent time in Toledo and that she had only returned recently to Roundstone Harbor. That she helped with the lighthouse chores. She was not specific about the four years away from her family, of her four years spent in Toledo married to George.

Arden's parents, he told her, were also adamant that he be well-read. He had bristled as a child, but now he was glad, as books were the best way to spend time on the long hours at sea. When he had time in a large enough port city, he would search for a bookstore to add to his book collection on the *Jenny Marie*. History. New advances in science. Explorers traversing the globe, going up the Amazon and the Nile. Did she know there were plans to explore, of all places, the Arctic?

For a while in her teens, Meggie had been tutored in French. Arden's uncle, he told her, had also spoken the language. Arden had learned the language from a sailor on one of his ocean crossings, so they laughed at their attempts to speak a few phrases together. When she asked more about his uncle and his parents, he grew serious.

"My uncle was my mother's brother. Warm. Full of laughter. He took me on short runs at first for a day or two at a time when I was as young as nine. The summers I was 12 and 13, I was with him almost every day. But then he was away on a long sail. When he left, he said it might be as much as three years. We had no way of telling him that my mother was sick or that five months later, she died. I was 14 at the time. My sister, four years older, had just married and moved away.

"And your father?" Meggie asked.

"My father was cold in every sense of the word. He did not care what I did or where I was. For months at a time, he was in England." Arden was evasive about the years that followed. "He and I were estranged for some years. But I reconciled with him before he died, so I am glad for that."

Arden asked about Jack. "And your father? He was kind to me when I talked to him a while ago in the harbor. He is almost a legend, it seems, in town."

"About the Madeline rescue, you mean?"

"Yes, a dock man told me about him, how your father saved eight lives a few years back. They are quite proud of him in this harbor."

"I was away and living in Toledo when it happened. My mother wrote me about it, but he downplays his part. He says he was only doing his job. My mom admits that she was terrified. He was out for hours and hours in high winds and waves. He brought one man and then another from a wreck caught on a reef. My father kept going back in the small skiff to save them. One man was lost but the rest were saved. He has pain in his back now that plagues him. The injury came from that night."

By late afternoon as they were finishing, the three other McGinn children came running up the path and across the yard toward them.

"We're home!" yelled Gillian, always talkative. She launched into the day's narrative. "Corina's uncle came to visit, and he brought her a real porcelain doll. She brought it to school, but Jessica started playing with it, and they fought over it and the dress tore, so all day Corina was crying, and Jessica was crying because Mr. Stangl made her sit in the corner, and her father told her she'd get a whooping if she ever sat in the corner at school."

"Goodness, I've never heard a child talk so fast! What's your name?" Arden said, laughing.

"Gillian."

Meggie immediately interrupted. "We're forgetting our manners! Let me introduce you to Captain Anderson, of the *Jenny Marie*."

Gillian curtsied.

"I've never in my years on the Great Lakes had a lady curtsy to me," said Arden seriously. He bowed back to Gillian then kissed her hand. Gillian squealed with delight and ran to tell her mother.

"You've given her something to talk about at school tomorrow!" Meggie laughed. "And this is Philip," she said, "and Peter," introducing her two brothers. "That's all of us, except Frank, who's in college in the East, and Father."

~

Kate came back outside when she heard the voices of her children home from school. This was the first year the village had school, and part of her missed the hours she spent with her children in books and study. She was always thorough with her questions about homework and lessons and subjects they covered at school. When she at last released her children to their chores and to play, she walked over to the storage shed where Arden and Meggie sat resting in the sun. "Captain," Kate asked, "I expect Jack home any minute. Dinner will be ready soon."

Arden smiled. "I can't remember the last time I've had a home-cooked meal. Thank you, Ma'am."

"Meggie, perhaps you and Gillian want to show Captain Anderson the rest of our property? Could you gather some wild-flowers for our table?" She smiled at them, called Philip with her into the house, and sent Peter on the chore of drawing more water from their well before supper.

As Meggie, Arden, and Gillian walked out of the yard and down a path to the north of the Light, Arden paused. "Thank you, Meggie, for this afternoon. It has been…unexpected. On a ship, we have only each other. I have a lot of time alone. Then I come into towns and people have nothing of significance to say except just little chit chat about unimportant things. But talking to you this afternoon was different."

Meggie nodded. "People *do* spend a lot of time talking about things that don't matter, don't they? People and their tedious conversations! It is tiresome to talk only about the weather or the price of grain for the cows or whether the newest house in the village should be on the north or the south side of the street."

Gillian was characteristically chatty and pointed out every feature of the path as it wound through the woods. "We once saw a five-point deer at this spot. When my brother Frank came back to visit us at the Light, he once built a whole hut out of branches washed up from the lake. Here's the place where, if you aren't careful, you could slip and fall down the bluff. Mother told me never to walk there when the rocks are slippery."

Although Roundstone Light was perched high on a promontory overlooking Lake Michigan, the land to the west of the lighthouse had been cleared, and the property, which belonged to the United States government and was maintained by the McGinn family, extended far inland. The government had purchased the land from a settler who had stayed only a few years but had planted fruit trees and raspberry bushes. Now in their fifth summer at the Light, the McGinns had plans to clear more of the land near that small orchard to plant a second garden.

The woods had been recently white with trillium that grew everywhere in the spring along with the small purple flowers in the shape of stars, a flower whose name Meggie couldn't remember.

"There's something we want to show you in this direction." Meggie said as they walked. She turned to Gillian, "Let's keep what's at the end a secret."

On the way, Meggie pointed out the thimbleberry bushes that covered the area and told Arden that "Thimbleberry Light" had been another name proposed for the lighthouse, but that "Roundstone Light" just made more sense. It was aligned in such a way to warn ships of a shallow reef just north of the entrance of the harbor. The addition of the Light had been a boon for the town, and now that ships could more safely navigate in and out of the port, the town had grown quickly.

As the path wound out of the trees and into the next clearing, Gillian stopped him. "Close your eyes, Captain." She laughed. "Come on, close your eyes, I'll lead you. It's only a few more steps." Gillian put her small hand in his and walked him slowly into the opening. Arden dutifully kept his eyes closed, playing along until both Gillian and Meggie said, "Open your eyes now ...look!"

It was the perfect week to show off the meadow. Like a snowstorm in summer, the short grasses were covered with thousands of daisies. A blanket of mostly white petals spread before them; spots of yellow and pink dotted the scene as well. Not only were the flowers plentiful, the air was permeated with the sweet fragrance of wild pear trees. All of them stood still for a moment. They were close enough to the lake to hear the lapping of waves at the beach; the sun was warm but not hot. Meggie and Arden were both quiet, aware they were witness to something not ordinary. Neither felt the need to comment on the beauty of the scene until Gillian spoke to the captain.

"Don't you like it, Captain? Isn't it beautiful? How many flowers do you think there are? Do you think there are more than a thousand? Can you count as high as a thousand? Have you been to other fields as pretty as this?"

"Gillian!" Meggie scolded laughingly. "Stop asking so many questions! Not everyone is used to your chatter!"

She began to fill her arms with flowers, and when Gillian had trouble breaking the stems to pick some of her own, the captain helped her. When all of their hands were full, they turned around and headed back through the path lined by cedar trees, past the rocky ledge, and into the yard of the Light.

22

"I MET SOLOMON today," Jack began as the family passed food around the table, soon after he had said grace to bless the meal. "I applaud you for taking him on as first mate. You must know he is a rarity among Great Lake sailors."

"What does *rarity* mean?" asked Peter.

"Not common, unusual."

"What is unusual about your first mate?" Philip asked. He was always all-ears when conversations turned to shipping.

"For one thing," Arden answered, "his skin is black. That's probably what your father is referring to. He is a man who went from slave to freedman to slave and back to freedman again. But here's another thing that is rare among sailors. He has memorized long passages of Shakespeare and can recite them on demand. He has read more books than I have, which I must say is a lot. And he knows every stitch of my sails and every inch of my lines. He also is older than he looks. It's a hard thing for my men to guess his age."

"Can I go see him tomorrow?" Gillian said. "I want to see a black man!"

"Gillian!" Kate quickly corrected. "Solomon is a man, and no matter what a person looks like, a man is not something to gawk at."

She turned to Arden. "Forgive us, Arden. I am embarrassed. There have been no blacks at all who have come to settle in the village, and I'm afraid that this very white-skinned place is the only life Gillian knows."

Jack added, "We have had an influx of new people here, but they tend to come with each other in groups: Swedes, Germans, Norwegians. And despite a war that supposedly made all men free, I am sorry to say that attitudes change slowly. I would like to say there would be no prejudice for a family with dark skin who moved to Roundstone, but the fact is, I doubt they would be treated well."

"Solomon has spent his life being wary," Arden mused. "I don't think he expects life to be otherwise. He has earned the respect of my crew, and he rarely has problems at the docks because of that. Well, that and his large size. He doesn't go in or about the towns when we come into port, and he says he is content to stay on the ship when we dock. This is convenient for me to have a man I can trust who can stay with the ship. Solomon is more than a first mate to me; he is also a friend."

Arden said this last sentence quietly. Jack nodded in response.

Kate was quiet for a moment. "I'm glad to hear words like this, Arden. I grew up in a family of long-time abolitionists," she said, "and we had so much hope that when the North won the war, freedmen could come and go as they pleased. We rejoiced at Emancipation. We celebrated the victory that slaves would no longer be 3/5 human but all five of those fifths just like everyone else. But here it is, nearly seven years later. Lincoln is dead. Already the south has put into place measures to prevent former slaves from being educated, from traveling, or even searching for their loved ones. We read stories in newspapers that black businesses are burned. Some former slaves are so hungry that they are asking to go back to the masters that mistreated them before they were emancipated. When I read these things, I'm discouraged. But I am heartened today that you call a black man a friend."

"Well, can *I* guess how old?" Gillian asked.

"Do you mean Solomon?" Arden laughed.

"You said your men can't guess his age. Can I try? Can I guess a hundred?"

Arden answered her, smiling. "He is half of that, exactly half. He is fifty years old."

Kate then switched the conversation back to Baltimore, and she and Jack asked more questions about the city they had lived in as children. The children sat around the table listening to names and places that did not interest them. However, when Arden mentioned having sailed to the Bahamas, it was Peter's turn to question the captain.

"The Bahamas? Isn't that where pirates are?"

"I have seen a few ships that were used in piracy," Arden told him. "And a few times we had to outrun a suspicious ship that we thought might be coming to do us harm. I have to tell you that pirates are not nice people."

"I know, I know. But please, tell us what you saw! And where else have you been?" For the next several minutes the family's atlas was out and open. Arden showed them the places he had traveled. The children crowded over Arden's shoulders as he pointed on maps to the countries he had sailed to, the ports he had entered, the waters he had crossed.

As the night carried on, Philip asked about the size of ships, about the differences between single masts and double masts in sailing. Gillian wanted to sing a new song she had learned at school. She kept repeating the same words over and over, having forgotten the right ones, and Philip had no patience for her mistakes. Jack asked his family to recite Wordsworth, one of many poems he had helped his children memorize around the dinner table over the years. Arden impressed them all when he was able to join in on a few lines.

As was their custom, the meal ended with their father reading a chapter of Scripture.

Arden got up from the table. "Thank you for dinner, Ma'am, and thank you all for a wonderful time. It's been a perfect day. He turned to Jack and Kate, "It has been a very long time since I have felt the warmth of a family. Thank you for including me this evening. I'm very grateful."

As he said this, Peter had been pulling on his father's sleeve, trying to interrupt.

"I told the captain about the old Indian settlement and the cave and the arrowheads, and he said he'd like to see them. Could he come back tomorrow, and we take him there?"

"Well, Captain?" Jack asked. "Is Peter planting ideas in your head, or does this truly interest you?"

"Thank you for asking. I'd be glad to see these historical sights, these "diggings" as your son calls them, if it's really alright that I impose another day of myself on your family. The ship will need at least another day, so I *will* be free tomorrow, but only if it wouldn't be asking too much of you."

"Jack," Kate interrupted, "you and I promised to spend the day helping the Baxters tomorrow. But the children have been wanting to go on an outing all spring. If Arden doesn't mind rowing the boat, and if Meg and Philip don't mind watching the younger children, it's a fine plan with me. I'll pack a picnic."

"You mean no school, tomorrow, Ma?"

"I'll catch the ire of Mr. Stangl, for sure, but it was a very long winter, and you have all worked hard at your studies. Heaven knows Captain Anderson shouldn't be this close to the old Indian settlement grounds and miss them."

Peter clapped and hugged his mother. Gillian talked a mile a minute about what to bring, and Philip went to check his fishing lines.

"Thank you again for the dinner, and for your kind hospitality. I should be going before it's dark. Tell me the way to the steps?"

"I'd show you myself, but it's time for me to light the Light," said Jack.

"I'll walk you back down to the beach. I love the water at twilight." Meggie offered.

Kate had not been slow to catch the way the captain's eyes kept coming back to rest on Meggie's face when she wasn't looking, or the way that Meggie, usually talkative, seemed more self-conscious than usual as she spoke.

The stairs were steep, and there were a few places without a railing. They moved slowly down them, and when they came to the first platform, Arden stopped.

"I will see you tomorrow, Meggie. Can I call you that? Or should it be Margaret?"

"Meggie is fine."

He did not continue down the steps. "I think I'll like having more time with you tomorrow." He turned to go, then turned back. For a brief moment, he raised his hand and touched her face, then let it fall to touch her hand. He started to say something else, but he turned away from her and went hurriedly the rest of the way down the stairs.

He shouted a goodbye when he reached the beach. She watched him stride out along the water's edge. He turned one more time and waved, then walked quickly and steadily away into the coming night.

Meggie's Diary *June 10, 1872*

I look back at my entries that are full of resolve. "I will not marry again," I wrote, so full of certainty. Captain Anderson intrigues me. He is a man that I could be tempted to love. Still, I have not forgotten that men want children. Would he be one of those men? Probably.

A sailor, a captain? Why do I even allow these thoughts of attraction? He would be gone two-thirds of the year. And all of that time, if I had grown to love him, I would fear in every storm that his ship would go down.

Who knows, is he married already? Would he have told me? Should I have told him about George? I am foolish, I think, to imagine. Still, I find my mind cannot help but to go down those paths. Those Arden-together-with-me paths.

23

"I DIDN'T GET a chance to tell you this before dinner last night, but at the ship yesterday, the captain and I talked about religious matters," Jack McGinn announced to his daughter and wife when he came down from the Light and said good morning to them in the kitchen.

"Arden Anderson?" Kate asked.

"Yes, I like him. Especially after last night. He was an entertaining guest."

Kate chided him. "Oh, Jack. Must you be so eager to proselytize? I hope you did not come at him too strong."

Meggie nodded. She had cringed slightly at her father's words. "I agree with Ma. You make assumptions that people want to talk about God. And sometimes, they don't. I hope you were kind about whatever it is that he believes."

"I asked a small question about church, and he was happy to talk."

"I suppose I *am* a little curious about his position." Kate said after a pause. "Surely a sailor doesn't have much chance to attend church."

Jack smiled. "I know I embarrass you both with my religious talk. And to be sure, your voices were echoing in my head as I spoke to him. I merely asked questions."

"Did he give answers?" Meggie asked.

"Not many. He said, though, that he believes he is unlovable to God."

"Did he say why?" Kate asked.

"He didn't, Kate. I told him that it was impossible not to be loved by God. God in His nature can only love. And then Captain Anderson had no answer to that. He obviously didn't want to go further in our discussion. You both will be glad to know that I left it at that," Jack reported. "But still, Meggie, you might keep that in mind today. It appears the man is parched for some kindness from God. Perhaps you might have further conversations."

"Well, *I* am not the one to do any instructing. Why would you ask that of me?"

Kate came to her daughter's defense. "Jack, this is a conversation between you and Arden. You shouldn't expect this of Meggie."

But Meggie was already riled. "Has it occurred to you that I am also 'parched for some kindness of God?' That not everyone finds God as easy to love as you do?"

Kate and Jack exchanged glances and were quiet. Neither said anything in reply.

Meggie continued. "*You* are certain of things, Father. *I* am not. Not anymore."

Kate answered before Jack did. "Meggie, you are right. What you have been through makes everything come into question. Neither your father nor I fault you for that. Jack, I don't think this is the time for this discussion."

But Meggie went on. "It is the God-is-love talk that I can hardly bear. I haven't told you that after the funeral—with both coffins closed and me barely able to hold myself up—a pastor told me that God wanted Jamie and George in heaven with Him, so that's why He took them. What am I supposed to do with that? Is *that* the God I am supposed to love? If so, I can't do it. I *won't* do it. I won't be speaking about religion to Arden today. Not today and probably not any day." She sighed and was quiet. The words had poured out, and the anger that was with them gone.

Jack crossed the kitchen and took his daughter in his arms. "My Meggie. Forgive me. George dying was a bitter thing. Your baby dying was a tragedy. We never saw that little baby—our grandchild, and we grieve him. We grieve him, too, for the pain that his dying puts on you. I pray that what is askew will be put right over time.

"I am sorry, too, for what I said about Arden. Your mother is right that this is my conversation with the captain, not yours." He defended himself with a smile as he let her go from his hug. "Truly though, I only wanted you to know what we talked about."

Meggie smiled at her dad. She turned back to the counter where she and her mother had been wrapping their food for the outing.

"And just one more thing," her father added. "What that pastor said is hogwash. Worse than that, it's wrong. He had no business saying that to you. If I had been there, I would not have let those words stand."

Meggie was about to answer when the younger McGinn children burst through the door. "He is coming! We can see a man walking the beach from the town. It must be Captain Anderson!"

Kate answered her children with a list of orders and questions. "The sandwiches are ready, as are the scones. Do you have mittens, Peter? Do you have your scarf, Gillian? I'm thinking it will be cold on the water." Their mother eyed the kitchen to make sure she had not forgotten anything.

"We'll be down in a minute," Jack said to the children. "We'll all meet him down on the beach when he gets here."

The clean and mended clothes had been carried down the stairs by Jack and Philip earlier that morning; Jack and Kate would take them to the *Jenny Marie* on their way into town. Meggie carried down the food they had packed for their picnic; Peter had a fishing line. Philip's job was to gather the blankets and any supplies they needed for the day.

Arden and Peter were deep in a rock-skipping competition while they waited for Kate and Gillian to come down the stairs. Jack had carried down his gun to pass along to Arden for the day; there was word at Cana Light of several deer that had been downed and devoured by a larger animal—possibly bear or wolf. Cana Light was several miles south of them and they would not be heading that direction. Still, there could be danger. Jack and Arden spoke about it in low tones, a distance away from the children. Then the two men pushed the keel of the old, heavy rowboat partway into the water.

One at a time the children climbed into the boat. They had been out only twice since the winter, and they all were looking forward to being on the lake. Gillian sat on Meggie's lap in the front of the boat, Peter and Philip in the back, and as Jack and Arden heaved the boat forward, Arden hopped over the side and settled himself onto the middle seat and took up the oars. Within moments they were away from shore, gliding out past the breaking waves and looking down into clear water. Arden was strong, and the oars cut quickly through the water, despite the weight of five of them in the boat. A gentle breeze blew, and although the sun was warming, the temperature was not as high as yesterday.

At Meggie and Philip's direction, Arden stayed close to shore around the bluff, then made a bee line straight across a narrow bay on open water, around a second bend in the land until they reached a sandy inlet. Their destination was a well-protected cove with land that curved in a big semicircle. At the closest end was a small creek that flowed quickly into the big lake. On the north end, a rocky point protruded far out into the water. Today, as they came near, a large flock of gulls lifted and circled in the air above them, squawking in protest of people disturbing this quiet and desolate place.

The trip had taken just under an hour. On the way, there had been more stories about pirates. Although Arden had only one story about his own pirate encounter, Peter wanted to hear it more than once. Gillian explained in great detail the children of her school, including their typical lunches and their favorite recess games. Philip took a turn at the oars, and Arden feigned gratitude for the break from rowing which in fact, he hardly needed.

Meggie watched Arden's back as he rowed. With his back to her, she did not try to talk, except to Gillian, who had grown uncharacteristically quiet. The steady rhythm of Arden's oars was lulling. Meggie looked out at the spring green leaves on the trees, the occasional fallen birch, the blue water splashing on the alternating rock and sands.

In the clear of the morning, Meggie was more practical in her thinking than she had been in the previous night. *It makes no sense to think more about him,* she told herself. *He has come suddenly to town, but just as suddenly he will leave. Within days he will be nothing more than a man whose ship I watch sail by on the water every few weeks. The shipping season is short; business owners have deadlines, and companies have profits to make. Captains cannot linger in ports.* By the time they neared the spot where they would beach the boat, Meggie was resolved to put away romantic thoughts about the man who was spending the day with her family. *Nothing more than common courtesy is required,* she told herself. *Just ordinary conversation with a family friend.*

As they approached the shore, Arden beached the boat, then he and Philip hopped out to steady it and pull it up on the sand so the rest of them could get out without getting their feet wet. Meggie lifted Gillian into Arden's arms, and Peter scampered out easily. Arden gave Meggie his hand, and she took it to steady herself. She could not help but look him in the eyes briefly as she thanked him.

Within minutes their little group left the beach and crossed into the hollow of land which held clues of another time. The area was set back from the water and further protected by a high sand dune. It was quieter away from the lake, and the breezes and winds that blew across the sand and sea grass inside this sheltered spot felt soft and haunting.

"We've met some Potawatomi people," Meggie said, "and they know of this place from their tribal elders. It used to be the summering ground for hundreds of their tribe who came here to fish and roam the beach. They say they came here for hundreds of years. Then, for the winters, they migrated to a place not far from Green Bay. They stopped coming only forty years ago or so."

Philip and Gillian and Peter had begun sifting through the sand to look for chippings. The boys had each found more than one arrowhead here over the years, and plenty of rock chippings remained that had been used in the process of making sharp weapons for hunting. This kept the children occupied for quite some time. Meggie and Arden sat on the sands several yards away.

"You've lived elsewhere. Do you like this life here, Meggie?" Arden asked.

"I am not planning to stay. I *have* lived in other places, and I think I wouldn't be happy if I were here forever." She paused. "But how could a person not be happy here for a time? I think it's the most beautiful place in the world. The water is solace, with colors that change and waves that sing. Sometimes the water is so calm it seems like I could write my finger on it and the letters would stay, and then within hours a storm can blow up and the waves are pounding and we worry about sailors like you being tossed about as if they were toy soldiers in toy ships. Wildflowers paint the fields all around me with color in the meadows of summer. Herons and egrets and cormorants fly overhead. At night the moon shines a path on the water, and sometimes the moonpath crosses paths with the Roundstone Light as it shines out its beacon. We live in the middle of wonder, Arden."

Arden was quiet. Finally, he spoke. "I don't know if I've ever heard a woman talk like you do. The girls in the cities talk about clothes and parties, and maybe the better ones talk about history or a novel, but you are so … so wholesome."

Meggie laughed. "I don't know if that's a compliment or not."

"It's a compliment," he said quietly, but did not look in her eyes.

24

"COME ON, CAPTAIN! Let's go to the cave!" Peter called out to them after only a few more minutes of digging in the sand. Meggie's siblings were already heading up a dune and into the trees. Philip was leading the way. Meggie and Arden hurried quickly to follow the children.

"There's a big rock ledge about a half mile inland. It's over the next dune and through woods," explained Meggie. "At the base of the ledge there's a small cave, and we've found artifacts inside. There are more chippings, and sometimes we've found bits of pottery. We've been told those pottery shards might be hundreds of years old."

"Wait for us!" Meg called. They caught up with Gillian, but Peter and Philip were ahead by several yards. "It's thick forest, this next part. We'll have to hold back the branches for Gillian."

"How 'bout I carry her?" Arden said. He slung the rifle over his shoulder and lifted Gillian on to his back as she giggled with the fun of being lifted high.

Meggie called again to the boys ahead, "Boys! Wait!" but they were already out of their sight. Her brothers were farther ahead than she liked. It was best to stay together in woods, not spread beyond earshot. Arden, however, chatted with Gillian while they walked. He kept a steady pace and did not seem to be worried.

It took effort to push through some of the undergrowth, as the place they were heading toward had no trail. In a few minutes, they found the boys waiting for them in a clearing.

"It's the cathedral," Peter told Arden. "I remember you named it that, Meggie, the first year we came here." They all stood for a moment, looking up at the tops of white pine trees and hemlocks which were tall and stood in an almost perfect circle around them.

"I remember this place, now!" Gillian started her chatter. "We came last year, Meggie, when you were gone in Toledo. Papa said that you started calling it the cathedral. I have never seen a cathedral but Papa told me that the ceilings in cathedrals are tall, just like these trees that go up to the sky."

"It is quite beautiful," Arden said. Light streamed in at all angles to the clearing at the forest floor. "I *have* been in a cathedral, and they *are* tall. Meggie, you are right. There is a resemblance."

"Who wants a snack before we head to the outcrop?" Meggie asked. Her siblings nodded, and soon they were sitting in various places among the trees munching on scones.

No one was in a hurry to move. Each found a patch of sunlight where they could sit, and they were out of the wind. Meggie closed her eyes and breathed in. The white pines were fragrant and the sun warmed her face. She sat on the soft pine needles in the circle of trees with her back against one of the enormous evergreens. Philip had brought a whittling knife and was working with a branch to make a sharp point. Peter was chasing a chipmunk and moved steadily farther and farther away in the trees. He had taken apart a meat sandwich and left a piece of it on the ground while he used crumbs from his scone to lure in the small rodent.

Meggie was only half listening to Gillian tell about Robbie Johnson who hit Elias Timmons at school, and about her friend Samantha who needed a new bed because hers was broken and Samantha was sleeping on the floor next to their dog and the dog kept licking her face at night. Her sister's small chatter was easy to ignore, and she closed her eyes in the sun. But just as Gillian had begun telling about her teacher's hat that was lost in a rainstorm, a horrible, loud crack of gun fire made Meggie jump and Gillian shriek and start to cry. A loud crack, the smell of gunpowder, and the fierce snarl of an animal transpired simultaneously. Meggie felt terror in an instant. The idyllic afternoon had turned suddenly awful, and it took a moment for her to take in what had happened.

Arden had crossed the small clearing and his attention was focused on something in the trees. With a strong push, he had rushed first to a terrified Peter and shoved him toward Meggie and toward the center of their circle. Peter was crying and gasping for breath between sobs. Gillian was wailing from the loud explosion, scared from the sudden noise, and Philip was still. As Meggie gathered her siblings close in a protective hug, she watched Arden reload the gun and stand poised with his rifle in ready position over the body of a large animal. When it didn't move, Arden kicked the huge, fallen creature, and waited several moments while he watched to see if the animal would remain motionless. Meggie stayed close to the children, but she could tell, even from a distance, that the body on the forest floor was that of a large, gray and white wolf. Finally, when Arden was convinced there was no life left in the animal, he hurried back to Peter who was now next to Meggie. Arden bent down to embrace him in a strong hug, and Gillian eventually quieted when she realized the danger had passed. Even Philip had been standing motionless at a distance. His pale face was regaining color.

Arden's attention was still on Peter, who was trying to be brave but kept wiping his eyes and gasping for air between sobs and the words he spoke to Arden. "I heard it snarl, sir… I felt its breath when it was behind me."

Meggie shivered at the words of her young brother. The body of the wolf was less than twenty feet away from where the small boy had stood moments earlier.

"It's rare that they attack, unprovoked," Arden said, finally rising from where he was kneeling with Peter. He turned to Meg and the others. "But his leg is all bloody and torn, so he must have been injured," he added soberly, "and hungry."

Gradually their terror subsided, although neither of the younger children moved more than a few feet away from Meggie and Arden. Peter kept turning to watch the woods. Fear had immobilized Philip for a few moments earlier; now he walked away from his family to look carefully at the dead wolf. "Dang, Captain. You shot it right between the eyes!" said Philip. "It was a perfect shot."

Meggie was keenly aware that she should keep her own fear hidden from her younger siblings. She was badly shaken and struggled to think clearly about what they ought to do with the wolf carcass, or whether they should continue on to the cave with its artifacts where they had first been headed. Arden, however, with the practiced ability to maintain cool nerves in a difficult situation, decided immediately that they should return to the beach and their boat. He was quick to instruct the children to gather up their things, and Meggie was grateful for his clear head and his willingness to take charge. Meggie and Gillian were very quickly leading the way back to the boat. At Arden's direction, Philip and Peter came next, and Arden followed last.

There were few words and no laughter as they made their way back through the woods, staying mostly along the creek's bank. It was a relief for all of them to see the tall sand dunes in front of them, and to hear surf in the distance, and then, the blue-gray lake. The sky was now overcast, and the temperature had fallen. No longer a bright, sunny day, the weather paralleled their mood: somber and wary.

When they reached the dune and Meggie felt it was safe to let the younger children run ahead to the boat, she held back for a moment and talked softly to Arden.

"Arden, how did you see it? How did you shoot it in time?"

"I thought I saw something moving in the woods while we were eating our scones in the trees. Your eyes were closed in the sun. I looked away from watching you to see that Peter had moved farther and farther from us, and I realized immediately that he was in trouble."

"Arden, I'm scared and relieved and so .. grateful.. I can't bear to think what would have happened if you hadn't been with us."

"Well, the worst didn't happen, did it? I'm glad I was with you." They were still walking quickly toward the lake, but he paused for a moment. He held out his hand to her. She had been holding back her fear, steeling herself not to cry. She took a step toward him and he held her for a moment in his strong arms while she took a deep breath and steadied herself. Then Arden moved away and motioned for them to move on.

"It is a good thing we came back when we did," Arden said, eyeing the water. "The weather is changing." The children had moved ahead of them and were close to the dinghy, but waves were splashing not far from the boat they had pulled up on the sand. As can so often happen on Lake Michigan, a storm was blowing in, and the wind had roughened up the waves.

"Would anyone mind if we waited to eat the rest of our food?" asked Arden, as he and Meggie came close to the children. "It might be a good idea to be getting back."

Meggie agreed. "It's fine, Arden, I don't think any of us are particularly hungry right now, and if so, we can eat in the boat on the way home."

It didn't take long for Arden to get Meggie and all the children settled in the boat and to cast them out into the water. The waves were choppy, and the wind was against him. Meggie reached under the seat and found blankets to cover her siblings. This time she sat across from Arden in the back. Peter and Gillian sat scrunched close on either side of her. She threw Philip the second blanket as he sat hunched, alone in the front.

Arden's arms strained against the oars. He made progress, but the boat did not move as quickly along the shoreline as it had earlier that day. Spray from the large waves splattered them. He and Meggie decided they should not head across the open water, but rather hug the coastline, adding additional time and more work for Arden's arms.

No one in the boat spoke for several minutes. Meggie wanted to ask if they were in danger, but she couldn't think how to ask Arden without alarming the children.

As if reading her thoughts, Arden spoke loudly and cheerfully above the wind, "It's a strong wind, and it's cool, but we're not in danger. It's a good craft we've got here, and we'll be home in no time."

Meggie nodded at him and mouthed "thank you." None of them talked much. She watched the shoreline and the water and was quiet with her thoughts. A few hours earlier she had resolved to have no personal feelings for the man who sat across from her at the oars. But here was a man who had saved the life of her brother. Who took action against danger. Who cared for the feelings of children. Who knew that she needed, for a moment, to be wrapped in a hug so that she could be strong for her siblings.

"Gillian, do you know what would help me to keep my rowing steady?"

"What, Captain Arden?"

"I think I would like a song. I think I need the McGinns to sing us home. How about I teach you a song? If I sing it a few times, will you all join in?" Arden began singing in rhythm with the strokes he took on the oars:

Come all ye young sailors and join me in song,
I've a story to sing ye, with a tale that's not long.
It's a story of sailing the deep ocean wide
It's a story of love, of a lad and his bride.

Meggie had often teased her husband George about his endearing tendency to be "over-serious." George had admired her father's profession, and told her that there was "nobility in lighthouse keeping." He went on with a metaphor. Their light on the high promontory, he said, brought a "sense of security to men in dark nights. Just being there for others can make all the difference. We can all be light like that." She had laughed at him when he said it, calling him melodramatic. *He was right,* she thought now. *It's important to just be there. All it takes is a song to cheer shaken children. Or to be the right man at a picnic.*

It took over two hours for the small boat to make the return trip to the rocky beach below Roundstone Light. Kate and Jack, home from their day's business, had begun to worry as they waited on the beach for their children to return. At last they saw the boat come around the point, and as the family grew close, they were grateful to hear the music of sea shanties and their children's voices in song.

25

THEY WERE CHILLED to the bone. Kate hurried her children up the stairs into the warm kitchen for hot tea. Jack and Arden tied the boat and followed soon behind them.

"I've only got time for a quick warm up." Arden said. "I'll have to go back to my ship soon to check the progress of the repairs."

Arden related to Jack the incident with the wolf, understating his quick instinct and dead-on aim. Jack listened intently and thanked him repeatedly not only for his help with Peter, but also for the difficult job of getting the boat home in rough seas against the strong winds that had risen so quickly.

By the time the men reached the warmth of the kitchen moments later, there was no other talk except Arden-the-hero. The children were spilling over with reports of Arden's various strengths and wonders. "Captain," said Kate as they entered the kitchen, "it appears we have several reasons to be indebted to you today."

Arden was clearly embarrassed by the excessive praise. "No ma'am, please don't say indebted. I was there at the right time is all, Mrs. McGinn."

Meggie joined them in the warm kitchen, having changed her clothes. Arden turned to her as he stood up from the kitchen table. "Meggie, might I ask you to walk me out to the stairs?"

Jack interrupted before Meggie could answer. "There's one other thing, Captain. I'm thinking of our talk the other day. I assume that you own a Bible? I've written some passages that I'd like you to read, if you would." Jack handed him a piece of paper.

Arden nodded his thanks, took Jack's list, and went out the door. Meggie borrowed her mother's cape and followed him outside. They walked across the yard to the steps at the bluff.

"I can't stay long, Meggie, but I have a question. I expect that we have one more day in the harbor. Could I spend more time with you tomorrow? Would you be willing?"

"Captain, my feelings about you are complicated. Haven't you heard that I am a widow?"

"I have, Meggie."

"And that doesn't stop you from an interest in me?"

He shook his head. "It does not. Maybe I am being selfish, Meggie, but I'm thinking only about tomorrow. Nothing more or beyond. I'd simply like more time with you."

"I am conflicted, Arden, but yes. Shall we have our own picnic? Can you come here in late morning?"

"I can and I will, Meggie." He smiled. "Now I am sorry to hurry, but I must be off." With that, he went quickly down the steep stairs and was gone.

Meggie found herself thinking of the times she had been in bed with George, of the times her body had risen with desire. The way her body hungered. How right it had felt to be filled with a man. She was not ready to go back inside to the chatter of her siblings. She instead pulled her mother's cloak around her and went with her longing to the overlook where she sat in the mist of the coming night.

~

But there was no late-morning visit, no extended conversation, no talk, no picnic. After breakfast, Meggie walked the path to the overlook and realized the *Jenny Marie* was not tied up at the docks and not in the harbor. The *Jenny Marie* was gone.

Jack had seen it sail out at dawn. After a short nap, he walked into town early to learn news. There was plenty of it. Mr. Lewis had badgered the carpenter to spend the entire night on repairs, so by four in the morning the sails were fixed in their rigging, and preparations were being made to sail. Additionally, word was all about town that Lewis' laborers had started a brawl in the tavern the night before, and Mr. Lewis and Captain Anderson had been called at one in the morning to settle Lewis' men.

Mr. Temple, the tavern owner, was a good storyteller, and as Jack sat at a table with others, the barkeeper imitated Mr. Lewis, causing laughter in the room. After ordering his men back to the ship, Lewis had cursed the town and insulted its people. He had come to the bar angry that he had been called and had left even more livid that there was no police force to handle the town's disturbances. There had been damage done in the tavern, but Lewis had offered neither help nor an apology for his men's behavior.

"And then Mr. High-and-Mighty, the man who could buy each of us a hundred times over, leaves my bar acting as if it was *my* fault that his men broke my chairs and my mirror. No apologizing—just complaints." Mr. Temple shook his head, "Well he ain't heard the end of it from me." It was clear that Mr. Temple did not like the man. Like all the other inhabitants of Roundstone Harbor, he had been curious to see and meet the famous man from Chicago who, rumor had it, was one of the ten richest men in the Midwest. In the span of a few days, Lewis' demanding temperament and condescending insults had created more enemies than friends among the people of Roundstone. Even in a pioneer town with strong spirits and no shortage of courage, it was still human nature to be intimidated by power. To his face, the residents of Roundstone were polite and even obsequious, but now that he was gone, they were quick to criticize.

One of the other customers who had been listening broke in. "I don't envy that ship captain at all. He'll be mighty glad, I reckon, to drop off his blueblood cargo and be on his way!"

"Now *that* is a man I'd welcome across my bar anytime," continued Mr. Temple. "They wasn't his men that was the problem. But he came with the big manufacturing man, and then stayed hisself and helped me clean up the glass that was shattered. He sent a man back with some money and the address of a shipping company where I should send the bill if that money ain't enough."

"Makes no sense that a man with all that money doesn't pay a dime, and a captain having to cover for him." This came from a woman seated at the bar behind Jack.

Mr. Temple answered. "Captain said he'd be back in this town sometime or other, and didn't want no hard feelings."

"I'd say he'd be back in this town." They turned to Jack. "Rumor is he spent more than a little time at Roundstone Light."

"Aye. That he did, and he's a fine man."

There was high respect for Jack McGinn, and the patrons of the bar knew better than to ask the question they were all wondering, if Margaret McGinn-Ford was part of the reason the captain spoke about returning. They would wait to talk of that when Jack was gone. The talk returned to Lewis and his money. "Still doesn't seem right, that rich man paying nothing."

"Rich people are rich because they don't part with their money, but they sure as hell make us part with ours."

There was plenty more talk at the bar that afternoon, more about Lewis, more about Captain Anderson. When the conversation shifted to the new machinery that was being delivered to help in the lumbering camps, Jack paid for his tea and went out into the late morning sun. Meggie and Kate would want to hear the news. He had watched his daughter go out to the overlook in the morning and could see her gasp when she saw that Arden's ship was gone. She had run up the stairs to the Light to see, he assumed, if she could get a glimpse of the ship sailing north. She said only a few words to him, then had gone back to her room. *Yes*, he thought, *Meggie especially will want to hear the news the whole town was talking about.*

~

She wrote more than once in her diary that day. Disappointment when she realized Arden was gone. Anger at herself for her unrealistic hopes. Confusion as to why Arden had broken his promise. Bitterness about her status in life: unmarriageable, alone.

Late in the day, when her siblings returned from school, they carried a letter for Meggie. The school was close to the dock, only three buildings away, and in the moments of early dawn, right before sailing, Arden had instructed one of his men to leave the letter in the dark and empty school room with instructions that it was to be delivered, via Philip and Gillian and Peter, to Meggie McGinn-Ford at Roundstone Light.

Although they begged her, she would not read the letter in her siblings' presence. She took the letter and an extra shawl and went back to the orchard where she could sit undisturbed in the beauty of the blossoms. There was sweet fragrance and the memory that she had been there with Arden and Gillian only three days before. She was half hoping Arden's letter would be business-like. She half-wished, in fact, that there had been no letter at all. In that case, she might be able forget all about him.

Arden's handwriting was strong. Clear to read and lovely to look at.

Dear Meggie.

The Jenny Marie will sail within the hour. I regret my promise to return to you this morning, for I am not a man who breaks promises easily. But I regret my broken promise more because it means I will not see you on this morning, or, in fact, for many more mornings. For the summer months I cannot see you at all. Already these three days lost have put me behind in the schedule my clients expect me to keep.

When we sail up and down the coast of this beautiful and tempestuous lake, I will think of you often, but especially when we pass by Roundstone Light. I will stand out on the deck and I will imagine you there in the yard with laundry, or on the beach, or in the orchard. I will remember when you sat in the boat holding your little sister, and you were strong and beautiful despite your cold and fear. Remembering you will make me glad.

I ask for no promises from you, Meggie. You say that you think you are not able to marry, and I think it is true for me, too, so I am foolish to write. There is a past I have not told you. I write only to tell you that I will be thinking of you.

Arden

P.S. I plan to return to Roundstone Harbor in late fall.

26

HER SIBLINGS BEGGED her to tell them what Arden's letter said. Her parents must have agreed with each other not to ask. Meggie was especially quiet for the next few days. Slowly, the busy-ness of the summer kept each of them distracted. Visitors came to the Light, and it was expected that a keeper would give tours, answer questions. Their garden was big and needed weeding.

The summer sun rose out of the water with long dawns and colored sunrises. The lake was blue for swimming and fishing and sailing and play. On breezy days, the sun dazzled the water and diamonds danced on the white caps. The McGinns gathered buckets of wild strawberries, then raspberries. Soon after came the thimbleberries that bore fruit in such abundance that for eight days the McGinn children took buckets into town and gave berries away. In mid-to-late summer there were cherries, then green beans and carrots from the garden. Their brother Frank came home for two weeks.

"I know that our brothers and sister adore Captain Anderson," Frank asked Meggie on an afternoon when the two were alone. "Our parents say there might have been something between you. Was there?"

He was one of only a few people Meggie confided in. "Yes." She paused. "Maybe." She paused again. "No."

Her brother laughed at her. "Well, which is it?"

"Truthfully, Frank, I don't know. I can't deny that I felt myself drawn to him. After George, I had resolved that I could never love someone else. I'm no longer sure that's true."

"I am glad to hear that, Meggie," her brother told her. "I think this is good news."

"Or maybe it *isn't,* Frank! Arden is a sailor. Sailors make horrible husbands! Gone all the time, and every day of their lives in danger. I tell myself I should forget all about him, that I should carry on with my plans to live alone for the rest of my life."

"Yes, what about that? Are you still thinking you'll go into business? Leave here?"

"I think so. I have friends in the village who are making nice things like dresser cloths and home goods. They are knitting mittens and shawls and sweaters. They are making candles. I think there may be a way I can sell their products in stores in the cities."

"I like living in a city, Meggie. I would help you however I could." Any further conversation was interrupted by Gillian, who wanted to show them the rocks she found on the beach. When Frank told her there were fossils in the rocks, there were only more questions. He had to reach for ways to explain to his five-year-old sister about ancient small crustaceans in an eons-old sea that once covered the place they now called home.

Frank returned to school in August. There were medical calls for Kate. Philip had turned thirteen and was now working as a dock hand for the harbor master. Ships that came to load and unload cargo often needed extra hands. The lifting and hard labor made him strong, and more than once Kate and Jack commented that the summer was changing him from boy to man. He usually returned to the Light late after supper, and his words to the family were few.

Jack was busy at the Light and still went almost daily to talk to the captains of ships at the docks, but now Philip was the family's best source of shipping news.

"I've news of the *Jenny Marie*," he said, one evening at a rare supper when they were all together.

"Captain Arden's ship?" Peter interjected, "tell us, tell us the news!"

"They say that it is lying idle and unused in the Chicago harbor. The crew was sent home. Captain Anderson has not been seen."

Meggie's face went white. Kate looked at Meggie. The kitchen went dead quiet. No one in the family said anything. "If a captain had been lost at sea, that would have been big news," Jack said slowly. "And if the ship's been seen, then it couldn't have been wrecked."

"But, why...?" Meggie said quietly, trying to keep emotion out of her voice.

"There's any number of reasons, Meggie. Sometimes a captain loses too much money and can't continue. Sometimes a captain sells a ship and works instead on land."

"None of those things happen silently, Pa, especially without people knowing the reasons."

"No, they don't, Meggie. You're right. This news has got me mighty curious myself."

Meggie's Diary *August 12, 1872*

This is the reason it is good that I did not spend a third day with Arden. I would have liked him even more, and then I might have begun to love him, and then I would spend the rest of my life like this: worrying.

I think of him often, but I do not know him well enough to love him. Even so, my mind can't help but imagine the worst. What is this news that there is no *news of him? Sailors talk when they come in to ports. What of his crew? Is he sick? Is he bankrupt?*

And what did he mean in his letter when he said he, too, should not marry? What is in his past that prohibits him from love?

27

BY LATE AUGUST there had been no further news concerning Arden. Fewer ships came to the harbor each day. With the number of ships dwindling, Philip was able to join them more often for dinner.

"It shouldn't have everyone talking, should it, Father?" Philip asked Jack as the McGinns sat down to dinner one night. They were continuing a conversation they had begun outside in the yard.

"What are you talking about?" Peter asked as he came down from his room.

"There were black people on a ship that docked for a few hours today in the harbor," Jack answered. "They are passengers, heading for a settlement on Washington Island."

"If their skin had been white, not one thing would have been said," Philip continued, annoyed by the interruption of his brother. "It bothered me, the things that people at the dock were saying about them. I was surprised, and not in a good way."

"Like what?" Peter asked.

"Like *I'm glad they're not getting off here. We'd have to start locking our doors.* And Mr. Jenkins—Mr. Jenkins who is a deacon at church—said he knew for a fact they were dirty and bringing disease. A black woman on the ship heard him say that and she told him that they were all quite well. That none of them were sick. She was polite to him, but he was angry that she dared to speak back to him. And the look on his face when he turned away from her was just mean."

Jack was quiet for a moment. "Well, it appears you have seen prejudice up close and personal this afternoon, Philip."

"But from people in our church? I thought we were all abolitionists here."

"It's a legitimate question, Philip," Kate jumped in. "And not a new one. In every place your father and I have ever lived, we have gone to church with people who preach "love your neighbor" but somehow think that does not relate to neighbors with black skin. And southern churches went a step beyond and justified slavery for over two hundred years."

"I'm glad we live in Wisconsin," Peter said. "Our teacher told us we were one of the first states to let Negroes vote."

"Voting means nothing if you can't come and go," Meggie said. "The newspapers are reporting that many Wisconsin towns have begun to enact sundown laws. What good is a vote if you can't move about as you wish! Isn't this why people died in a war?"

"It will take time." Jack told her. "My parents didn't own slaves, but they knew people that did. And those people weren't horrible people. What's considered acceptable in a place can change, but it can't change immediately. Attitudes don't change overnight."

"It's *not* overnight! It's been eight years since Emancipation! And even before, how could people live with themselves? How were people allowed to treat other humans as people beneath them, or even worse, as not human?"

"We are blind to our own hypocrisy, that's for sure," her father said. "But when a whole group of people thinks something is acceptable, it is hard to believe otherwise."

"You are too forgiving, Father. People who kept slaves are despicable."

"That might be a bit harsh, Meggie," her mother said. "The entire society's thinking needs to change, and change takes time. Perhaps your job when you leave here should be mayor, or politician!"

"Don't we wish, Mother? How long will it take before *that* happens? A woman politician? A woman in office? Maybe I *will* think about joining Susan B. Anthony. Get us the right to vote. Women in charge would never enact sundown laws!"

Gillian needed explanations about Susan B. Anthony and the word *politician* and if black people could go back into town at midnight because they weren't called midnight laws and what happened if they needed a doctor in the middle of the night?

Despite the lengthy conversation that extended almost to dusk, Jack insisted that they carry on with the nightly practice of scripture reading. He read quickly, then went upstairs to light the lens. Kate, Meggie, and Philip talked for another half hour about the freedmen and freedwomen who had settled in western Wisconsin, the blacks that were now languishing in the south under new laws, and the ways they themselves would react if a family of freedmen came to live in Roundstone Harbor.

"I wonder where Solomon and Arden are right now?" was the last thing that Philip said before he opened the door to the light tower and went up the winding stairs to take something to his father. Meggie did not admit out loud that she had been wondering the very same thing.

~

Summer spilled over into most of September. The days felt lavish to Meggie. There was beauty all around and plenty to do. Her body had healed. Her daily walks to the village and her work at the lighthouse grounds made her body strong. Kate was busy dealing with medical needs, so she and Meggie rarely took in laundry, and Meggie was all too glad to give the work to others. She helped with the garden and played with her siblings. Meggie joined the small church choir and liked attending practices. She was helping to gather books and set them up on lending shelves in a church alcove that would be available for anyone in town. She spent a few hours each week in the homes of her friends.

Kira was unstoppable as a knitter. Not only was her work beautiful, she was fast. She knit hats, scarves, shawls. She took orders for sweaters. In June, Meggie had written to her sister-in-law in Toledo and asked her to be on the look-out for a small storefront in the fashionable section of town that might be a good place to open a shop. As of yet, she had heard nothing, but it was still something Meggie thought about. What else might she sell besides mittens and scarves? A woman in Egg Harbor had a loom and was weaving. Meggie had seen her tablemats and decided others would like them and buy them. A farm wife in their church kept bees and made candles, but only a few at a time. A newly arrived wife was making an interesting kind of art out of Lake Michigan stones. Could all these things together: candles, knitted pieces, vases and weavings, be enough to put in a store, to fill shelves so that there would be enough for people to buy?

Charlotte's baby Adeline was born. She was healthy and a good sleeper at night. It was easier than Meggie thought it would be to hold her. Adeline was Adeline, not her Jamie, so she did not compare the two children. Still, more than once she was glad for the long walk back to the Light after a visit with her friend and new baby so that she could be alone. What could anyone have told her as comfort? It was a grief she had to carry alone. It was *her* body that could never birth another child. It was *her* mind that remembered George's face when she told him she was pregnant. She remembered the joy of it and his silly fear that he was hurting the baby when hours later they made love on the couch with sunlight streaming in through the window and the smell of lilacs outside. Everything so full of promise and spring. It was *her* arms that ached to be wrapped in a hug, to fall into bed with desire.

Charlotte was back at her sewing just a few months after Adeline was born. "Of course I will make things for your shop," Charlotte had told her when Meggie first thought about opening a store in Toledo. The subject came up again as they talked. There had been a storm in the morning, then a stunning full rainbow over the water. When Meggie stopped in for a visit with her friend in mid- afternoon, the ground was already dry from the warm summer sun. They lay blankets on the ground, put Addy between them, and watched as the baby kicked and cooed. Charlotte's house had a good view of the village, and they watched people come and go from the general store and the blacksmith's and the bar.

"I've been thinking about your store in Toledo, Meggie. Would it *have* to be there? Couldn't you open a store here instead?"

"I doubt there would be enough customers. And is it right to open a store while the one store is here already?"

Well, yours would be different. You could sell all the crafts from the women in the town. Think of it. Jenny Alden's flowers. Lois' candles. And Kira's mittens and scarves! My sewing. Maybe jams, apple butters? Preserves? We could find more, I'm sure!

"It *is* a thought. And just when I think I am ready to go back to a city, I find I am also not ready to leave here yet."

"Is there any reason you *must* leave this fall?"

"No, it's only the time period I put on myself to say that I need to be finished with my grief. I can't bear the thought that I will do nothing with myself except be a self-absorbed, crying widow for the rest of my days."

"Meggie, you aren't that way at all! You are full of life, not death. And look at the good you are doing here by staying! What would I do without you? You've become my best friend!"

"I suppose staying one more winter wouldn't hurt anything. I don't have a clear plan what to do next. It's true that I haven't heard back from my sister-in-law in Toledo, though I believe she is looking. And maybe by next year it will be more obvious whether a store here is a good idea or not." She talked slowly, pausing to think between sentences, and Charlotte did not rush her. "My mother is busy with medicine and needs me to help with Peter and Gillian when she's called away. Maybe it makes sense to wait here in the winter at least, to not begin anything new until spring. You have given me a lot to think about."

Meggie did not mind taking her time as she walked the long stretch of stone beach that evening. Gulls soared and squawked. Terns dove for fish. She took off her shoes and waded at the water's edge. By the time she made it in to the house and apologized for missing dinner, she had made up her mind.

Although she had little doubt of their reaction, she wanted her parent's permission to stay on through the winter. Kate and she went up the stairs to discuss her news with Jack. He climbed down from the lantern room to the small landing. Kate sat on one stair. There was barely room for Meggie and Jack to stand.

"We would never say what you should or should not do, Meggie. You are your own woman. But, of course you can stay here! And it's good news for us! It is what we both secretly wanted!" Jack smiled at Kate. "If there were more room in this lantern room, I would hug you both just now!"

Before following her mother down, Meggie went up with her father to the top windows to watch the sun set.

"Four ships still in view," Jack murmured. They were silent for a moment. "And that sky, Meggie! Aren't you going to miss that sky when you go?" They both watched the clouds where the sun had sunk below the horizon. The colors deepened from lavender to deep gray-purple as the sky behind them turned black.

28

THE CHILL OF fall, then snow. There had been dangerous October storms but no deadly shipwrecks nearby this year. Dark, long hours without sun. Philip and Jack asked more than once for news when a ship came in from Chicago. No one knew anything about Arden, but there were rumors about a black man asking questions about the *Jenny Marie.* Kate was busy treating coughs in a logging camp on the other side of the peninsula. One week in November she was gone four nights out of the seven. Both she and Jack said more than once how glad they were that Meggie was staying with them through the fall and winter.

The Light closed on November 1 and the family adjusted to the slow pace of winter. The addition of the piano made a huge difference for Kate. In her first years at the Light, she found herself sinking when the sun set before four in the afternoon, but now she went to her piano at sunset and played. Meggie was willing to cook, and she was good at engaging her siblings in the supper preparations, better than Kate had ever been. The family settled into a pattern, and the music carried them through December and January. Each of the children was learning to play. Peter, it turned out, was quite good. On some evenings Kate would go back to the piano after the dishes were done, and they'd gather and sing folk-songs together.

~

In February, a village resident named Daniel Jarls started visiting Meggie every Tuesday. She was cordial at best, rude at worst. He either did not notice or was not rebuffed by her coldness. He came like clockwork, about four in the afternoon. His actions were predictable. He knocked on the door, greeted Kate or Jack, asked what they thought of the weather. He nodded at Meggie, then stood stilted and awkward in the kitchen. He was most at ease with Gillian, and usually asked her a question about whatever toy she had in her hand. After a moment of conversation with her, he returned his attention to the adults in the room. He routinely refused an offer of tea, then nervously asked if he might "spend a few minutes visiting with their daughter, Margaret?" Jack and Kate took the other children upstairs and left Daniel and Meggie alone.

He had children of his own. Daniel was a widower of three years, his wife having died only months after their second child was born. Now he was here in Roundstone Harbor on land next to his brother. His sister-in-law took care of his children during the day while the brothers cleared land and built sheds and barns. At night he took his children to his own house, fed them supper, put them to bed, tried to be a good father. The exception was Tuesday, when he came to the Light and asked to sit with Meggie "for a spell" in the living room.

He was a quiet man who spoke in short sentences. He was stocky and strong, not particularly handsome but not particularly unattractive either. Freckled. His hair had a tinge of red. There was always a faint odor of soap and hay and manure surrounding him. Daniel seemed able to talk about three subjects only: the weather, his farm, and a farming manual he had read about cows. He had plans to buy twenty dairy cows of his own in the spring. He would need to order feeding troughs and milk buckets. He would learn to make butter. He had grown hay in the summer. His barn was nearly ready for the cows when they were set to arrive in April.

Meggie did not encourage him. He never mentioned his late wife and said little about his children. The few times she attempted to ask about books or politics or places he had been, he had nothing to say. She did not want to be rude, but after a fifth Tuesday when her replies to him were shorter than his own attempts at conversation, she opted for honesty.

"Daniel, I'm afraid that you are here to court me. You are kind to show interest in me. But I have to tell you honestly that I do not return your interest."

He avoided her eyes. "I did not expect you to right away. I know I'm not anything special, like your first husband was. I hear he had education and money and looks, all the things I don't have. But here's something I want to say. I am not a bad man. I would take care of you and give you a good life. Please, let me keep coming so that you can change your mind."

It was more words and more honesty in one paragraph than Daniel had spoken in all of his visits combined. After such an impassioned request, Meggie could not turn him down.

"I make no promises, Mr. Jarls, but I will see you again next Tuesday."

Meggie's Diary *February 20, 1872:*

I know that I am a snob. George had class and education; Daniel does not. How quick I am to say in discussions with others that every man is equal, that we are all the same despite skin color or creed or money. Yet, look at my own hypocrisy. I was proud to marry George. But Daniel? Why do I feel myself thinking of him as a man lower than I am? Why should it matter that a man doesn't read books? Or that a man smells of cows? Shame on me to think I am above a dairy farmer, that a woman who lives as a dairy farmer's wife is less than a woman married to someone like George, a man with a factory. I see my own arrogance, and I am not proud of the ugliness inside.

Still, it will take me a while to consider him seriously. Of course, there is something quite practical about the prospect of life with him. I could stay in Roundstone, close to my family. Close to my friends. Charlotte and I could open a shop here. I would be mother to his children. But all this assumes he is a man I could marry, a man I could live with.

Am I wrong to hope for love again? I have had one man to love. Maybe that was enough. I know some women never have love in a marriage. Why should I think I am entitled to it twice? I might possibly grow to appreciate him even if I could not grow to love him. Or would I grow to resent what he does not give me? To resent that he is not more than he is?

And now, why at all times, do I think about Arden? Why do I imagine what Daniel's arms would feel like compared to the time at the beach when Arden wrapped me in his and I felt happy? Is Arden well? Is he even alive?

29

MEGGIE WAS AFRAID Daniel would propose marriage. He made hints. "Once the cows come, I need to figure out about milking them in the mornings," he told her. "The children will be alone. It would be good to have someone else in the house."

It would not be love, Meggie thought, but maybe it would work. Meggie had told him her idea of opening a shop in the village. He nodded, but did not offer any opinion. He said only that his own mother had sold eggs and sometimes a few vegetables. At least he did not object as a matter of principle to a woman selling things. She doubted that there would be *any* issue on which he might take a stand. When she had asked whether he would have fought in the war if he had been older, Daniel had just shrugged.

"Don't you think it wrong that people were enslaved?" she had asked.

"I am a simple man," was his answer.

Could she grow to appreciate his calm? Or would she grow to resent his complacency, become discontent? Her answers to those questions changed daily. She was not ready to make such a decision, and she feared it was coming sooner than she wanted.

Meggie was cautiously excited about the idea of a shop, however. Earlier she had wondered if there were enough customers in town to buy the products she might sell, but there were plenty of signs that those fears were unfounded. Kira sold her mittens as fast as she could knit them. She asked a high price and she got it. The yarn that Kira used was spun from a farm in Fish Creek across the peninsula and was lusciously soft. Kira had already asked, and the spinners there seemed amenable to having Meggie sell the yarn in her store, should she open it. She could sell Kira's mittens, perhaps ones from other women, too. Eggs, soap made from goat milk, honey. Dyes from botanicals for homespun cloths. She could gather together the things people wanted. The early settlers to the town were spending money throughout the year. It was not like the early days in the town, when every penny went to survival. They were beginning to want pretty things for their homes. Farmers' wives, especially, had become industrious, and Meggie decided a shop might actually work.

⁓

She found herself dreading Daniel's visits. On a Tuesday night in March at dinner, after Daniel left, her brothers teased her. "Your "boyfriend" might want you to milk cows. Don't dairy farmers smell?"

Gillian asked innocently if Daniel's children would be called her sisters or cousins. "In school," Gillian reported, "Daniel's daughter Melissa is quiet. When the teacher calls on Melissa, she is so shy that she only whispers. Mr. Stangl tells her to speak louder, that she can barely be heard. But she stays quiet. And sometimes she cries when he asks her a question."

Kate and Jack told the children to stop asking questions and stop teasing, but it was too late. Meggie's face streamed with tears. She left the table and headed up the stairs to her room. Kate gave her a few minutes to cry, then followed her up the stairs.

"I try to make myself think I could grow to be happy with him." she told her mother, through tears. "I try to make myself believe I should be grateful for a man who would want me, a widow. I try to convince myself how convenient it would be to stay here in Roundstone, close to you and Father and the boys and Gillian. I ought to be able to make myself happy with Daniel. But no matter how hard I try, I can't do it."

"I don't believe a woman should ever marry someone she doesn't want to marry, Meggie. Has he asked you?"

She shook her head and blew her nose. "I am afraid it is coming."

"Meggie, just over a year and a half ago you were bereft." Her mother sat next to her on the bed, an arm wrapped over her shoulder. "Your grief was so thick it was heavy. Then you began to heal. You started smiling again, and then laughing. But so quickly, you had plans for a future as a single woman with no need of a husband. You talked of leaving here and living alone. And now you are crying because you feel guilty saying no to a man you do not love? That is a lot for a year. Can you slow down? Let there be time in between all these changes? Not move so quickly?"

Meggie laughed through her tears. "You're right. I *do* seem to keep changing my mind." She took a deep breath and wiped her face.

Her mother waited a moment before going on. "One last thing, Meg. Say no to Daniel. Soon. Nothing good will come of trying to talk yourself into a marriage you don't want."

As they talked more, Meggie didn't mention the other name that should have been added to her mother's list of her continual vacillations. She had kept every thought of Arden to herself. When she tried to talk herself into a life with Daniel, it was always Arden that came to her mind. It was a life with Arden that she imagined more than a life as a wife of a farmer, with cows. Yes, he would be away in the summer, but in the winter they could sit in front of a fire, read books, talk of history, make love. He would want a house by the water, and they would not grow tired of watching gulls fly over the waves.

~

There were continual snows in early March. At the end of the second week, the temperature finally rose above freezing, but the melting snow froze again overnight and made walking on the ice difficult. Kate complained that the ice from those re-freezings made March worse than February. The children said school was boring. Even Gillian came home with few stories; nothing new happened day after day.

Suddenly, in the last week of March there was a packet of letters. A large envelope held three separate, smaller envelopes with letters inside. It came in the post, addressed to Jack McGinn at the Roundstone Harbor Light. Jack stood in the street outside of the grocery where he read two of the three. Moments later, instead of going directly home to the Light, he went first to the stables and arranged for horses to be readied.

He burst into the kitchen, told Kate that he and possibly Meggie were needed. "Could you please help me pack, Kate? Would you gather some food for our travels?"

"What has happened? It's not Frank, is it? Will you be gone long?"

"No, it's not Frank. It's our friend Arden Anderson. He's in Chicago, and he is in need." He explained quickly that they might be gone for quite some time. She should hire any help that she needed. Not hesitate. There was money enough. And if the man who had saved the life of their son was in trouble, how could they not go to help him?

He called Meggie down from her room and gave her the third letter, unopened. "If it's what I suspect, then I'm guessing you might want to come with me, Meggie. But we'd need to leave soon. We have to leave here within an hour to get to Sturgeon Bay by dark." He gave the other two letters to Kate to read while he went upstairs to gather his things.

The first letter was short, written on high quality paper. The hand writing was formal and the envelope was stamped with an elegant letter D, sealed with wax. Two other envelopes had also been in the packet: one addressed to Jack McGinn and the other to Meggie McGinn-Ford. Kate read the larger one first:

Dear Mr. McGinn at Roundstone Light;

I am taking the liberty of sending these letters to you on behalf of Captain Arden Anderson. I believe that you might be interested in knowing his whereabouts and that he is not well. He was reluctant to write you, but has done so at my urging. I visit him weekly, but as you might imagine, I have little recourse or resources to help him. He has little hope.

Solomon Dupree

The second letter was written with soft pencil on paper that was not well designed for it. The words were smudged and difficult to read.

Dear Mr. McGinn,

I write from jail. I am accused of a crime I did not commit, yet I am here nonetheless. I was told for the longest time I was forbidden to make outside contact. I have no access to my bank account, but finally I have legal counsel. In the last nine months, attorneys have been assigned to me, but each has quit. I fear those in power have sway.

I wanted to tell you that your list from the Scriptures has been comfort to me. (They do allow me a Bible in jail.) I think I am in good company with Joseph, a man falsely accused.

I write also to give regards to your family. The two days last summer with your family at Roundstone Light are memories that burn warm and happy for me in this cell that is cold and without life. I hope you are all well.

Arden Anderson

Upstairs, Meggie sat at her desk, tore open the envelope, and read the short letter from Arden.

Dear Meggie.

I intended to see you last fall, to come again to Roundstone at the end of my season. I hope that my words to that effect in my last letter did not offer you false hope for further contact with me. If that is the case, please forget me. There are serious, false charges against me, so I am imprisoned. However, on other scores, I am not an entirely guiltless man so perhaps it is here I belong. I was foolish to imagine that I could further a relationship with you. Please, find happiness with a man better than me.

Arden Anderson.

Within the space of an hour, she and her father were hurrying to the stables in town. Jack and Meggie rode horses to Sturgeon Bay where they stayed overnight. The next day they rode in a stage to Green Bay. The following morning they traveled by train to Chicago and were comfortably settled by early afternoon in the guest rooms of old friends of Jack and Kate. Soon after arriving, Jack went in search of Arden's lawyer. Jack and Meggie planned to be at the jail for visiting hours at 10 a.m. the next day.

30

MEGGIE WAS NOT a particularly squeamish person. Her brother Philip had become interested in hunting in the last year, and Kate often chided him for the messes he left on the lighthouse grounds, but Meggie was not bothered by animal blood or entrails. Additionally, Meggie had occasionally accompanied her mother at the sick beds of villagers, and in that regard had seen vomit and blood. She was not usually repulsed by the smell of human waste and urine.

But Meggie was not prepared for the stench and the dirt that overwhelmed them as they stepped into the visitor waiting room at the jail. Families crammed the room with dirty, undiapered children, many of whom appeared to be ill. Men lay on the floors smelling of alcohol; a man close to the chairs where Jack and Meggie waited had fresh vomit on his coat. A middle aged man who sat near them had a festering wound on his hand. His fingers were gray.

Finally they were called into a different room, a long corridor with cubicles. Each cubicle had two chairs in front of a wall; in the wall there was a small window with iron bars. They were told to sit in one of the cubicles, and as they waited, they could hear the murmurs of voices and conversations through adjoining small windows.

Arden had not known who his visitors would be. A smile lit his face, followed by a look of self-conscious agony, as he reached up to push his fingers through his long, unkempt, filthy hair. Meggie smiled at him, trying desperately to hide any shock she felt at his appearance.

Jack spoke immediately. "I wish we'd known earlier, Captain. We came as soon as we heard."

"It is such a long way, and I am chagrinned to think that you have made the long trip on my account. Now I regret that I wrote you, as this is way too much for you to have done. I do not deserve your kindness."

Jack dismissed those thoughts with a shake of his head. "Arden, that is of no matter. Don't think about us right now. We have only a few minutes. Tell us what you are accused of and how you came to be here. We want to help."

"I am accused of theft and attempted murder. Neither is true. However, it is Archibald Lewis that is convinced of my guilt, so he has made it nearly impossible to refute the charges. As you know, he is a man of considerable power and sway."

"How are you here? Where did this happen?"

"On Shallow Island, last summer, when I was delivering supplies. It was right after I left you at Roundstone Light. As you know, I was carrying Mr. Lewis and four of his men, as well as hardware and building materials, north to his building site. He was visiting his island to check on the progress of the big house he is having built there. There was a shooting at night on the island—an attempt on Mr. Lewis' life. Sometime earlier, someone stole money from Lewis's safe and put the money in my cabin. I was accused of both crimes. No one could vouch for me, as I was on the other side of the island alone when the gun was fired. I had no alibi and, due to the lack of any constables or police force, Lewis and his men took the law into their own hands. They locked me in my own cabin on my own ship and made my crew sail me to Chicago. I was immediately arrested and have been here in this awful place ever since."

The bailiff came behind them and told them their time was up.

Meggie spoke to him quickly as they got up to leave. "Arden, have you been sick? You don't look well."

"Yes, I have been. It's cold in the cell, and there aren't enough blankets. I think I may have gotten pneumonia a few weeks back. I feel better now."

Jack said the final words as they were ushered out. "We'll be back, Arden. I'll meet soon with your lawyer, and we will help however we can. I'm praying as well. I believe that God is on the side of the innocent. Don't lose heart."

Meggie cringed slightly at her father's words. It was characteristic of her father. He meant well, but empty platitudes were no help at all. She hoped that Arden would not be offended. Her father's religiosity bothered her, but judging from the look on Arden's face, he had not minded. Arden seemed grateful for their visit, despite the look of hopelessness which he wore as if it fit.

The situation, however, was *not* entirely hopeless. Solomon had also written Sally and John and they had recently sent money from Ohio to hire a defense attorney. John-Paul Stewart had just taken Arden's case; he was young and inexperienced, but he was also determined and idealistic. He had gone into law with the hope of fighting corruption.

Additionally, Jack had both connections and expertise that might help. He had a few friends in Chicago who he hoped might prove helpful. In particular, he had an old friend who was a newspaper editor. And in the war, Jack had served on court martial boards and knew something about legal proceedings. A legal provision allowed Jack to sit in on the client/attorney meetings with Arden as John-Paul prepared for the upcoming trial. It was arranged that the two men together would listen to Arden's story.

That afternoon, Jack and John-Paul were back at the jail, and this time they were allowed more time to talk. Meggie sent an extra blanket, a sweater and scarf, and homemade bread. Their friends, the Ingrams, assured Meggie and Jack that they should feel at home, that Meggie could bake or cook whatever she'd like. She and Jack could come and go as they pleased.

The Ingrams were older and slightly infirm. Their house was large enough so that Meggie could visit with them if she wanted, but be on her own, too. When Meggie offered to prepare all the dinners for the four of them while they stayed, the couple was happy with the arrangement. They were ideally located, only a few blocks from the jail, and close also to shops where Meggie could provision. Each time that Jack went to the jail, she planned to send food for Arden.

~

In a small, private room at the jail, Jack and John-Paul sat across a table from Arden. "Tell us everything that happened after you left Roundstone Harbor," John-Paul instructed. "Please give as many details as you can."

Arden took a bite of the cake that Jack had delivered from Meggie. After he swallowed, he began.

When I returned to the ship after I left you and your family at the Light, Jack, Solomon met me with a troubled look. Lewis had been disgruntled all day. 'He convinced the carpenter to hire another pair of hands,' he told me, 'and they plan to work through the night. I hope they aren't cutting corners.'

I went immediately to the hold to inspect the repairs. Two men were hammering and a third was sawing. The largest hole had been repaired adequately, not perfectly, but it would suffice. They were working on a smaller hole patch. It wasn't the complete repair as I had hoped, but it would do. The carpenter told me he had decided against the design of dovetailing the lumber in a more crafted manner and had opted for a patch, as he knew we were in a hurry.

"We didn't agreed to that," I told the carpenter, but at this point I could see that the ship would be fine. The sails were ready, and truthfully, Mr. Lewis was hovering and angry, so I decided that we could sail safely when the carpenters' work was complete.

There was the matter of cost, of course. I needed to pay the sailmaker and the carpenters, and I had barely enough in our coffers to do so. I carried some insurance, and felt confident that my new sails would be paid for. But if human error had caused the damage to the structure of my ship, then I reasoned it was humans that needed to pay. If Lewis' men had not secured those rods properly, Lewis should reimburse me for the repairs. I broached the idea with Lewis when I met with him and the carpenter, but Lewis was dismissive. He said he had no reason to pay, but that I'd get my money when we made it to Shallow Island. So it seemed right to sail on and get the man to his house as soon as possible. I did not want my funds to shrink any further, and every day that I did not haul cargo was money lost.

Now, months later, with all this time to think, I wish I had been more watchful as Lewis' men loaded their supplies in Chicago. Ethan Boggs, a man I knew from the year before, was supervising the offloading from wagons of the cargo and was there at the dock and then below deck hovering around the men. In my experience, Mr. Boggs was meticulous, and I did not double-check the supplies to make sure they were secured. The crates, it turned out, were bound tightly, but the bindings around those metal rods were worthless. Not much more than cording, not even strong rope. But all the crates were stored in front of them, and the rods were not in plain sight. The storm was a vicious one, and perhaps none other than the wind and the lake were at fault. Still, in the aftermath, it was pretty obvious that those loose rods were to blame. Simply put, the rods put the holes in my ship.

"So you were already having difficulty with Lewis?" his lawyer asked.

Yes, I am getting distracted. This matter of the ship damage was only one among many unpleasantries with the man. After my morning and afternoon with your family at Roundstone Light, we gathered final supplies throughout the evening and repacked the cargo as soon as the carpenters finished. We readied the Jenny Marie for an early morning departure the next day. We hoped to make it all the way to Shallow Island in one sail. It had been a long day for me—including the excursion with your children, Jack. I had given orders that my men must be back on the ship by eleven, and all had obeyed except two who came straggling in sheepishly just a few minutes late. I was tired, and I went to sleep quite easily about midnight.

Lewis' men, though, were a different story. Lewis was in charge of his men, so I let him set his own rules for them. When they were told that we would sail in the morning, they headed for the town's tavern. Shallow Island has no amenities, of course, so like lemmings they followed their foreman into the bar when he offered to advance them the night's drinking money against their first week's wages.

Shortly after I had gone to sleep, probably about 1 a.m., I was awakened by shouts and calls from the shore. The barkeeper in Roundstone Harbor had sent men to the ship to summon Mr. Lewis and me because his men had been brawling with some men in the village. There was damage in the bar. They were calling for us, hoping that as their superiors, we would have sway. Mr. Lewis took his time. He complained about there being no constable or police force. Finally, we arrived at the bar together where he threatened his men. "I'll dock your pay, gentlemen, if you aren't on the ship in ten minutes. If you aren't back in fifteen, you can stay here and rot in this town, and you'll never see a penny of the money that you had planned on from me." And then he turned around and left the bar, leaving all that damage that his men had caused without a word of consideration to the tavern owner.

His men left quickly. Not one of them was walking straight. They followed their boss to the ship, more than a few steps behind him. He is not the kind of man that would walk with them to the ship. I stayed for half an hour or so, helped to clean up. There was a broken mirror, broken chairs, broken glasses. The tavern owner wanted payment for damages, so I offered some money—almost the last that I had—as partial compensation. It seemed the right thing to do as it was the men on my ship who had caused the problem. I figured Lewis had left the tavern quickly to make a point, but that he would see his responsibility for the damages as well and reimburse me. I was wrong about that, too. He said he wasn't going to cover anything.

Arden looked at Jack and John-Paul, his lawyer. "*I admit I was furious.*" He paused. "*I did not harm Mr. Lewis, but I can understand why someone would.*"

John-Paul Stewart jumped in. "Arden, if we have you on the witness stand, please don't say anything like that."

There was a nod and a half smile. Arden continued.

I was back on the deck of the ship about 3 a.m. Before I went to my cabin, I went down to the crew's quarters to see what I could learn about the fight and to make sure all the tempers were calmed. As I held up the lantern to survey the scene, I could hear only snores and see passed-out bodies of men who had drunk more than they could handle. Included in these was their foreman, who, if he been in my employ, would have been fired right away and relieved of his duties.

A few hours later we were on our way to Shallow Island. My men worked hard to hoist sail; in contrast, Lewis' men rose slowly throughout the morning with complaints and nausea. They were unpleasant and smelly, but I consoled myself with the knowledge that the trip would be ending soon and I would be rid of Lewis and his men. The winds were with us and we made it through Death's Door by mid-afternoon. A few hours later we were able to dock and begin the unloading.

There was impressive progress on Lewis' building since the end of the previous fall when I had last seen it. Lewis was in a good mood as the mansion came into view. I made the mistake of bringing up finances again as we approached. I wanted to settle the two matters that I expected extra money for: the damage done to my ship caused by his metal rods, and the damages I had paid for at the tavern. But he dismissed me. I

> *admit there were sharp words from both of us when he told me he would pay neither. I raised my voice and I am sure there were men that heard me do so.*

John-Paul had been taking precise notes. He asked the occasional question, but mostly listened. After thirty minutes, the locked door opened and the conference was stopped. Arden was taken back to his cell, and the two other men left with the promise that they would return the following morning.

31

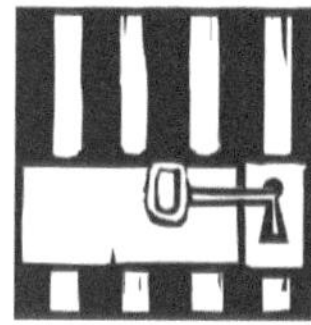

JACK AND JOHN-PAUL had to wait. There had been a fight in the yard, they were told; the guards were busy. Finally, Arden was brought in, this time in leg shackles.

"Are those necessary?" John-Paul asked.

"On everyone today," was the answer the guard gave. Arden looked at his visitors and shrugged, as if he was unfazed by this latest indignity.

"The fight wasn't even in my building," he said quietly as soon as the guard left the room. He sighed, then picked up his narrative where he had left off the afternoon before.

As I said, there had been progress on Lewis' buildings. The smaller outbuildings were roofed, and masons were at work completing the high outside walls of the second story of the huge mansion. The space inside would be big enough for a banquet size hall and kitchen as well as six upstairs bedrooms. Adjoined to the large house was a nearly completed room that was to be Lewis' office. It had a desk already set up, book shelves, and a comfortable chair. The Jenny Marie carried with it an expensive carpet that would be laid out on the wood floor that had been completed only the previous week. There were to be windows, but when we arrived, there were only openings. Some framing had begun, but as yet there was no glass installed yet.

It took some maneuvering, but the Jenny Marie accessed the dock. The cargo was impressive: besides the rug, there were fancy oil lights, beveled mirrors, and an elaborately carved mantlepiece. Lewis was particularly proud of an imported marble countertop, which, thankfully, had survived the storm's jostling. There were barrels of nails, tools and hardware, furniture, linens. Both my men and his were involved in the unloading. Lewis was everywhere on the building site. He flitted from his office to the ship to meetings with workmen. Though we could tell that he was pleased with the progress, I observed that most of his questions were negative. "Why isn't the oil for the lanterns stored more safely? Why was the tallest tree felled for stove wood instead of lumber for building?" By the time the unloading was finished, he had compiled pages of notes for his foremen.

It was evening when we finished. I was not about to sail through Death's Door at night, so we intended to spend the night at the island. We were offered a meal by the cook and we contributed food from our ship. It was late when we gathered to eat in the yard with all of Lewis' men. The work crew by that time was 29 men.

"Are you certain of that exact number?" John-Paul asked. "How do you come to that number?"

Arden thought for a moment. "There were four of his men on the ship with me, and Lewis had told me more than once that there were 25 there already. He was proud of the fact that his project was so large."

"Does that number include the foremen?"

"I am not certain, but I assume that it does."

John-Paul again made a note. He went back and underlined it as Arden continued.

We were all weary from the heavy lifting, and we were mostly quiet in the yard as the cooks finished preparing supper. Lewis came out of his office, caught my eye, and beckoned me over to him. I expected that he was going to pay me for the delivery of his supplies as we had agreed. Instead, the conversation was not good news.

'My foreman tells me that the one small boat that we have on this island has been ruined in a storm,' he said. 'My builders use it to make short trips to the neighboring islands—even as far as Washington Island—if we need certain supplies. It was also the boat I intended to use to get home. My men were to take me to Rock Island five days from now and I will be picked up there. So we must have a small boat here, not only for that purpose but also for the needs of the men on this island. Our boat is not salvageable. But I see that you have a small boat on the Jenny Marie that would be adequate for our needs. I would pay you, of course.'

'I'm afraid that's impossible,' I told him. 'It is dangerous to sail without a lifeboat. I won't attempt it.'

I was incredulous that he would assume he could take what was mine. He was insistent. He said that the lives of thirty men (he included himself) on an island were more important

> *than the seven lives of the people aboard my ship. He would pay me and I could get a new one at any of the shipbuilders located in the cities where I was headed.*

Arden looked at Jack and John-Paul.

> *Once again, I was angry. Over my lifetime, I have seen men who believe they can do whatever they want to people beneath them. To me, it is the greatest example of evil, the worst character trait of all.*
>
> *'When I refused, he told me that our whole agreement was null. He said he would not pay me at all for the delivery of the very supplies we had spent the day unloading. I was livid and we argued. I told him that what he was proposing was bribery, and asked how he could do business in such an unethical manner.*
>
> *'I have been doing business in the wilderness for quite some time now,' he told me. 'In 1850, Chicago was the country's 29th largest city. Today, it is the second largest. Do you think it's grown because people like me are kind and genteel? Because we are gentlemanly? No, it is all 'survival of the fittest.' It is 'take what you need however you can.' Captain, give me the boat that I need, and all will be well.'*
>
> *'We are not done with this conversation,' I told him. I needed to calm down and consider my options so I walked away from his office. Truthfully, I wanted to discuss this development with Solomon who I could trust to look at the situation logically. But I was certainly not in favor of giving Lewis my lifeboat and putting my own men's lives in danger.*
>
> *I walked away from the house and back toward the summer kitchen. I have had a lot of time to think about the words I*

said to Mr. Lewis as I was walking away from him. A lot of time to realize that there were many men who likely overheard the exact words that I told him. He looked intensely at the two men across the table from him.

I said, 'I am not done with you, Mr. Lewis. You will have to pay for this.'

All three were quiet for a moment. Jack continued by asking a question: "What did you end up deciding about the boat?"

I decided to give it to him. Or to sell it to him, rather. Solomon, as he always does, asked questions that made me realize I was more ready to be done with the man than stick to my principle. Most of my crew had heard about our disagreement by then and they let me know through Solomon that they were with me, lifeboat or not. If Lewis paid me, it was true that we could purchase a new boat in Algoma or Sheboygan, only a few days sail south.

However, Lewis never heard that was the conclusion I had come to. We left it that we would talk again before we sailed in the morning. But that talk never happened.

"So you never got paid?"

"No."

"For any of it?"

"No, Sir, I did not."

Dinner was long in coming and it was nearly dark when we ate. I sat with a large group of men at the tables and Lewis did not come out of his office. We watched a cook carry a plate across the yard for Lewis, and he ate by himself. I headed back to the ship about half an hour later. The winds had come up and the waves were loud, but the night sky was clear. More and more stars had come out, and instead of going directly to the ship, I walked north along the shoreline. Cassieopeia was out. The two twins, and in fact all the constellations of stars in the northern sky were about as bright as I have ever seen them. The Milky Way was a river. I saw fifteen falling stars. I stayed for almost an hour, I'd say, before I turned back to the ship and walked along the shoreline. I had a lantern with me, but I didn't need it. After my eyes adjusted to the dark, the stars gave off enough light for me to see my way back to the Jenny Marie. I walked on to the pier, and went into my cabin.

I had been reading less than twenty minutes or so-

"What time was that, do you think?" John-Paul asked.

"My guess is a few minutes after 11:00."

John-Paul nodded for him to continue.

I was reading when Tim Fowler, one of Lewis' foremen, and two large men who accompanied him burst into my cabin. Fowler had a gun. They started searching my cabin, opening drawers and unpacking my luggage. It all happened suddenly, but they found an envelope with $1200 in my map drawer. I only keep money in my safe, and would never have put money with the maps. I don't know how it got there or who put it there. It could have happened anytime in those hours after the loading stopped and we were all in the yard. We had no reason to have anyone stay and watch the ship. The Jenny Marie was tied up and secure. We were all away in the yard until well after supper.

"Was your cabin unlocked?"

"Yes, I rarely lock it. And there was no reason to lock it on Shallow Island."

Not only did they find the envelope with money in my cabin, they talked repeatedly about a shot that had been fired. Apparently, it had happened during the previous hour, when I was on the north side of the island and the wind had carried the sound the other way. Mr. Lewis had been fired on as he sat at his desk. There was a hole in the wall right above where he had been sitting. Someone had fired at him from the outside but had missed. The shot was heard by the men who were sitting around the fire right next to the bunk house and summer kitchen. Lewis cried out and ran out into the yard to call for help. Men ran across the yard to the office when they heard the gunfire. Nobody had seen who fired the shot as it was already dark.

I was told that after the gunshot, two things happened. Lewis went back into his office and opened his desk drawer to get out his own gun, and he found that his money was gone. Secondly, everyone was gathered together. They accounted for everyone except me. Some people had been in their bunks, some people at the privy, and some at the fire. But Fowler gathered them up and deduced that everyone was there except for me. I was, according to them, the only one that had not been seen during the previous hour.

Solomon told me that my men protested when I was blamed. Someone suggested that we had all been in on the plot together, so we were all under suspicion. I was locked in my cabin. Fowler and his strong men with their three guns made my men sail the Jenny Marie to Chicago. Without a lifeboat, of course. They made sure they lowered the lifeboat and tied it to their dock before leaving Shallow Island. As soon as we landed in Chicago, Fowler got the police and I was arrested.

Lewis must have sway with the police force. The police told my men they should not make noise, that they should keep quiet. That they could tell their story at a trial, but they should stay away from the docks, keep it all quiet. They were threatened, according to Solomon. I was in prison, so I guess they could see what they were up against. I don't fault them for leaving as they weren't going to be paid. Solomon did what he could, tried to contact a lawyer. But no one much listened to him. So there was not much to do except wait. I have had two public defenders. Both have resigned from my case.

Arden was done with the account. He paused and looked at the men in front of him.

I did not shoot at Archibald Lewis. I did not steal any of his money. Yes, I was frustrated with him. I do not think he is ethical or fair in his business. But I did not steal. I am not a man who steals. I did not try to kill him, as I would not ever try to kill any man.

That is all that I know. Solomon spent his own money, paid to have the Jenny Marie put into the river over the winter. I don't know what will become of her. I have few resources, as all of the money I had was invested in my ship. I appreciate your taking my case, John-Paul, but I do not believe I will ever go free. I wish I believed, as you do, Jack, that good wins over evil. But I do not.

Jack was ready to engage in a discussion on the topic, but John-Paul Stewart had been reviewing his notes. Before Jack could talk, John-Paul spoke.

"I have to ask: did you kill men in the Civil War? The prosecutors will want to know."

"No, Mr. Stewart, I did not. In the Union Navy, I sailed on ships for five years. I hoisted sails. I pulled lines, steered around hurricanes, bailed water, drank horrible coffee, and delivered ammunitions to our troops past enemy lines so that we could win the war. I was crew and then first mate. We maneuvered against Confederate ships and dodged cannon fire that came at us. We were in danger when we unloaded our supplies in Southern ports. I know how to use a gun and it turns out that I had steady aim, but no, I did not kill any man in the war. I smelled the stench of wounded men that we hauled back on ships when we sailed North. I saw what gun shots can do to the body of a man, and I have no desire to see that again, even in a man I loathe."

"And how long have you been here in this jail?"

"Eight months."

Do you know the whereabouts of your crew?"

"I was taken off the ship by Chicago constables and brought here. Solomon has stayed in Chicago but he says the rest of my crew were told to leave town and not to sail on the ships out of Chicago harbors. It was grim business, and Solomon does not fault them for scattering."

"And what has life been like for you in this place?"

"Occasionally a pastor visits. Once I was given a light blanket. Once a week some water to wash. I was sick in the winter. There is barely enough to eat. I have been in the same cell, sometimes with a cell mate and sometimes not. In August, then again in September, I met lawyers, each of whom gave me less than a few minutes of time, no longer. This is the first time I have told anyone the whole story.

"Solomon has come to see me, but no one else. He has contacted my sister and it is she, as you know, that hired you, John-Paul, to defend me. Jack, I thank you for coming, but I am doubtful that any defense will succeed. Archibald Lewis is a man who gets his way. Especially if he has the law and the police with him, I have little hope that I will be anywhere than here for a very long time."

The following day, when the two men came back to discuss details of the trial that was to start soon, Meggie sent three books with her father to give to Arden: a copy of *A Tale of Two Cities*, a newly released book entitled *Middlemarch,* and a blank diary and a pen. She sent soup and bread as well.

Arden had been allowed a Bible in the jail, but he had had access to no other books. He was hungry to read. After reading several chapters of the first of the two books, he set that aside, then opened the blank diary and wrote.

Arden's Diary *March 28, 1872*

It feels a relief to tell my story to someone. I told them what I have told myself: it is hopeless. Still, I see in their faces they believe there is a case to be made for my side. But how can John-Paul Stewart and Jack McGinn be a force equal to Archibald Lewis? Is it like David and Goliath? I doubt it. I am no David.

Jack did not talk religion to me today. It is just as well, as I am unsettled. 'God cares for the innocent,' he said. But I am far from innocent. Perhaps judgment has finally come to me. I am accused of stealing and attempted murder. Aren't those my exact crimes? I didn't commit those crimes on Shallow Island, but didn't I steal lives away from the people squeezed below deck on the Flying Falcon? Didn't I attempt their murders when I transported them to their certain deaths on cotton fields? Is this my right and fitting punishment for what I did all those years ago?

Strangely, I have had fewer nightmares here in this prison. All through the war and for all those years after, whether on the ship or in the orchards at Sally's, I'd wake up in the night to those cries of the people below deck. But here, it is waning. Perhaps I am finally assuaging the guilt.

Jack McGinn is well meaning, but all wrong. God has nothing to do with it all except to say here, take your punishment. I am wishing now that he and Meggie had not come. I can hardly bear to look at Meggie. How dare she hope? How dare she make me hope along with her, to think there is even a chance that I could walk free with her in a world beyond these walls and bars? I almost do not want them here.

And John-Paul Stewart? He will be no match for Lewis' lawyers. All this do-gooding of others will be for naught. I will lose the trial. I will likely die here. Or I will be old when I see water again, when I will walk under blue sky. But at least then I will say I have paid for my guilt, for the evil I did.

Tomorrow I will ask John-Paul to sell the Jenny Marie. Solomon did the best he could do to preserve her over the winter, but he cannot be captain. With a new season starting, someone will surely have an interest in buying her.

32

ONLY A FOOL would say the cards were not stacked against Arden Anderson on the first morning of his trial. In the courtroom, Mr. Lewis appeared confident, even smug, accustomed to having his way. He was well dressed. Whether unconscious habit or intentional, he periodically took out an expensive gold watch to glance at, as if to call attention to the gold chain fob that hung in an arc from his pocket. He sat next to his attractive wife who was dressed in a pale green, fashionable dress. They sat immediately behind two prosecutors and their two assistants.

On the other hand, Arden's defense attorney, John-Paul Stewart, appeared disheveled, even motley. Arden had been allowed to shave, but the suit that had been found for him by the Ingrams was ill-fitting. His face looked gaunt. Eight months in jail had taken its toll; he did not look like the confident captain Meggie had met the summer before.

The charges were read: attempted murder and theft of twelve hundred dollars.

"How do you plead?"

"Not guilty, sir." He said this with deep conviction. Even the court reporter looked up to glance at his face.

Charles Albion, lead prosecutor for the state, was a personal friend of Archibald Lewis. He, too, was well dressed, past middle-aged, and experienced in court proceedings. He began his opening arguments with a long introduction to the description of the events that had unraveled in the hours of the July summer evening nearly eight months before.

"Many of you may know of my client, Mr. Lewis. He has worked hard on behalf of the city of Chicago and it can be argued that he and a small number of other fine individuals have been the reason this city has grown to become the wonderful metropolis that it is today. He has worked hard in industry. He has worked hard in commerce. He has brought prosperity to Chicago. I will remind you there are public parks which exist in the fair city of Chicago today because Archibald Lewis donated the land.

"What you may not know about Archibald Lewis is that he loves the water, as many people in Chicago do. In fact, I would wager to say, that many of you fine gentlemen on the jury enjoy strolling along the Lake Michigan shore. Mr. Lewis is in his fifties, and he has begun to plan for a future of less work and more leisure. He has been endeavoring to build a home on an island in Lake Michigan. He purchased the island six years ago. He hired architects and surveyors to draw up plans. For the past three years he has been in the process of building structures there. The court and the jury can imagine that this is a lengthy and complicated process.

"In the construction of this impressive residence, a great number of people have been involved. Workers are hired, and supplies must be procured and transported. Mr. Lewis tells me that it is a beautiful place. However, it is remote. There are no stores or roads, no markets or butchers or tailors. There is no grocery filled with baking supplies or fresh fruit. Mr. Lewis is a self-reliant man, capable and competent. But in the matter of this building project on

Shallow Island, he must rely on ships. He must rely on captains and sailors and the boats they handle to transport everything possible to survive on the island. He must put his own life into the hands of others who are more familiar than he about the ways of our great Lake Michigan.

"Last July, after many weeks away from the project on his island, Archibald Lewis did this very thing: he put his life into the hands of Captain Arden Anderson. Archibald Lewis scheduled a trip to Shallow Island. He is a very busy man, but he planned to take two weeks off of his remarkably full schedule to check on the status of his building project. He made arrangements with the captain of the *Jenny Marie* to deliver himself, four laborers, and numerous building supplies to Shallow Island. The sailing trip was to take three days. He procured passage home on a different ship. He arranged to be picked up ten days later for his return trip back to Chicago.

"It should not have been a difficult job. It should have been a straightforward sail. However, the sail was anything but routine. Mr. Lewis was subjected to one problem after another. Bad weather is of course out of the control of a ship captain, but a ship captain should *do his job* in bad weather. Instead, on a late afternoon of rough winds and high waves, the sails on the *Jenny Marie* ripped. Additionally, the ship started taking water as two substantial holes emerged in the side of the ship. Before continuing to sail further north, the captain of the *Jenny Marie* insisted that repairs must be made. They were waylaid in a small village for two extra days. The captain would not hear of speeding the repairs or of sailing the ship in its slightly impaired state. He was insensitive to the needs of Mr. Lewis who had nothing to do in a small town in the Wisconsin wilderness except wait. A sailmaker and a crew of carpenters were called in, but they did not start immediately. It was several hours before the work began, and the captain was gone for the better part of the two days, unconcerned, it seems, about the pace of the repairs.

"Objection!" John-Paul stood up, and the judge nodded.

"Sustained."

"When they arrived at Shallow Island, Mr. Lewis was happy to see that in spite of the storm, most of the supplies had arrived undamaged. He was glad to be on the island and to see the progress that had been made in his absence. The unloading took until evening, and as winds on the lake were picking up, Captain Anderson made the judgment not to sail out immediately but to harbor there through the night and sail out in the morning. Mr. Lewis granted that permission and even extended the generous offer to provide supper for Captain Anderson and his crew.

"There was, however, a problem on the island. His foreman told Lewis that the building site's only boat had been damaged in an earlier storm and they were in desperate need of a new boat. The extensive work crew on the island used this boat to make runs to neighboring islands for supplies. As many as thirty men were on the island and though supply ships like the *Jenny Marie* came and went every five or six days, it was vital to have access to their own boat for emergencies. It was a matter of life and death. I bring this matter up here to the court, because it is important on this point: Captain Anderson could have helped with this matter. The *Jenny Marie* carried with her a small dinghy that would have sufficed. Mr. Lewis offered to pay a good price. Sadly, Captain Anderson refused. It seems inhumane that he would not take into account the needs of the many men on the island. Instead, he was inexplicably angry, and everyone on the island heard the two men arguing.

"In fact, this was not the only argument that he and my client had engaged in. They had argued much of the way up the coast. Anderson felt that Lewis owed him more money. There were disagreements about the way cargo had been packed. There were disagreements about the speed of the repairs. It seems that Anderson had a pattern of problems with Mr. Archibald Lewis and that he was not an easy man to do busi-

"Objection!" John-Paul rose from his seat. "Mr. Albion is not presenting the facts. He is defaming the character of the defendant."

"Sustained." The judge turned to the jury. "Please disregard the previous statement. Mr. Albion, please carry on, but stick to what is known."

"I apologize," said the prosecutor. "I will rephrase. I will state only that on more than one occasion, it was observed by several witnesses that Arden Anderson and Archibald Lewis argued."

Albion took a drink of water before continuing. He seemed in no hurry to finish. "Now, on the night of the crime, Captain Anderson and all of his ship's crew and all of Mr. Lewis' workers had eaten at tables in the worker's yard. It had been a good workday and the men were relaxing in the summer night. Then, in the dark of that peaceful night, a horrible sound rang out. A gunshot! Can you imagine, on this beautiful, peaceful island? A gunshot shattered the quiet of the night. Multiple sources have told us that several minutes of commotion followed. The sound had come from Mr. Lewis' office, and most of the men ran across the yard toward the sound. Mr. Lewis had been sitting in his office with the lantern lit, an easy target for anyone to see through an open window. He shouted out and came out of his office. One of the masons in charge told his men to search the property for whoever it was who had shot the gun. When they went back into the office to investigate, they examined the room thoroughly. It was grim. A bullet was found lodged in the wall just a few inches above where Lewis' head had been hunched over papers he was examining. It was clear that this had been an attempt on Archibald Lewis' life. Thankfully, the attempt was unsuccessful. For whatever reason, Captain Anderson was not able to follow through on his evil intention."

"Objection!" John-Paul jumped up. "There is no evidence that the perpetrator was Captain Anderson."

"Sustained."

"Again, I'll rephrase. While Mr. Lewis was sitting in his office, a gunshot rang out in the night. Someone fired a gun and the target was most certainly my client. We are all glad Mr. Lewis is alive and with us today.

"It was dark by this time and the foremen rounded up all of the men; every man was asked to come to the yard. Many had gathered together after they had eaten around a fire pit. A few were in the privy, a few were in their bunks. They were all instructed to gather and be accounted for. Each man, it seems, had seen another, and everyone could vouch for another. There was only one exception. Arden Anderson was not in the clearing. He was not in the yard; he was not on the grounds. His crew said he had gone back alone to his ship, and in fact Mr. Lewis' men found him there several minutes later. Arden Anderson was the only possible culprit; all others had been together at the workers' yard.

"But I have not yet told you the most damning evidence. Mr. Lewis was rightfully skittish after having just survived an attempt on his life. He had a personal gun that he kept in a locked drawer in his desk; he opened the drawer to retrieve it. In addition, he had brought with him a large sum of money. He intended to use a portion of that sum to pay Arden Anderson for his passage and the transport of supplies. In addition, his foremen would need funds to pay the supply ships that were scheduled to arrive throughout the summer. Mysteriously and troublingly, that money was missing. Not only had there been an attempt on his life, at some time earlier in the day, he had also been robbed.

"I will say to Captain Anderson's credit that his crew was loyal. They objected to the accusations that were made about their captain. They insisted he would not have fired a shot at Mr. Lewis. They were angry that he alone was accused. Someone in Mr. Lewis' employ suggested that maybe they were all in the scheme, that somehow they were all complicit. Sadly, it meant that the entire crew of the *Jenny Marie* was suspect.

"Imagine yourself in Mr. Lewis' position. I will remind the gentlemen of the jury that there was no police force on the island. There were no constables or lawyers or judges. However, there were crimes committed against Mr. Lewis. Someone had to take charge. Anyone in his place would have felt the need to do the same. He directed his foremen and two others to go to the ship to look for Captain Anderson's whereabouts. When they came to the ship, they reported that he was reading calmly in his cabin and claimed to be unaware of any commotion on the construction grounds.

"When they searched his cabin, though, Lewis' envelope with $1200 money was found. It was stuffed in a drawer full of maps. Captain Anderson claimed to have no knowledge of that money or how it came to be in the drawer. Because he denies his guilt, we have not ascertained how or when Anderson could have stolen the money, but it is clear that he is guilty of horrendous, immoral, and violent actions.

"We will show in this trial that Arden Anderson is indeed guilty of the crimes of which he is accused. It could be asked why Mr. Lewis is pursuing this case. His money is recovered, his life is intact, his beloved building project is continuing. However, Mr. Lewis was wronged. His money was stolen, and an attempt was made on his life, and he does not want the perpetrator to go free without consequence. It will not be difficult for you, the jury, to come to the conclusion that Mr. Lewis willingly put his life into the hands of Arden Anderson only to be returned with betrayal and conniving and anger and evil. We believe this will be a quick and easy trial, and we will not need to waste a lot of the court or the jury's time. Thank you."

Mr. Albion sat down. The jury shifted in their chairs and watched as John-Paul Stewart got up from his chair.

~

Jack and Meggie had been sitting spellbound, as had most of the jury and all of the spectators who watched from the gallery. Had they not known Arden, it would have been easy to conclude his guilt. The district attorney was well practiced, a good story teller, and expert in his craft.

Despite Archibald Lewis' fame, there were few other spectators in the court-room. Lewis desired that the case not draw attention, and it appeared he had managed to fulfill that aim. There was one unexpected exception. Jack had alerted his friend Ollie Danielson, an editor at a medium-sized newspaper, that the trial was beginning, and Ollie had sent a reporter to observe the proceedings.

In contrast to the practiced rhetoric of Lewis' lawyers, John-Paul Stewart was young and inexperienced. He appeared slightly nervous as he rose for the first time to address the jury. He began with a murmur, and the audience strained to hear what he said. "Innocent until proven guilty." He repeated the phrase, a little louder this time. "Innocent until proven guilty." He looked at the jury. "Please indulge me while I say this phrase a third time: 'Innocent until proven guilty.'" He continued. "I have only recently graduated from law school. To be honest, I will admit to you that I have tried less than ten cases in a court of law. But I'd like to remind everyone in this room of a principle so crucial to the proceedings here that I truly think it can't be said often enough. In this country, accusations are one thing. Assumptions are another. But to ascertain the guilt of a man or a woman, we need proof. We need evidence. Without it, we cannot convict. This is written into our Constitution, and it is the heart of what makes the legal system in this country admirable. It is the reason that there will be justice accomplished in this court whether I am on my third case or my three thousandth case, whether I have riches like my esteemed colleagues here whose job it is to prosecute crimes or whether I am a young attorney struggling still to furnish a meager apartment. In this court of law, only one thing matters. Justice. And justice is accomplished through this principle alone: a man is innocent until he is proven guilty.

"Now, sirs, let me remind you of the facts of this case. A man has been accused of a crime by people who have, it will be proven, treated him ill. He did *not* aim a gun at Mr. Lewis or fire it. He did *not* have any intent to do so, and he does *not* have the character to do so. He did *not* steal money from Mr. Lewis, and he has no idea how that large sum of money came to be on his ship. By all accounts, Captain Arden Anderson is a man of good reputation and integrity. He treats people fairly. He is honest in his transactions in commerce. His crew likes him. You will learn in the course of this trial that there are only accusations and assumptions, not facts and evidence. We accept that crimes were committed. But it is not true that those crimes were committed by Arden Anderson.

"It is your duty to examine the evidence, to see if there are facts that prove the guilt of Mr. Anderson. The gun that fired the shot has not been found. There was no gunpowder on the hands or the clothes of my defendant. No one saw him outside the window of Mr. Lewis' office. No one watched him—or any other of those thirty men on the island that night—shoot a gun and attempt to kill Mr. Lewis. The only evidence the prosecution offers is that Arden Anderson was not on the grounds. Was there a police investigation? Were all the workers on the island questioned? Were everyone's whereabouts verified? And is it not likely that in a close-knit community like the one that these island workers had created, a man might stick up for his friend? If a man were off having a smoke or a drink somewhere on the island, might it be easy to take his friend's side, to not tell the whole truth?

"Let us turn to the alleged robbery. My client denies the charge. I can present to you the books which Captain Anderson keeps. They are impeccable. He keeps careful records of all his commercial transactions, and he is honest, and generous, I must say, to a fault. There is a safe in his cabin. If he had money, it most certainly would have been inside that locked vault. We will get to that fact later. But let us return to the principle I attempted to emphasize earlier. 'Innocent until proven guilty.' Did anyone see Captain Arden Anderson go into Archibald Lewis' office, find a key to a desk, open a drawer, take money out, return to his ship cabin and stash money inside? Was anyone watching the ship throughout the evening to see him do this? And if not, couldn't any *one* of those thirty people on the island that evening have planted that money on the ship with a plan that is yet to be understood? In fact, doesn't it make more sense to reason that it was one of Lewis' men who knew that his boss had a locked desk and would likely have brought money with him? Isn't it more likely that one of *them*—not a person who had spent only an hour on the island—would have known the location of a key and would have known there was money inside?

"Gentlemen, you will find there is no solid proof against my client. I do not deny that there were serious offenses against Mr. Lewis. But Mr. Lewis was wrong to conclude without evidence that those offenses were committed by Captain Anderson. You, as jurors in a court of law, would be wrong, too, to make those same conclusions.

"Finally, gentlemen, let me remind you that wealth and power do not equate to justice. The person that attempted to take the life of Mr. Lewis should be found. The person that stole Mr. Lewis' money should be prosecuted. But that person is not Arden Anderson, and just because a man of privilege and power believes him to be guilty does not make him so. Thank you. I look forward to examining further the details of this trial."

With the conclusion of both the prosecution's and defense's opening arguments, the judge pronounced that the proceedings would resume Monday morning. The one lone reporter returned to his desk at the paper. He was glad that he would be able to make the deadline for the small story that would run in Saturday morning's edition.

33

JACK AND MEGGIE were finishing their Saturday night dinner with Lillian and Byron Ingram in the comfortable kitchen of the Ingram's home. Byron told them news of the great fire that had destroyed so much of the city the year before. Their grown son and his wife and family lost their home, as had one-third of the city's inhabitants. The fire had been so hot that, even three days after it had burned itself out, the embers were too hot for rescue efforts to begin. The church building where the Ingrams worshipped was gone. The congregation was raising money for a new building, but this time it would be built out of brick. Building prices were high. Some businessmen had lost everything. Others were making a fortune this year. Between price gouging and the need to rebuild quickly, the rich just got richer. Corruption had only gotten worse in the city after the fire.

It was about 7:00p.m. and had already been dark for over an hour. The Ingrams did not live on a street that was electrified; their neighborhood was quiet, so it was unusual to hear a knock on the door.

Ollie Danielson, Jack's journalist friend, came into the dining room where he was welcomed and was offered a chair at the table.

He came with interesting news. "At about two o'clock this afternoon, an envelope came to the newspaper with $200 toward the defense fund of Arden Anderson. By about an hour ago, three additional couriers had delivered letters with money totaling an additional $150."

"Who were they from? Why did they come to your paper?" Meggie asked.

"One donation was from a name I recognized. The other three were anonymous. It is not unusual for us to receive donations for this fund or that. But this, I will say, *is* unusual. The story we ran was small. It ran on the fourth-page of our newspaper without a big headline. There was no mention of a fund. If there is this much money already, I would not be surprised if more comes in to us on Monday."

"What do you think this is about, Ollie?" Jack asked.

"The wealthy men of this city did not make their money by being nice guys. That is no secret. One of the anonymous donations included a note intimating that Lewis has not been ethical in his money dealings. His words were something to the effect of, 'Lewis has cheated, stolen, and connived his way to the top. It is time for the big man to come down and let the little man rise.'"

"Is that something we could use in court?"

"Doubtful, without a signature. It could be used by the prosecutors as nothing more than the ramblings of a man seeking revenge."

"Still, it shows that there is a pattern to Lewis' actions."

"I'm afraid that until we know more, it won't do any good. However, this money might help you. I'd recommend hiring private investigators who can dig into what really happened on that island. I don't think the whole story is being told."

Jack and Ollie hurried out the door to discuss this new development with John-Paul, and Meggie and the Ingrams were left to wonder about this turn of events.

Meggie knew that her father would adhere to the sabbath the next day. There would be no meetings, no new action until Monday morning. They wouldn't go to the jail and visit, so Arden would be unaware of this new development even though Meggie wished she could tell him. She was glad to have her knitting for the rest of that night. After they attended church the next day in a temporary building, she tried to content herself with more knitting and with reading, but she was restless. Meggie wanted her father to do something more than sit in the parlor and read. Finally, at about four o'clock, during the last hours of daylight, Jack walked with her to the lake and back. There was fog and chill in the March air. Still, it was good to watch waves. Lake Michigan was a steely, impersonal gray.

There were more questions than answers. John-Paul would ask for more time from the judge, but if more time was not granted, all this new-found hope would be useless.

The mood in the courtroom was far different than the one that had prevailed on Friday. This time, there were reporters from three newspapers. The seats in the court room were full and more chairs were brought in for spectators. Still others were standing around the edges of the room when the court was called to order.

Lewis, who apparently had not wanted this trial to attract attention, seemed bothered by the increased number of spectators. Thankfully, John-Paul Stewart was not a man who shrank from performance; he was buoyed by the crowd. Armed with the information from Ollie, who gave him hope that the crowd was on "his side," he carried himself with more confidence than he had on the first day.

Minutes after the court was called to order, John-Paul asked for a continuance. "Your honor, new information has come to our attention. We would respectfully ask for an additional two weeks to prepare our defense."

"What is the nature of this new information?"

"We cannot say at this time, only that it is pertinent."

"That's not enough, Mr. Stewart. We will continue for today. However, I am willing to consider your request if you can give me a better reason than the fact that you are unprepared. Mr. Albion, I believe the prosecution is ready to call witnesses?"

"We are, your honor. We call George Hermann."

George Hermann was the foreman of the masons on Shallow Island. He had been one of the long-time laborers, one of the first crew there at the beginning of the project, and the man who was most familiar with the men on the island the night of the incident. He had met Arden Anderson each time he had docked and delivered supplies. He reported his version of the gunshot they had heard, the call to gather all of the men to the open yard, and the fact that he had been instructed to find Mr. Anderson. It was he, along with Tim Fowler, who had found the money in the map drawer in the captain's cabin.

"Can you tell us what Mr. Anderson's reaction was when the money was found?" John-Paul asked when it was his turn to question the witness.

Hermann paused a moment. He looked at Arden before continuing. "I wouldn't have taken that man for a liar," he said. "But he sure proved to be a good one. He acted like he'd never seen the money. He acted surprised. He acted like he didn't know anything about the gunshot."

"Mr. Hermann, I'd like you to think back about the weather that night. Can you describe it for us?"

"Well, windy. Surf was up. I remember the ship crew saying they hoped the winds would die down before they had to sail through Death's Door the next day."

"Thank you. So is it possible that Mr. Anderson was telling the truth that, with high winds and crashing waves, he had not, in fact, heard a gunshot?"

"Well of course he heard the gun shot. He *shot* the gun shot!"

"I understand that is your belief, Mr. Hermann. But let me ask this question another way. What sounds did you hear when you were on the boat?"

"Waves, Mr. Stewart. High surf and winds." He understood the line of questioning and spat out his answer.

"Do you think the sound of a gunshot would have carried over the sound of the surf?"

"I don't know. Maybe not."

"Thank you. Mr. Hermann. That will be all for now."

Albion's team called three more witnesses. All were men who had been on the island. All had remarkably similar stories. *Anderson and their boss had argued. They had eaten. Everyone was in the yard by a fire. They heard a shot and Lewis had called out. No one saw who had done it as it was already dark. When they were called together, Captain Anderson was the only one not present.*

Under their cross examinations, Jean-Paul got the witnesses to admit that "everyone" had in fact *not* been at the fire when the shot had been heard. The cooks were cleaning up after dinner. A few men were already in their bunks. There was often a line at the privies, so of course there were probably a few men there. The fire where many of them sat didn't burn all that long because the winds were picking up.

Late in the afternoon, a fourth witness was called with a similar story. At a specific point in his story when he was testifying for the prosecution, Arden leaned over to John-Paul and whispered something emphatically.

When it was John-Paul's turn to question, he rose quickly. "Mr. Lems, you have testified that you worked as a mason on Shallow Island and were there at the night in question."

"Yes, sir."

"Mr. Lems, when you were asked by the prosecution what you were doing by the fire on the night in question, you told us that you were using the firelight to write a letter."

"Yes, sir."

"Mr. Lems, you may not be aware of this, but Captain Anderson is a very literary man. He values words, books, and letters. He tells me that he made it known to men on Shallow Island that he would be happy to take letters to post. But he also distinctly remembers complaints from other laborers who told him that there was no paper to be had on the island. That a few men would have liked to have written letters for the captain to post, but in fact *no one* could write any letters because there was no paper available on the island."

"Objection! What does this have to do with this case?" Albion for the first time in the trial looked flustered.

"Over-ruled."

"So let me ask you another question, on an unrelated matter. You have heard a few buildings referred to in these proceedings. Can you tell me if the bunk house was constructed with wood or with stone?"

"Objection! What is the relevance? There is no need for us to know about the buildings on the island."

"Your honor, please. There is a reason for this line of questioning."

"I'll allow it. Just get to the point, Mr. Stewart."

"Thank you, your honor." He turned back to the witness. "Mr. Lems, you are a mason. You certainly know the difference between wood and stone construction? How was the bunk house constructed?

"I don't know. I didn't pay attention."

"I see. What about the office where Mr. Lewis was working that night?"

"I don't know."

"What about the tool shed?

"I don't know. I think wood."

"The tool shed, Mr. Lems, is in fact made out of stone. This is a fact that I would think you would know, especially as you are a mason. Mr. Lems, were you even *on* the island on the night of June 28th? Let me remind you that you are under oath to tell the truth."

Lems paused for a moment. He glared at the team of prosecutors. Albion, in return, avoided his eye. "No, I wasn't. But I had a friend who was, and he said I could go as him, get some money."

"Your honor!" John-Paul exclaimed, along with murmurs and exclamations from the audience in the room. "I move that this witness be removed from these proceedings and that he be charged with perjury. And this relates precisely to the kind of information that I referred to in my request for a continuance."

The judge banged his gavel to quiet the room. He addressed the prosecution first. "Mr. Albion, I am unsure who is behind this perjury, but I will warn you that it will not be tolerated in my court. If you thought for one minute that this would be an easy and quick trial, you must know it has just become more lengthy. I will direct the district attorney's office to charge Mr. Lems with perjury. I will direct them to investigate whether there is further criminality involved."

The judge turned to the defense. "Mr. Stewart, I will grant your continuance. If you find further evidence of witness tampering, you will bring that evidence directly to me. This court will reconvene in fourteen days' time."

34

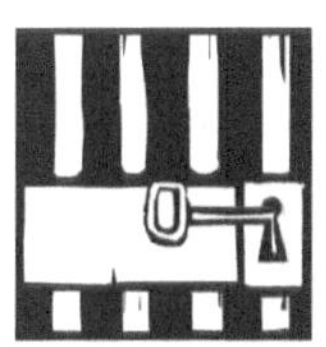

JACK COULD NOT stay on. He needed to return to Roundstone Harbor as the Light would be lit for the season on April 20, only two weeks away. Meggie would stay in Chicago with the Ingrams and wait for the trial to resume. With the money from the donations that continued to come in after more newspaper coverage, John-Paul brought on a retired criminal lawyer as a consultant and hired three private investigators.

The new lawyer was a good strategist. He had experience and could give good advice and direction to John-Paul and the team of investigators. It was decided that they would not call Solomon to testify; a black man's word would be discounted. However, Solomon helped them find Ossy, the ship's cook, and Conrad, a crew man who had been on the *Jenny Marie* and at Shallow Island. Both men could speak about the events on the island. They could provide character witness for Arden.

They sent an investigator to Roundstone Harbor to talk to the sailmaker and carpenter to learn about Lewis' interactions with them while they'd worked on the ship. He was instructed to talk also with Owen Temple, the tavern owner in Roundstone. It was that investigator, a man named Barnes, who made the decision to transport Temple to Chicago to testify in court. He sent a telegraph to Jean-Paul saying he had important information and that he and Temple would be coming by ship. They hoped to be in Chicago by the time the trial resumed, but the travel time was uncertain. It was anyone's guess when the two men would arrive.

Jack returned to Roundstone feeling more confident now that Arden had a team on his side. Ollie Danielson was following the case. There were people watching, and Lewis with his friends in high places could not as easily work outside the law.

The Ingrams were of the same religious ilk as Jack. Prayer before each meal. Lillian was active in her church's missionary society. She read very little other literature besides her Bible. Byron was a deacon at their church. While in their home, Jack and Byron discussed Bible passages. They shared an admiration for the street preachers in Chicago who evangelized both clients and ladies of the brothels of the red light district in the city. Meggie heard the two men praying for Arden on the night before Jack had arranged to leave. She waited for them to finish, then came in to the kitchen to listen to their conversation.

"There was no question that I wanted to help Arden when the letter came. The man saved my son's life, and I felt compelled to at least hear his story."

Byron nodded. "It was asking a lot of you to come."

"Oh, he never asked it. Not in his letter. Not at all. He never expected it either. Our coming was a surprise to him. Sure, it was a bit of a slog to come here with Meggie and leave Kate and the others at home. But now that we are here, it has become more than that. I believe in his innocence. I know in my bones he is not guilty of these crimes. And somehow I feel we are a meant to be a part."

"One of us will try to go with Meggie each day to the court. We will pray. We can't do much, but whatever we can do, we will, as God allows. And Meggie is welcome here as long as she'd like."

"I am grateful for that, Byron. And now I must leave Arden in God's hands. And Meggie in yours. Thank you. My ship sails early, so I may not see you in the morning."

Each of those next fourteen days while the investigators dug for more information, Meggie waited her turn in the crowded waiting room of the jail so that she could talk with Arden for the few minutes that the prison allowed. It was arbitrary. Some days she had half an hour with Arden. Others, only five minutes. One day, she waited and was never called.

She and Arden talked about the books she brought him. She asked, so he told her of the orchard in Ohio, of his niece and his nephew. His gratitude to Solomon and his worry how, without funds, he could pay his friend back. His worry about Solomon's health. But all of their conversation was only report. There was no reason to look forward, to think of a time when they could talk in open air, in a forest of green or by a beach with stones. They avoided conversations about Shallow Island, about the trial, or any mention of life in the future. Arden believed he would never be free. Meggie came to distract him, not prod him to some hope she was unsure of herself.

She also went often to a stationery store around the corner from the Ingram's.

Journals, diaries, pens and inks. There were shelves of greeting cards and stationery with envelopes. Imported wrapping paper for packages. Dyed paper from the new mills in Appleton. The store owners, a young husband and wife were friendly. They had only recently set up their store in a new building constructed just after the fire. The wife was chatty and willing to give Meggie details about finances and investments and inventory. They gave her the names of their suppliers, told her there was good profit and that people were buying.

"They are nothing but encouraging to me," she told Lillian. "I was afraid they would see me as competition when I said I had dreams of opening a store like theirs. But they only laughed at that, said there were plenty of people that wrote letters."

"Are you still thinking of a store in Toledo?" Lillian asked.

"No. And not here in Chicago either. I'm thinking more and more about Roundstone Harbor. Or perhaps somewhere else in Door County. I would not live *with* my parents, but I could be somewhere nearby.

"Being in a port town is important, I should think."

"Yes, and now that I know the names of suppliers, all I would need is a ship that can deliver the supplies to me. And if Arden goes free...I would know a ship captain. Is it too much too dream?"

"I pray for him daily," was the only answer that Lillian gave.

In the two week's recess, one of their investigators began asking questions about the business dealings and patterns of Archibald Lewis. He had to make his inquiries quietly. It appeared that there were police and strong men who did Lewis' bidding. There were accusations by plenty of people he had wronged, but no hard evidence. Nothing that could be proven. It was all vague hints that the man held sway through the power of his money. Also, the investigator learned, the hard way, that Archibald Lewis employed men who were good at intimidation. Men who were persuasive when they said a man should stop asking questions.

There was little help from the law. Immediately after Franklin Lems was charged with perjury, someone in the district attorney's office had been given the task of investigating the charge of witness tampering. That was hopeful. But that individual had conveniently gone on vacation the following week. When a reporter questioned the timing of that man's vacation and asked why the investigation wasn't a priority, he was told only that the office was understaffed.

After the explosive revelation that Franklin Lems had lied about being in Lewis' employ, the courtroom was even more crowded when the trial resumed on Wednesday, April 15. Immediately after the judge gaveled in, Meggie was the first person to be called by the defense. She wore a gray-blue dress. Characteristically, her hair did not stay pinned back, and the few wayward strands of hair across her face were endearing. She answered questions without hesitation.

"How do you know the defendant?"

"I met him last year, when his ship was in Roundstone Harbor for repairs."

"Can you describe your interactions with him? In what context did you meet?"

She described the afternoon visit regarding laundry, the dinner at the lighthouse, the nature of their conversations.

"Objection, your honor. How is this relevant to this case?" Mr. Albion stood.

"Sustained. Mr. Stewart, please get to the point."

"Mrs. Ford, I would like to ask you about an incident the following day, the second day that you and your siblings spent with Mr. Anderson."

Meggie nodded and continued. "I have three younger siblings, sir, and it was a spring day. We had planned a picnic excursion to an interesting landmark in Door County not far from the lighthouse where our family resides. It had been a summering ground for Indians for as many as several centuries—

"Your honor? What is the reason for this questioning?" Albion objected again, and again the judge urged Stewart to get to the point.

"We were there enjoying the day, and though it's a long story, I will try to make it short by saying that on this otherwise very pleasant day in the woods, my younger brother was startled and nearly attacked by a wounded wolf. I had been totally unaware of the danger, but in one terrifying moment, Captain Arden Anderson saw the wolf and acted quickly by shooting the wolf dead between the eyes just as it started to spring on my brother."

"At what distance?"

"Probably fifty feet or more."

"Were there obstacles in the way? Would it have been a difficult shot?"

"Yes, certainly! Yes, there was an obstacle in the way—my young brother! If the Captain's aim had not been so sure, he might easily have shot Peter. Captain Anderson was across a clearing where we were sitting after having something to eat, directly across from Peter. We were in the woods, sir. Trees all around. My brother was wandering off at a bit of a distance from the rest of us, chasing a squirrel or a chipmunk, I think, when the wolf came at him."

"So is it your testimony that Arden Anderson is an excellent shot with a rifle?"

"I don't know about his aim in general, sir. I only know that in this one instance he was remarkably accurate."

"Thank you, Mrs. Ford. That is all."

Mr. Albion rose and spoke in a condescending voice. "Mrs. Ford. You are a widow, I understand."

"That's correct, sir."

"Just over one year since your husband's death?"

"Nineteen months, sir."

"I am surprised that in your recently widowed state you were so willing to spend time with a bachelor."

"I am not sure what you are asking me, Mr. Albion."

"Is it true that you have a romantic interest in the captain?"

"Objection!" John-Paul stood.

"Sustained."

"We know that the captain spent two full days with you when he was in Roundstone Harbor. We know that you have visited him several times here in the Chicago jail. I am merely pointing out to the jury that a woman with a romantic interest in a defendant may not be the most reliable witness."

"Objection!"

"Sustained."

"I have no more questions for the witness, your honor."

"You may step down from the stand, Mrs. Ford."

Meggie knew that all eyes were on her as she walked back to her seat. John-Paul and Emmett Grayson, the newest lawyer, had warned her to expect the prosecutors to be harsh. She knew to keep her composure, to try not to show how they had rattled her. Thankfully, Lillian Ingram was in court with her that day, and Meggie was glad for a friend to sit next to when her time on the stand was completed.

The afternoon was spent questioning two crewmen from the *Jenny Marie*. In the exchange back and forth of the prosecution and defense, a picture emerged that was different than the one presented by the first set of witnesses who had been called by Albion. According to the crew on the *Jenny Marie*, after the sun set and it had grown dark, only a few men were still at the fire. Many had left the yard and were in the process of retiring for the night. With the strong winds, it had been decided that no more wood should be put on the fire. Less than five men were left around the fire ring watching the last embers burn themselves out when the gunhot was heard.

Additionally, there had been drinking. Kegs had been brought in on the *Jenny Marie* and delivered that day. There was some arrangement that Lewis' laborers could buy drinks against their pay, and some had chosen to spend down that pay on the new beer.

"Was there excessive drinking? Were men inebriated?"

Both men acknowledged that not all, but that several of the men had drunk heavily.

"Were the foremen nearby?" Stewart asked.

"No," they reported. The foremen had their own section of the bunkhouse and spent most of their nights apart from the workmen. It was Conrad's impression that the island men were left to themselves in the evenings.

John-Paul asked, "It is your testimony, then, that not all of the thirty men on the island were nearby when the gun shot went off?"

Ossy replied that he had been helping inside the kitchen and that men had come in and gone out. He remembered the door slamming loudly many times as they cleaned up. There were four men or so in the bunkhouse, maybe five. He remembered that a few others had come in with wet hair. They had been washing or possibly even taken a dip in the lake.

Conrad said under oath, "They were all over the island, Mr. Stewart, sir. The place was all new to us, and *we* didn't go wandering much from the yard or the fire. All of us crew, we were waiting for Ossy here so we'd go back to the ship together. But I saw the island men go this way and that way after supper, and I remember asking myself where they were going. Latrines certainly. One of them had a lantern, and I think some might have been playing cards in a shed, but I'm not sure about that. All I know is that they weren't all in one place. I *am* sure of that."

~

The papers were full that night of Margaret McGinn-Ford, an attractive young widow who took Arden Anderson's side. She had been a strong character witness for the defense. She had been poised, articulate, confident. Even though the prosecution tried to intimidate her, to accuse her of flirtation, she had met the captain for the first time just a few days before the incident on Shallow Island; it was wrong of the prosecution to badger her, to treat a young widow condescendingly. She was only a concerned citizen, trying to tell a story that might help a family friend. One newspaper interviewed her at length about the incident with the wolf. They wrote the whole story, including the hike to the former Indian settlement and the moments of rest to eat a snack in the woods. The account included that the waves had come up as the captain rowed the children home. It was good narrative writing, a story that readers would love. The article ended with questions. Why would a man who enjoyed nature, who owned a ship of his own, who was competent and successful, stoop so low as to shoot a man who angered him? And how could he, such a quick-thinking, accurate marksmen, miss an easy target? Was the wrong man on trial?

35

JOHN-PAUL CALLED ARDEN to the stand the next morning. Judging by the reactions of the people in the gallery watching the proceedings, sentiment was on his side. "Can you explain for the court the nature of your disagreements with Mr. Archibald Lewis?"

"The first was in Roundstone Harbor. Our ship was listing, and we were in danger. Our main sail was ripped and we had holes in our side. The ship could not sail on in this condition. The previous afternoon and evening we had been battered by winds and waves. Long metal rods, supplies for Mr. Lewis' new mansion, came loose from their bindings and burst holes in our hull. Think of them as battering rods. With the particular movement of the waves in that storm, the rods rolled about in such a way that they broke holes through the ship. Mr. Lewis' men were very particular about loading their own supplies; they wanted to handle the crates and do the storing of their supplies themselves. They didn't want advice from me or my crew. I contend that the way they secured those rods was insufficient, and therefore his company bears some responsibility for the costs to repair the ship."

"And what is Mr. Lewis' position on that question?"

"He refused to address it. He dismissed my request for sharing the cost of carpenter repairs, saying I surely had some kind of insurance. I admit his dismissal was frustrating."

"And do you have insurance?"

"Not for damages such as these. And I am of the belief that if human error or negligence caused the damage, then the person responsible should pay for the repairs."

John-Paul nodded. "That seems about right, Mr. Anderson." He asked a follow up question, "You had other arguments?"

Arden nodded. "Our second disagreement was regarding the bar fight in Roundstone Harbor."

"Would you explain?"

"I had initially been told that the repairs would keep us in Roundstone Harbor a third day. That is one reason I felt free to spend the day with the McGinn family on the second of those days. The carpenter told me he would be finished late in the day on Wednesday. I am a man who does not feel comfortable hovering over someone else's work. I left him alone to do it, under the worthy eye of my first mate. I was surprised to return to my ship on Tuesday afternoon to hear that the repairs were almost completed."

"Were the repairs done well?"

"I was not delighted with the quality, no. But they were adequate. I knew Mr. Lewis was eager to get to the island, and in contrast to me, he *had* watched every move of the carpenter closely. The carpenter said he was finished and I saw that the ship could sail. We made plans to leave in the morning.

"However, when the men in Mr. Lewis' employ (the four men we were taking up to the island) learned that they'd be leaving the next day before staying on Shallow Island for the next several weeks, they went—all of them, including a foreman—to the bar in Roundstone Harbor. Not long after midnight, Mr. Lewis and I were summoned to come assist with a bar brawl and to escort the workers in Mr. Lewis' employ back to the ship. I was dressed and ready to respond immediately. In contrast, Mr. Lewis took his time.

"There was extensive damage to the bar. Chairs were broken, and a large mirror and a huge number of drinking glasses were shattered. Bottles of liquor were broken, spilled. The bar owner was furious. I stayed to help clean up and I sent money an hour later from the ship's coffers to help compensate for the extensive damage that Lewis' men caused. In the morning, though, Lewis scoffed at the fact that I had compensated the bar owner. He said he would not even consider reimbursing me for the damage his men had caused at the bar. I think his words were 'It's their own fault for not having a constable. Why should I pay for anything? I'm never coming to this town again. It's a lousy little town anyway.'

"So yes, Mr. Stewart. We argued about that in the morning. In front of the men. I said I expected payment, and that it should be part of the final costs that he planned to give me on the island when the delivery was complete. I told him he owed me two additional charges that were not in our original contract—those being the damages to my ship as well as the damages in the bar caused by his men."

"And the final argument?"

"It was about the lifeboat, sir."

"The lifeboat?"

"He wanted my lifeboat. The small craft they had on Shallow Island which was used for small trips to the neighboring islands was ruined. He wanted my lifeboat to replace the one that had been destroyed. I understand needing a boat on the island. But to tell you the truth, I'm surprised that they had only one. You'd think if they'd planned ahead to have thirty people on the island at a time, they would have had more than one little dinghy for emergencies. But that is not pertinent. He told me that their boat was inoperable, and that he wanted the dinghy that we have at ready on the *Jenny Marie.* He said he would pay me for it.

"I told him it was a lifeboat and that I wouldn't risk the lives of my men to sail without one. I told him I would *not* sell it to him, but that I could stop at a town in Door County and make arrangements for another small craft to be delivered to him. Additionally, I could arrange to have someone else come pick him up and take him to Rock Island on the date he desired."

"What did he say to those offers?"

"He refused them. It appeared he had his mind made up that he wanted *my* boat and would not hear of any alternative. And it bothered me that he thought he could just take what didn't belong to him."

"Of course, Mr. Anderson."

"What he said next was worse, though, Mr. Stewart. He said then that he wouldn't pay me at all. That if I was going to leave men stranded on an island, I didn't deserve to be paid. I was angry that he'd twisted my character into something other than it was. I do not believe I am a heartless person for ensuring the safety of my crew on the *Jenny Marie.* I decided that there was no need to talk more that night. Truthfully, I was tired, and I assumed we would talk more rationally in the morning light.

"I told him the conversation wasn't over and that we'd have to settle things before we sailed out the next day. I admit I was angry. I admit that I raised my voice. Truthfully, by that point I was considering letting him go ahead and buy my lifeboat, but I needed to ask my first mate's opinion. As a sailor, it doesn't feel right not to have a lifeboat, but I was also quite ready to leave the island behind."

"And then?"

Arden was not sure what John-Paul asked.

"And then what did you do after you argued?"

"I went back across the yard. I ate dinner quickly and talked for a few moments with my crew. I intended to head straight back to my ship. But despite the wind, the stars were coming out, and I found that the island had particularly good viewing of Cassiopeia that night."

"Excuse me?"

"Cassiopeia, the constellation. And the Ursa Major and Minor. Orion's belt, of course. And meteors were falling. The stars were spectacular that night. The moon was barely a crescent, and as you might know, the lack of a bright moon makes star- gazing more brilliant. I walked around the west shoreline, away from the ship and the building site. One of the planets was low in the west, and I was able to see its bright light quite easily just over the horizon. I believe it was Venus, although it might have been Jupiter."

"How long were you out watching the stars?"

"Well, I suppose at least forty-five minutes. I returned to my cabin right about 11:00 and began reading."

"Did you notice anything amiss when you returned to your cabin?"

"No sir, I did not."

"Do you ever lock your cabin, Captain?"

"Rarely. I have a safe in the cabin that I *do* lock."

"And what do you keep in that safe?"

"The present contract I have regarding a current journey and any money that I have on board at the present time."

"Did you receive any of the money owed you from Mr. Lewis?"

"I did not, sir."

Thank you. Mr. Anderson. Is there anything else you would like to add?"

"Only that I am innocent of the charges. I will not say that I approve of Mr. Lewis' business practices. In fact, it surprises me that he can continue to treat people so callously. I still believe he should have offered me recompense for my ship's damages and the damage in the Roundstone Harbor bar. And I would have let him pay me for the lifeboat, even though it was wrong to threaten to withhold my payment in order to get it. That does not make me a thief, however. I did not steal Mr. Lewis' money. I also did not make an attempt on Mr. Lewis' life. I anticipated only to get up the next morning, engage in a rational conversation to settle our differences, then raise our anchors and sails and be on our way. I expected to spend the rest of the summer making hauls up and down the Lake Michigan coast. Not only have I been accused of crimes I did not commit, I have been unable to earn a livelihood. I am a seaman, Mr. Stewart. I love the lake and the feel of a sail. I was building a business of hauling cargo up and down the coast. Instead, the *Jenny Marie* sits idle. I am unable to sail her, as I sit here in a prison for crimes I did not commit."

Mr. Stewart sat down. People shifted in their seats as they waited for the cross examination. Mr. Albion seemed in no hurry to get up from his seat. He rustled through a pile of papers on the table in front of him. He sauntered up to the witness box, smiling.

"Mr. Anderson, you make us believe you are a man of fine character."

"I have tried to be, Mr. Albion."

"You read books. You watch stars. You rescue children from danger. You convince us that you are quite the hero."

"I was there at just the right time, I believe, if you refer to the incident of the wolf at Roundstone Harbor."

"You served in the War Between the States."

"Yes."

"Were you a great soldier? Did you kill people while fighting for your side, Mr. Anderson?"

"I was a sailor, Mr. Albion. I served in the Union Navy and did what I could to help the Union side."

"What about killing people in war, Captain? How many people did you kill? How many did you shoot with a gun?"

"I personally killed no one. If the cannons that were fired from our ship killed or wounded soldiers from the Confederacy that were shelling us at the time, I cannot say a specific number."

"Oh, again you portray yourself as so good. Such a humanitarian. Such a hero."

"I don't believe you have heard me boast, Mr. Albion. I have never said that I am a perfect man."

"Oh good, Captain. I'm glad you admit that, Mr. Anderson, because I was just about to bring that up. I have in my hand a certain manifest from a particular ship that might be of interest to you and to this courtroom. He held out the paper. Does the name the *Flying Falcon* mean anything to you?"

Arden gasped. He turned white and put his head in his hands.

"Can you answer the question, Mr. Anderson? You are clearly upset. I will give you a minute to answer."

Arden was quiet for a few moments before he lifted his head. He looked at Meggie who was watching him closely, waiting, as was everyone in the courtroom, on words that were clearly difficult for Arden to say. Finally, Arden spoke. "You have found out something about me, Mr. Albion, that I am loathe to divulge."

"I will help you out, then, Mr. Anderson, so that the jury and the viewers in this court room can learn the exact nature of this document that I hold in my hand. It is a manifest of a ship named the *Flying Falcon.* Can you at least tell the court what a manifest is, Captain?"

"It typically lists the cargo that a ship carries."

"Cotton, it says. And here is another section of this same document, I believe with your name on it. It is a listing of the ship's crew. Arden James Anderson. Is that correct?"

"Yes, it is sir."

"Now I have another document, here, a document from the court of South Carolina that maintains in the year 1855, the owners of the *Flying Falcon* were *not* in fact hauling cotton, but instead they were hauling a far more nefarious cargo. Am I right, Captain Anderson? Were you in fact working on a ship that was hauling slaves?"

"Yes, I was, Mr. Albion, though I am ashamed to admit it." There were murmurs in the courtroom, exclamations of surprise.

"Here, Mr. Anderson, you had us believing you are such a hero. You save children, fight on the side of the Union against the "evil, slave-holding" Confederacy. You have us believing you are so good, that when something goes wrong on the ship you are merely a victim of bad weather. You lead us to believe you are a gentle man who would never steal or use a gun in anger.

"But I think the truth is otherwise, Mr. Anderson. You are in fact, NOT a good person. You make us think you are good, when in fact, you are evil. You make us think you treat everyone around you well, and yet we find these facts about you that tell an entirely different story. We all know now the conditions on slave ships, the horrible cruelty inflicted on the poor souls. We know that such practices were outlawed long before the year 1855, and yet you were on board such a ship, presumably profiting from the horrible practice.

"You are not at all who you've made us think you are, Mr. Anderson. Tell us, isn't it true that you hated Mr. Lewis and wanted to kill him? Tell us, wasn't it easy to steal back from Mr. Lewis the money that you believed was rightfully yours? Weren't you the one that attempted to kill him, that stole his money and then pretended to watch stars and read a book in your cabin as if nothing had happened?"

It took Arden a long time to answer. "No, Mr. Albion, I did none of those things. I did not shoot a gun at Mr. Lewis, and I did not take his money. As to my time on the *Flying Falcon,* I was fifteen years old. I am not proud of the fact. In fact, most days, I hate myself for it. I cannot undo that evil but— "

Mr. Albion interrupted him. "That is all, Mr. Anderson. No further questions." Arden sat for a minute before getting up from the stand. The courtroom was full of chatter. The judge banged his gavel and called for order, then immediately said that the court would adjourn until 9 o'clock the next morning.

Reporters hurried out, eager to write about the latest development. Although they were quick to file out of the room, Meggie had been faster. She had been one of the first to exit. A reporter followed her, asking for comment, which she did not give. She could barely speak for the effort of trying to hold her composure. As soon as she turned onto the street that was a distance away from the courthouse and away from those who were watching, she burst into tears.

36

WHEN MEGGIE SWOOPED into the Ingram's kitchen, she was still crying. Lillian Ingram came in immediately with questions. "Is it over then? Did it go poorly for Arden?" Lillian limped slightly because of pain in her hip. Still, she hugged Meggie and put on a kettle for tea.

"No, it's not over. But there has been news that has changed everything."

When Meggie told Lillian of Arden and the *Flying Falcon*, Lillian said, "It is news you don't like to hear about Arden, Meggie. But it need not affect the outcome of the trial. From what I saw of the jury, the men were more old than young. They were surely not *all* abolitionists. They certainly are old enough to know people who enslaved others."

"It is unthinkable to me, Lillian. I thought he was a good man! I can't reconcile the Arden I know with a man who had anything at all to do with a slave ship." More tears fell and the women were quiet for a time. Lillian got up, poured tea for them both and sat down again.

"Do you know how long? In what capacity? Were there details about the ship? The conditions on board? Or the number of trips that were made? Or why he was there?"

Meggie shook her head. "Arden said only that he was young—just fifteen years old—and that he regretted his actions every day of his life."

"Well, that is something, at least." Lillian said. "I think you should hear more of his story before you condemn him."

Meggie's Diary *April 16, 1872*

Why do I choose men that die? For Arden is dead to me. As dead as my George. I was foolish to think of him, to begin to imagine that he would be a man I could love. He is not at all what I imagined. I was fool to begin to desire him.

When Arden wrote in his letter that he was unmarriageable, I imagined many scenarios. But never this. There are stories of the horrors of war, and I had thought that he might have been made to kill or maim or fight in cruel ways. Such actions are forced on a man by war, and I could forgive him for any of those.

But not slavery. It means in one's heart there is arrogance and cruelty. My parents have told me that attitudes change, that hearts change, that at one time the practice was acceptable and that society allowed it. That the commonplace-ness of it throughout the south means that I should not be so harsh to condemn those who practiced the cruelty. But for me it reveals a person's nature. I cannot see it another way.

George was with me in this. He hated the horrors of slavery. It was yet another reason I loved him. He had begun hiring freedmen at his factory. He was pushing for one lunchroom, not two. Not segregated. He and I knew it was possible.

Yes, Arden was young. But even a child knows that a black man is a person.

I am angry at Arden. I am angry at myself. And my father? Why did he drag me along? He told me he thinks God has put us in Arden's life to help him find peace with God. But where is my *peace with God? The men that God puts in my life are men that I love only to have them taken away.*

~

In the morning, Meggie could not bring herself to go to the trial. The absence of Margaret McGinn-Ford was noted by reporters.

Throughout that day, John-Paul brought in an expert on guns and much of the morning proceedings were about the angle of the gunshot and the type of gun that would likely have been used. Lewis himself was put on the stand and asked to describe the hole in the wall above his desk. He was asked how many guns were on the property and he said only "several."

"Can you tell us an exact number, please?"

"There were some for hunting, of course. Deer come to the island over the ice in the winter. If a man shot a deer or a rabbit, or a duck in the sky, for that matter, the cooks would be glad. The men get tired of fish. I pay a lot of money to feed the men in my employ. I am all too happy to encourage the hunting."

"What is your guess of the number of guns on your island?"

"I don't like to guess, Mr. Stewart. The honest answer is, I do not know. Maybe seven or eight."

"As we understand it, Mr. Lewis, on the evening of June 28, you were sitting at a desk with an oil lamp at your side. You were reading."

"Correct."

"Your office was unfinished. You will eventually have glass in that window, but on this night, there was only an opening where the glass will someday be."

"Correct."

"Did you hear anything outside your office before the gun shot?"

"Just the waves in the distance."

"After the shot, what did you do?"

"Well, I was startled, of course, as any man would be. I called for help, knowing there were men still sitting in the yard. I ran out into the yard. When the first man came, I told him to run and get Tim Fowler, my foreman."

"And Tim Fowler, where was he?"

"I assumed he was in his room in the bunk house. He has his own room partitioned off from the others. He usually goes to bed early, and I gave orders that he should be wakened."

"How long did it take before he came?"

"Several minutes. It was rather chaotic. The new foreman was also there, and I directed him to take a few men and lighted lanterns to search all around the house and the grounds. Being new, it took him some time to find lanterns. I had to direct him where those might be. And then, after a while, Fowler was there and he said we should gather the men.

"And when the men searched the grounds, they found nothing?"

"No."

"No gun, either?"

"No. We searched in the daylight the next day as well."

"Was a gun found in Arden Anderson's possession?"

"No, it was not."

"And yet you accuse this man and him alone?"

"He had my money, Mr. Stewart."

"How do you explain the fact that there was no gun?"

Lewis scoffed. "It is an island, Mr. Stewart. Mr. Anderson has strong arms. He could have easily thrown it into the water in a thousand places."

"And if another man had shot at you, could he not also have thrown a gun into the water in a thousand places?"

"Is that a real question for me, Mr. Stewart?"

John-Paul nodded, conceding the point. "Let's turn then, to the money you say was missing. When did you notice that it was gone?"

"I had just been shot at. After about thirty minutes in the yard while men searched the island and we were gathering the others, I was still, as you might guess, rattled. I keep a pistol in a locked drawer in my desk, so I went back inside and opened the drawer to take it out. That's when I saw that the entire envelope with all of the money, a considerable amount, was gone."

"When did you put it in to the drawer?"

"Shortly after we arrived that afternoon."

"While the unloading of the ship was occurring?"

"Yes, that's correct."

"Who has access to the drawer?"

"Only myself and my two foremen. We are the only ones with a key. I brought a lot of money with me, as the foremen need money to pay ships when they come to deliver supplies. Or when emergencies arise and they must provision off of the island."

"Mr. Lewis, how often do you come to your island?"

"This was the second time this year."

"So there are stretches of time when the office is unoccupied, and no one sits at your desk?"

"My foremen know to keep an eye."

"How many people were employed by you this past summer?"

"Between 25 and 30, depending on the week."

"These are men who are skilled in many trades, am I right? Some are carpenters, some are masons, some are skilled with iron work or small machines. Would it be a stretch to imagine that among those 30 men, one might have locksmith skills? That a man in your employ might know how to fashion a key or open a drawer with a lock?"

"Objection! This is conjecture." Albion shouted this without standing up.

"Sustained."

"A few final questions. We were told that all of the men on your island were gathered together and questioned about a half-hour after the gunshot. This would have been all of your laborers and all of the ship crew from the *Jenny Marie*?"

"That's correct."

"How did you go about questioning the men about their whereabouts at the time of the shooting?"

"Well, it was mostly the foremen who did it. Fowler and Hermann know their men best. They work with them every day. They use the same latrines, they eat the same fish from the lake. They know which men work harder than others, which men want to cut corners. I left the questioning to them."

"And you believed them when they said that every single one of their men was accounted for?"

"I trust my foremen, Mr. Stewart. It is not just anyone that could spend their summers on an island making other men work. I pay the two of them to know their workers and to get my buildings built. And I am not quick to compliment, but the house they are building on Shallow Island is impressive. To me this is proof that they know how to get good quality work from the men I employ. Despite this unfortunate incident with Arden Anderson, I am proud of the house I am building."

"Mr. Lewis, would there be any men on the island who might have wanted to do ill to you?"

"I assume so, yes. I am a wealthy man. There are *always* people who want to do ill to me. I have found that most men in this world are jealous. They are greedy. They begrudge the fact that I have money when they do not. They bear grudges for long periods of time."

"Grudges, Mr. Lewis?"

"I have factories. I have bought and sold land. I have made business deals that have favored some and not others. There are always people unhappy with me. It is the price of success. But on my island, I can't say of anyone specifically that hates me. They knew what they were getting, a job on an island."

"Do you feel that you treat those in your employ well, Mr. Lewis?"

"Objection!"

"I'll move on. We are almost finished. You mentioned that you had two foremen on the island. They have their own quarters?"

"Well, it's barely quarters. But yes, they each have rooms that are portioned off from the communal room of the bunkhouse."

"With separate entrances?"

"Yes."

"Can you tell us please, about the new foreman who accompanied you on the *Jenny Marie*?"

"Hans Holdt has worked for me for years. Mr. Fowler, the man he was replacing, had been on the island the longest, three summers already. He'd told me early in the summer that he only wanted to work through July. He was good at the rough build, the site planning and carpentry and masonry, but now that we were getting to the finish work, we'd agreed that he could turn over the supervision to Hermann and Holdt, let the two of them finish the job. I was planning a big opening in late August with guests from the city. I was pleased to see the progress in June and optimistic that we'd meet the goal.

"Fowler was going to stay on the island for another four days, then return to Chicago with me. We had it planned that he would spend time with Holdt, going over the details of the building and planning out the remaining tasks that needed completion before the house was finished. But when the captain here disrupted—"

"Objection!"

"When somebody shot at me and stole my money, Tim Fowler offered to take him back to Chicago, so it seemed the best way to handle the situation. I sent him and two other men—the biggest ones I had—to watch over the crew and get the captain into police hands."

"I think those are all of my questions for the time being, Mr. Lewis." He turned to the judge. "I reserve the right to recall this witness at a later date."

The judge nodded, told Mr. Lewis he could step down from the stand, and declared that the trial would resume the next morning.

37

ON THE AFTERNOON after Meggie's conspicuous absence from court, Solomon sent a letter by messenger to the Ingram's house. He asked if Meggie would be willing to meet him at a park on the lakefront. The two had not met in Roundstone Harbor when the *Jenny Marie* was in port, but on the first day of the trial Solomon introduced himself to Meggie, and they had conversed regularly since. At the adjournments or breaks in the proceedings at the courthouse, they had often spoken a few words. More than once they had seen each other outside the jail when she was leaving after a visit with Arden and he was coming in.

"This news has been a blow to you, Mrs. Ford," Solomon said after they found each other and walked toward a bench, then sat wrapped in their coats, barely protected from the cold breeze that blew off of the water.

"It is horrible news," Meggie answered. "I can't understand it. How could he have been a part of that despicable trade?"

"It should not be held against him," Solomon said these words quietly but emphatically.

"I can't think of anything worse that a man could do. And how could *you* not hold it against him?"

Solomon did not hurry with his words. His voice was raspy and he coughed several times when he spoke. "Arden Anderson has paid over and over for his sins. His story is his to tell, not mine, but he does not go a day or a night without regret for those actions. And though he has compensated for his sins on the *Flying Falcon* many times over, he still considers himself unforgiveable."

"But how do *you* forgive him?"

"I think the figures are these, Mrs. Ford: two million people were put in chains on ships and were brought to this country. For over a hundred years they came against their will across the Atlantic. After those ocean trips were banned, hundreds of thousands more were put on ships that carried enslaved people from the northern states to the southern ones *within* this country. By the time we were all pronounced free at Emancipation, the number of slaves in this nation was four million." Solomon stopped to excuse himself as he coughed before he continued. "Was the Captain wrong to be caught up in the storm and the winds of that evil? Of course. Do the great numbers of others caught up in the horrors exonerate him? No. But did he extricate himself from that evil? Yes, he did. Did he wrest himself free of those winds? Yes, he did. Did he help me and people like me after he left the trade? Certainly. I would not be here, a freedman, talking to you if not for the captain."

Meggie had listened quietly. The wind blew clouds quickly across the sky; overcast sky vacillated with a sunny one.

"Why didn't he tell me? Why did he hide it from me?"

"Forgive me, Mrs. Ford," Solomon smiled. "You were with him how long? Did you expect him to tell you everything about himself in only two days? Is it so wrong to present himself as the person he is in the present instead of the young man that he was in the past?"

She smiled back. "You are right, Mr. Dupree. We talked about a great many things at Roundstone Harbor, but not everything, of course." She paused. "And I understand why he could not have told me when we talk at the jail. It is too public. It is not a place to talk about much of anything."

"Arden carries much shame on the subject. It plagues him, and he carries that shame as if it is attached. In a misguided way, he says he has come to peace about being falsely accused by Mr. Lewis. Though he is innocent of the crimes on the island, he says he will accept it as punishment for his old actions, for the summer he spent in a horrible place when he was hardly more than a child."

"He said something like this to me, but I did not understand it." Meggie told him. "That though he was innocent, he did not deserve to go free. I don't know that I can accept his slave trading, but it seems odd for him to conflate it with this crime on the island. You don't agree with this thinking, surely?"

"I don't, and I have tried to convince him otherwise. But he has for years borne the secret about his time on the *Flying Falcon*. He doesn't see it clearly. I have wondered since the news came out, if the information that was meant by others to damn him might actually work toward his good."

"How?"

"He has no deep secret to hide anymore. Arden thought that the shame that he bore was un-shareable. The weight of that secret and shame has been heavy. But now that his actions have been brought to light, people will accept him or not, forgive him or not, ostracize him or not, judge him or not. He can carry on with his life with his own self-recriminations, but he is now free of the fear of what others will think when they know the worst of him."

Meggie had listened intently. They were quiet together. They watched a boat, early in the season, sail out of the harbor. "Mr. Dupree, I can see why Arden respects you."

Solomon looked at her and spoke again. "I don't know what opinion you will come to on this topic, Mrs. Ford. I hope in time you will judge Arden Anderson for the good that he has done as opposed to the evil. Your acceptance of him and your forgiveness of him would help him, I believe."

"I don't know that I am ready to do that, Mr. Dupree. Maybe someday, perhaps. I have always been an abolitionist. It is unthinkable to me that I could align myself with a slave trader."

He nodded. "Is forgiveness so hard, Mrs. Ford?"

She didn't answer.

"I am here only to tell you that the man, Arden Anderson, who you met last summer is far better than the boy who was fifteen years old, caught up in a practice he himself hated. I would urge you to consider finding forgiveness. And if you cannot do so, let us pray that he can find a way, with or without your help, to forgive himself."

The talking had not been good for Solomon's voice or his throat. Meggie watched as Solomon coughed and then fought to steady his breathing.

"Are you not well, Mr. Dupree?"

Solomon shook his head. "I have seen a doctor. He advises rest."

She turned her attention to him, to his needs. Meggie offered to arrange for a carriage ride to wherever he needed. Despite Meggie's insistence, Solomon refused her offer. After his coughing fit calmed, she watched him walk in the general direction of the docks. His progress was slow as he stopped to lean against a bench and then the wall of a building to cough and then catch his breath.

She realized, after he left, that they had not discussed the trial at all. She would have liked to have heard what Solomon had witnessed on the island, what his thoughts were about Archibald Lewis. Why did Solomon think Lewis was so quick to accuse Arden? The prosecutor was effective and had planted doubt. She would like help remembering the Arden who saved her brother, who listened patiently to Gillian, who talked of literature and stars. She considered going after him, but Solomon was in the distance now, walking slowly amongst boats on the pier.

38

SHE COULDN'T BRING herself to visit Arden in the jail, but Meggie, like so many others in the city, was curious about the trial. She owed Arden that much, she thought, to be there in the courtroom even if she would likely never talk personally to him again.

When she went the next morning, it would have been hard for her to get a seat in the courtroom except for the fact that she was recognized. People moved over to let her sit down. She was squeezed and uncomfortable, but as it turned out, it was not a long day. By eleven-thirty in the morning, the trial was over.

Owen Temple, the owner of the tavern in Roundstone Harbor, had sailed in late the previous night. John-Paul had only a few minutes to discuss with him the questions he would ask before the trial started for the day. It was risky, but the private detective they had hired to ask questions in Roundstone Harbor had insisted that the info he brought would be helpful.

Temple described in more detail what had been already presented: the bar brawl and the fact he had sent men to the *Jenny Marie* to rouse Captain Anderson and Mr. Lewis. He described the damages to his bar and his appreciation to the captain for assisting with clean up. "It was way past midnight, I tell you, and the captain asks for a broom! Can you imagine that other one doing that?"

He was asked about Lewis' men who had been in the bar. John-Paul asked him directly, "Did they talk about Lewis, about the job they were going to? Could you shed any light on the workmen or the situation on Shallow Island?"

"Well certainly. Men's tongues wag when they have alcohol. If you ask me, it weren't the captain at all, it was the people on the island that had it all planned."

"Objection! This is opinion!" Albion rose to object, and murmurs broke out through the courtroom.

"Mr. Temple, this is important," John-Paul told him. "You cannot simply give us your opinion. You were not there on Shallow Island, so your *opinion* about whether Captain Anderson is guilty or innocent does not matter to this trial. However, what you heard from Lewis' men in your bar might have bearing. Please talk only of that. Now, do you have any specific information about Lewis' men?"

"Well, sure I do, but nobody asked me before. Who was I going to tell anyway?"

"Mr. Temple, please, continue."

"Like I said, tongues wag. I suppose they didn't mind me overhearing, being so far away from where they were going. One of them was a big, brawny man, and I take it now that he was in some kind of cahoots with a man on the island."

"Objection!"

John-Paul jumped in. "Mr. Temple, please, tell us only what you heard, not what you think about the man who said it."

"Well, this big man said, 'just remember, follow the lead of the person in charge. If funny things happen once you get there, just follow along. Say what I tell you to say."

"And did you hear any specifics about this plan?"

"Only that it had something to do with all the money Lewis would be bringing to the island. That the foreman had a key to a drawer, and Lewis would be putting money in the drawer as soon as he got to his fancy new house on the island."

"And the gunshot, and the murder attempt?"

"I didn't hear anything about that. I only heard about the key and a drawer in a desk. And how there would be extra money if they'd go along with it. A nice little bonus for everyone, he said more than once."

"Mr. Temple, why have you kept this information to yourself?"

"How was I supposed to know what happened on that island after the *Jenny Marie* left last June, after the night my bar was all ruined? I didn't hear anything about any crime. Who knew *anything* about the ship and what happened? They kept it all a secret from what I can tell. I only just learned of it when the newspapers in Chicago started writing about it, just after Jack McGinn and Meggie left Roundstone Harbor to go down to Chicago a month ago. When this lawyer sent up his man asking questions, I was more than happy to tell what I heard. It seems all fishy to me, Mr. Lewis taking the law into his own hands, sailing the captain down here like a prisoner and making him sit in a jail all these months and none of us knowing anything."

"Objection!"

"Stick to answering the questions, Mr. Temple," the judge reprimanded him for the third time.

Temple's news had surprised everyone in the courtroom. Even John-Paul had not heard the extent of the words Temple reported hearing in his tavern. It was fortuitous that he had arrived back in Chicago in time for Temple to testify. John-Paul had not known just what a helpful witness the bar owner would be.

The prosecutors were definitely caught off guard. They had assumed that Temple had been called merely to be a character witness for Arden, that he would talk only about the help Arden had offered in the bar.

Still, Albion did his best to discredit Mr. Temple when he questioned him.

"How much money did the lawyers pay you to come testify today, Mr. Temple?"

"They paid my travel costs and are putting me up in a hotel."

"I see." He paused for a moment. "You had a complaint against Mr. Lewis, did you not? You would have liked to get some money out of him, and he refused to pay you, is that right?"

Owen Temple looked at Mr. Albion with some disdain. "I get what you are trying to do. You are trying to make me look bad. Like I'm trying to get something here for myself. This is not about me liking or not liking Mr. Lewis. This is about me doing my duty to tell you that I don't think the captain over there is the one that did any crime. I have a bar to run, and I would rather be there right now than here. I'm here because I heard things in my bar last summer, and I'm telling you that somebody other than the captain is guilty."

"You have not answered the question, Mr. Temple. How much do you think Mr. Lewis owes you?"

"Ok. I'll answer your question. It was his men that broke the nicest mirror I'll ever have. It was his men that broke chairs and drinking glasses and bottles. I had a bottle of scotch—75 years old that I kept high on my shelf—you know, just for show, and they broke it. I'd say overall, a couple hundred dollars for everything."

"So, the lawyers for Mr. Anderson sent a representative to Roundstone Harbor and offered to give you some money. They told you to come talk about Mr. Lewis and they would pay you some money if you do. They said it's a way to make Mr. Lewis look bad, and you'll get a nice little all-expenses-paid trip to Chicago."

"That's not how it was."

"Fine, Mr. Temple." Albion used a condescending tone with these last words as if talking to a child. But Albion had underestimated Mr. Temple. Owen Temple was not articulate, his teeth were bad, and he did not have a huge vocabulary. But he understood full well that he was being spoken down to.

"As I recall, Mr. Lawyer, I didn't say one thing so far this morning about Mr. Lewis. I don't really care whether he lives or dies. Some people have money and some people don't. But here's what I know. I heard his men talking about how someone on the island had a key to a desk drawer and they were all to keep quiet about it. How they'd get extra drinking money if they did."

"Oh yes, the drinking." Albion said. "This is all, as you say, drunk men talking. Did this man on the island with a plan have a name?"

"I don't know that I heard it more than once or twice. Mr. Stewart asked me the same, and I can't rightly remember. All I can think of is that it was some kind of a duck or a bird."

"Fowler? Not Tim Fowler!" This time it was Archibald Lewis who broke courtroom etiquette and yelled the name from the seat where he was sitting.

"Yes. Yes. That could be it." Mr. Temple said. The judge banged his gavel and asked for quiet in the courtroom.

Archibald Lewis was incredulous. He was signaling to his lawyer who was standing. He was frantically trying to talk to the additional lawyers at the table in front of him, and the judge gaveled again for him to be quiet. After Temple was released from the witness stand, Albion approached the judge and asked for a recess, which was granted. He gave him three days.

~

Soon after the recess was announced, Meggie packed up her things and booked arrangements to head back to Roundstone Harbor. There was no need for her stay in Chacgo. She had done what she could for Arden by visiting the jail, by testifying in court in his defense. There were others now who were helping him. Her part was over. She didn't go to the jail to see Arden, although she wrote a formal note saying that she wished him a good outcome and that she would be leaving Chicago. She would read in the papers of any developments in the trial, if there was anything to Mr. Temple's story, if anything more could be found out, and in the end, she would read of the jury's verdict. She spoke with John-Paul who was optimistic. However, he urged caution. He expected the trial to continue. Temple was only one witness; it might take days more of back and forth in the courtroom. It would still be for a jury to decide.

"And there is always the possibility that Lewis will pay off members of the jury," he told her. She was surprised that he said this so matter-of-factly.

As best as she could, she would put Arden out of her mind. The outcome might go well for him, but she was not ready to be there at the gates of the prison on the day he went free. She was glad that her father had gone there, had helped. Was she glad that *she* had gone to Chicago? She wasn't sure.

A newspaper reporter asked to interview Meggie as she left the courthouse when the recess was announced, but she refused. Instead, she found herself wanting to be back at her room at the lighthouse, to sit at the table with her parents, and to listen to the chatter of Gillian. She knew that it would be only a matter of weeks before there would be buds on the trees, paths muddy with thaw, ramps rising out of the snow, and wildflowers blooming in the woods. She was eager to busy herself with spring cleaning, with airing the house after winter. To turning over the soil in the gardens as soon as the frozen ground warmed. She was anxious to see how much Charlotte's Addy had grown in the weeks that she had been away.

She had plans, too, to talk to the bank in Sturgeon Bay and to Mr. Schultz who had built many of the houses in Roundstone Harbor. How much money would she need to build a small store? Perhaps with a room up above or behind where she could have her own living space? She had sketched in her notebook the shelving displays that she had seen and admired in the stationery shop. She had been thinking of what she might call her store. She liked the name *The Peninsula Pen,* but it was too limiting. Besides writing supplies, she was committed to Kira's mittens and scarves, to the handcrafts and art work of her friends.

Meggie hugged Lillian and Byron Ingram goodbye. She thanked them multiple times and promised to write, then she boarded a train to Appleton. Mr. Temple had offered to accompany her, but unlike her, he preferred traveling by boat, despite the fact that few boats were running. He was in a hurry to get back to his business. The ice had only recently come out, and it was not even certain that the Roundstone Harbor docks would be open, but he located a ship with a dory whose crew promised they would get him to shore. There was still money in the defense fund, and John-Paul was happy to pay for it. After the notoriety that this trial had brought him, new clients were seeking his help. He had multiple clients who were willing to pay.

Meggie liked the train. She liked being able to travel alone. She had money enough left over from George to afford the nice car of the train and the overnight stays in fine hotels. For part of the trip, a well-dressed, older woman sat near her. She was returning home after attending meetings in favor of woman's suffrage. "You'd be welcome to join us," she told Meggie. As the train slowed to her stop, she hurried to write down names and addresses for Meggie and told her to write. After that, the train car was quiet except for a few private conversations between couples. There were distractions enough for her, but her resolve to put thoughts of Arden aside were not successful.

Meggie's Diary: Appleton Hotel *April 19, 8 pm.*

I am settled into the hotel near the train station. There are lovely big homes here, high on a hill overlooking the river and near the campus of Lawrence College. I had thought I might write on the train, but the bumpiness prevented me. But I have, however, had time to think.

Solomon urges forgiveness. My father, I'm sure, would do the same. He and my mother, and most of Roundstone Harbor will have read in the newspapers by now of Arden's time on a slave ship. The boys will be full of questions. Philip is only a year younger than Arden was at the time. Fifteen is not very old.

I still can't reconcile how he could have been part of slaving. Even Lillian with her high morals doesn't condemn him the way I do. She says that I must find out more. She reminds me the year was 1855 in Baltimore, a place with slaves all around. But excusing it seems wrong. Doesn't wiping it all away with an easy forgiveness dishonor the people who suffered, the slaves that were killed on the ships, in the fields, in the cotton gins?

Am I supposed to pretend that it was nothing?

She wrote more in the morning while she waited for her train to Fort Howard.

Meggie's Diary: Appleton Hotel *April 20, 9 am.*

There are buds on the trees outside the window of this hotel. I am sure it will be weeks before we see blossoms like these at Roundstone Harbor.

Solomon says that Arden finds it hard to forgive himself. This means that at least he has a conscience on the matter. It is better, I suppose, than a hardened heart.

There were probably indiscretions with women when he was off sailing the world. The thoughts of these don't bother me. I am glad he would know how to hold me, how to lie with me. But why can I forgive him for those actions but not for the slaving?

I told Lillian that it is the horror of his actions that makes me wonder if I could ever love him. But really, I think it's Arden's pain that troubles me the most. That day in court, his pain was tangible. Pervasive. Between the two of us, don't we carry too much of it? I will never have a child to hold. Ever. I have a hole in me that is George. And Arden? He has been through war with shells falling around him and wounded men moaning on deck. He was orphaned. And now, his ship and his money and his reputation are gone. A trial has taken away his hope and broadcast his horrible past.

My grief. His shame. How can it not be too much?

Still, on the last day that I saw him in jail, before I learned of his time on the Flying Falcon, he asked about my brothers. And Gillian. We talked about Middlemarch, the book I gave him to read. He said he believed absolutely that women should vote. And he told me about the white buildings of Greece that overlook the blue Mediterranean Sea. That I should go there because of the beauty. Either with or without him.

Can two broken people be healed through love? Or would our brokenness make it impossible?

If Arden is free, he can find me. Solomon tells me he has a story worth listening to, so if he comes, I will listen. But I will not watch for him every day from the Light.

A short train to Green Bay, then a carriage to Sturgeon Bay. Finally, she traveled by horse to Roundstone Harbor. It was close to dusk when she arrived in the village. Meggie walked down the hill from the stable and past the dock in the harbor. There had been ice-shoves on the beach when she left, but now the ice was entirely melted, and the waves were soft and gentle as she walked onto the stony beach and headed home to the Light. Her family must have been watching for her. After ten minutes or so of her walking toward the Light, she saw two small figures leave the stairs and come toward her on the stony beach. Certainly, they were Philip and Peter. She saw them stop, then turn back to wait for a child who came running to catch up with them. A minute or two later, her parents followed.

She was not used to the uneven surface of the rocky shoreline. She was wearing her traveling shoes, and her feet were tired and sore. Was it those things that made her feel like it was taking forever, or was it only that she was eager—so very eager—to be home?

39

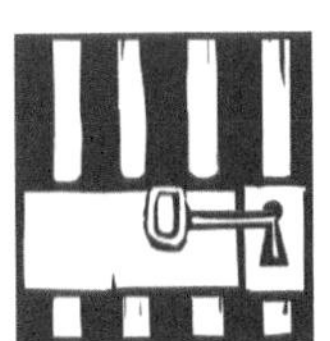

IT TOOK ONLY a day for detectives to locate Tim Fowler. He was no longer employed by Archibald Lewis. He had resigned from Lewis Industries six months before, only eight weeks after successfully depositing Arden in prison. Fowler had left on good terms with Lewis and had been given a nice send-off with thanks for his years of service overseeing various building projects for Lewis. "I want to retire early," he had told Lewis. "I have come into some money from my wife's side," he had said. "My wife always wanted to move west of Chicago; we have purchased a nice home outside of the city." Lewis had thought nothing of it, told Fowler at the time he was happy for him. That the countryside west of Chicago was nice.

But a ledger book found in Fowler's house when it was searched by police told a different story. He had been embezzling money from Lewis for years. And after that, it was not hard for the detectives to get a confession. Fowler admitted to firing the gun on Shallow Island, purposely missing his boss. When Lewis ran outside, Fowler had gone into the office through the inside door of the big house, opened the desk drawer and taken out the money. It had taken only a moment. He went back through the inside door and exited through the back of the building in the dark and made his way quickly to the ship. There was confusion, and men were running in various directions. He was met by only one other man who was easy to convince that he, Fowler, was also searching for the assailant. On the dock, he threw his gun into the water and even thought to dip his hands in the water to wash off any gun powder residue. He was in luck that Captain Anderson was not in his cabin of the ship. He had thought at first to just find an easy place to stash the money among the crew's clothes, but it was too dark to see below deck. At the helm he found a candle and flint, then it was only a few steps to the captain's cabin and the map drawer inside. By the time Fowler left the ship and ran into the yard pretending that he had been looking for the assailant, no one questioned where he had been.

With the gun shot, everyone's nerves were rattled. When Fowler had gathered them all together and asked if anyone was guilty, they were not lying when they each said *no*. When he asked them if they each had an alibi or if they could vouch for each other's whereabouts, it was easy for them to tell the truth and say *yes*. Arden Anderson was the only one missing. Fowler had been planning this for several months, but it all went off much easier than he had ever dared to hope.

Detectives pieced together the timeline. Fowler had had Lewis' confidence for years. During each year of the building on Shallow Island, it had grown easier and easier to tell Lewis that the supply and delivery costs were one price when in actuality they were another. In fact, as his ledger showed, in some cases Fowler told his boss the prices were double of what they actually were. He had accumulated more and more each year, but this was his grand plan to get out. He denied nothing when questioned. "What better way to get off the island than to volunteer to be the escort of a man who was a criminal?"

Besides that, he knew his boss to be particularly concerned about his own personal safety. Fowler figured that rattling him with a loud gunshot would have done the trick, and it did. Lewis ran out in the yard and Fowler ran in. It was easy to blame it all on the captain.

As to getting off the island, Fowler convinced his boss with only a few words that he was loyal and that he wanted justice done for Lewis. "I'll get him down to Chicago," he had said to Lewis. "I'll get him to our police friends."

And though he was good at deceit with his boss, he was forthcoming and cynical once he was pressed by detectives. His children were in the next room and his wife was crying. He held little back in his confession. He had continued to work for Lewis while Arden waited in jail; he lay low for a few months while things quieted down. He remained in Lewis' employ just long enough to make sure there was no suspicion, then he quit Lewis once and for all. He only wanted to live out a life with his family who always spent more than he made. "Lewis had plenty of money, and he was a stingy son-of-a-bitch that never paid me enough anyway. Why isn't a man entitled to a modest home when your boss has a mansion on an island?"

With the confession of Fowler, all charges against Arden were dropped. The next morning, Arden woke up inside a small cell as he had done for eight months. By noon, he was walking the streets of Chicago. Alone. It was not unlike coming into port after long months at sea.

Meggie had already boarded the stage coach north so she did not see the newspaper headlines announcing Fowler's confession. She was unaware of the news that Arden was free. Ollie Danielson's paper printed a long story with news of the investigation of Fowler, his indictment, and Arden's release from jail. There was a subtle bias against Lewis and the city's mishandling of the case.

Another paper in town published an opinion piece alongside their headlines in defense of Archibald Lewis. "It had been logical for Lewis to assume that Captain Anderson was the criminal," it said. "Anyone in his place would have done the same. In the absence of law enforcement on the island, what else was the man in charge supposed to do? His own life had been threatened, so it was understandable that Lewis had directed his men to keep the captain and his men under guard until they could be questioned by Chicago police." Unlike Danielson's paper, there was no call for a public apology from Lewis.

40

THERE WAS TO be a civil case. John-Paul insisted that Arden was entitled to money to make up for his lost revenue from the *Jenny Marie* while he sat in prison for those long eight months, falsely accused. If Lewis had been a good man, he would have publicly apologized once he learned that Arden was innocent. He would have offered restitution once it was clear that he had wrongly ruined Arden's reputation and livelihood. But Lewis was not the kind of man to admit his own failings. Court proceedings would be needed. Money that John-Paul Stewart intended to exact from Lewis would have to serve as the closest thing to any admission that the captain had been wronged.

On a large scale, Arden's case had highlighted how poorly "justice" was done in the city of Chicago. Not only the general public, but also the Governor's office had learned about Arden's "arrest" and incarceration at the word of a powerful, connected man. There were calls for change. The time when people could take the law into their own hands was over, folks were saying. The frontier was growing, and there needed to be constables and sheriffs. Jurisdictions needed to be formalized. Procedures needed to be followed. And why had the police not done a better job of investigating? Why had Arden Anderson not had due process of law? A new jail had just been built in Chicago. Who was deciding how the jail was filled? Who was watching the police? There would be reforms. Such a thing could not happen again. The newspapers were now watching. Politicians were debating how to codify it. The governor promised an investigation.

John-Paul was adamant that he could win a civil case and get recompense for the way Arden had been treated. But it meant that Arden would need to stay in Chicago. He could not spend the summer sailing on the *Jenny Marie*. Tim Fowler's confession and arrest had come in early evening, only a day after the trial had recessed. Word came to John-Paul of Arden's release in mid-morning the next day. He had only minutes to talk when he met Arden outside of the jail in the sunshine of the early afternoon; John-Paul was due in court for another case. He talked hurriedly with an apology for not being available that day. He said he'd be filing the civil suit soon and that Arden should not leave town. Then John-Paul pushed money into Arden's hands. "For food and clothing," he said, and, along with the money, gave him a business card with his office address. He asked Arden to come to his office the following day.

Arden walked away from the prison with no idea where he was going. It did not matter, only that he was walking. Clouds came in over the sun and there was chill off of the lake. He walked first one direction and then another in the streets around the jail. There was new construction all around; he found a diner and ate. Coffee. A roast beef sandwich with meat piled high on fresh bread. Mustard. A long gherkin pickle next to his sandwich on the side. Pie for dessert. A second cup of coffee, with cream and sugar.

When he passed a store selling clothing, he went in and bought boots, pants, a new shirt, and a coat to replace the dirty and frayed ones that he wore. He asked the clerk to throw the old things away, then he walked out of the building and headed toward the water and found his way to the docks. He was not eager for conversation and was glad no one recognized him when he asked directions to the small marina on the river where Solomon had told him the *Jenny Marie* was stored. Solomon had supervised, as best he could, the stripping down of his ship for the winter. She was now waiting idle and completely unprepared for the shipping season to come, and he was eager to see what state she was in.

He followed the Lake Michigan shoreline for the first mile. It was mid-afternoon, but there were patches of sun. He found a place with trees close to the shoreline, a park that was empty of people. When he was confident that no one was watching, he undressed and plunged into the ice-cold water of the lake. He wished he had bought soap at the store, but the rinse made him cleaner than he had been in months. With strong strokes he thrashed against the cold water with his arms, swam out deep beyond where waves were breaking. He swam hard against a slight undertow, treaded water, dove under again and again. There were no walls. No bars on windows. No metal door clanging hopeless and final and formidable. Floating, he looked up to the sky, big and expansive. Water, and the feel of the swirling around his body. The strength of his arms, the kicks of his legs, the power of it. To have power at all. To move however he wanted.

Arden came out of the water and saw two figures walking his direction in the distance so he dressed quickly. Hair dripping and body still wet and now chilled, he continued on his way, walking ahead of the couple so he would not have to speak.

It was after five when he arrived at the pier where the *Jenny Marie* was tied. Workers had obviously been at work on other ships that day as lines were uncoiled on decks. Mice were notorious for eating through lines in the winter and every inch had to be checked in the spring. Ships were in various degrees of preparedness. Some ships had all their sails back up on their rigging while others had only a few. He had expected to see his ship in a long line with others, but there were plenty of gaps, so it meant that many ships were out on the water already. It would be hard to get her ready in time for the season; work should have begun weeks ago.

When Arden had asked John-Paul to sell the *Jenny Marie* several weeks before, the lawyer had been reluctant to do so. And with the fast-moving developments of the trial, he had not had the time or attention to give to a sale. Now, Arden was glad John-Paul had waited. Whatever the next season brought, it was good to see that the *Jenny Marie* had weathered the winter.

He stopped in a small grocery near the marina and bought food for his supper. He bought apples, more than he needed. He took in the smell. He ate slowly to savor each crunchy, tart bite. He took those and the cheeses and rolls he had purchased onto the deck of the *Jenny Marie* where he sat until the stars came out. And then he sat longer.

The captain's cabin was locked, and he did not have the key. He was unwilling to force his way in. Instead, he found an unsecured axe on a nearby boat. He came back and broke through a clasp and a lock so he could go down below to the hold and spend the night there. Blankets were stowed in a locker. He cocooned himself into a small space which felt better to him than a large one. It was cold, in the forties, but the blankets were heavy, and he slept.

41

ARDEN RETRIEVED THE key to his cabin the next day from the harbor master. Olsen was a talkative man, and Arden was not used to conversation. Olsen had followed the trial, had read every word in the papers. This morning's paper, in fact, had featured Arden's release. "The captain had declined to be interviewed," one paper had written. But no one except John-Paul had been there when Arden walked out of the prison. No one had come looking for him; no one had tried to ask any questions. When Arden told that to the harbor master, he shrugged and said, "Makes a better story that way, doesn't it?"

On the pier, workers pointed and gawked. "It's not every day they see a celebrity, Mr. Anderson. Can you blame them? We realized pretty quick it was your ship that was here in our moorings once the news started coming. I can't say we weren't watching to see what would happen to the *Jenny Marie*. And to you, of course, Captain." He had followed Arden to his ship, watched him climb onto the deck. Olsen told him he'd wait to see that the key fit and to make sure that Arden could go into his cabin. But he kept talking, and Arden tried not to be rude.

Olsen did not come on to the deck, but he was in no hurry to leave, either. "Just what did that Mr. Lewis think he was doing, locking up a captain inside his own ship? And why didn't your crew just come to your aid? That's my question. Why didn't they overpower Lewis' men and just take back the ship?"

"Well, the short answer, Mr. Olsen, is that Lewis' men had guns, and my men did not. They expected to be able to tell their side of things when they arrived in Chicago, but we all were surprised about how things went at the docks when we pulled in. When the police came on the scene in Chicago, things did not go our way."

"Yep, there are dirty cops by the docks. We all know it. Why do you think I like it up here away from the downtown docks? Give me these piers on the river any day over the Chicago docks. And when the fire destroyed it all? I could tell you about the cops that made money after that." He was ready to launch into his new topic, but Arden interrupted him.

"Excuse, me, Mr. Olsen. I need to get inside my cabin. Thank you for holding the key and for keeping this ship safe over the winter. But I am afraid that I have much unsettled business. I'll check back in with you before I leave for the day."

He turned away from the man, unlocked the door, and went in. Solomon had done a good job of tidying the cabin for the winter. Everything was in its place. Books that Arden had reread many times sat on the shelf that he had built to hold them. When he had been locked inside this very room nine months before, he had tried to read *Gulliver's Travels* to distract himself. Arden threw off the unease that came back with those memories. He considered taking the book off the shelf and giving it to Olsen to get it out of his sight. His drawers held extra clothes: shirts, pants, a sweater he liked. He put on a warm hat and scarf as it had been drizzling this morning, and there was chill.

At his desk were a box of letters and a spotting scope. There was a picture of Sally and John and the children. He would need to write Sally soon. Hopefully, even this afternoon. She was reading the papers, he knew, so she would soon learn the news that he was free. He would return to her whatever money she had paid for John-Paul Stewart. She would be worried.

He opened the safe, and there was a small amount of money inside, just as he had left it. Solomon had put his important papers inside; the contract he had signed with Lewis was on top. He figured that the document would be helpful for John-Paul in the upcoming case, so he took it out of the safe and put it in a blank envelope. Writing paper and envelopes were stowed in his desk exactly where he had left them, back when he had had a life with envelopes in a drawer for the letters he wrote, and books on a shelf that he read and re-read, and clothes that he folded and put away neatly in a drawer.

He notified Olsen he would be returning, if not that evening, within a few days. When Olsen asked if he would ready the *Jenny Marie* for the season, Arden shrugged off the question and said only that he didn't know yet. He asked the best way to get back to the city; Olsen told him where he could pick up a carriage, so Arden walked the mile or so to that location, then rode into the city and was let off in front of John-Paul's office.

John-Paul was with clients when he arrived. His win against Lewis had given the lawyer instant celebrity, and it turned out that there were plenty of people who had scores they wanted to settle. He had already agreed to three cases and was turning others away.

Arden waited for John-Paul to finish, usher out his clients, and pull down his shade to indicate he was done with business for the day. He beckoned Arden to accompany him to the small room at the back of his office that served as John-Paul's living space.

John-Paul was lively, still buoyed by the outcome of Arden's trial. "Tell me what you think of this," he said. "I can afford something bigger now that money is coming in. I have found an apartment, so much better than this small room. It is almost brand new, has a nice kitchen and two bedrooms. Since you will need to stay in Chicago for a while for the legal proceedings, are you interested in sharing the rent on the rooms? There is money in the defense fund; it would not be unethical to use it to live while the next phase of the case is decided. And it would not be hard to buy a bed and new linens. It is one of the new buildings that has just been constructed after the fire. Would you like to see it this afternoon?" In his excitement, John-Paul kept up with more questions. Had Arden thought what he might do for employment? He had ideas. He had a friend who was looking for people. Also, what were his thoughts about his ship? Would he be keeping the *Jenny Marie*?"

"I can give you few answers." Arden told him. "I have thought for nearly nine months that I would be old before I ever saw water again. I used to dream of the waves. I imagined wind in the sails. I got to the point where I could hear the wind ruffling canvas and the ship rushing through water as if it was real. I believed it would be the only way I could hear those sounds as long as I lived.

"But now that I am out of jail, I can't think what I will do in real life when I no longer have to imagine it. It is all a tad disorienting, to be honest."

John-Paul's face changed. He sat down and motioned for Arden to do the same.

"Forgive me, Arden. Of course, this is too much to think about. I recall a colleague from my law classes once spoke of how people who are incarcerated react once they are free. You need time, I am sure, to adjust to the notion that you have agency.

"So let's do this instead," John-Paul continued. "I have a few numbers to go over with you in regards to the upcoming trial, and let's not make decisions about your next steps until later this week.

"And here, I almost forgot. This came for you this morning." He handed him a letter. Curiously, it was from Ethan Boggs. It was short. "*I am sorry for your misfortune. You did not deserve this injustice.*" Arden reread the note and put it down on the table with a shrug.

"I surely didn't expect that. Boggs never came across as a man with a heart," he told John-Paul. The men pulled their chairs up to the table and John-Paul added columns of figures and took careful notes as they discussed the details of lost revenue and the money that Lewis owed him for the delivery of last year's supplies.

And then Solomon was there at the door of the office. Knocking and coughing and Arden and he embracing. Arden weeping at the sight of his friend and Solomon with silent tears streaming down his old face. Solomon standing first at the door with his large frame, but hunched, and then his long outstretched arms that Arden came into like shelter. Solomon's large hand over Arden's head like a grandfather blessing his child. Sorrow. Relief. Neither man unable to do anything but cry. And then more coughing. Arden and John-Paul insisting that Solomon sit and asking if he needed a doctor. Solomon not talking for coughing. Silent tears that would not stop as Solomon held Arden's wrist while Arden stood at his side.

John-Paul poured a glass of water then stepped back and stayed silent. Who could not see the emotion that flooded the room? There was nothing to say. Words were too small.

"Now let your servant depart in peace." Solomon said finally, half smiling. His coughing had subsided. He had taken out a handkerchief and wiped his wet face. He turned to John-Paul. "I applaud you, Mr. Stewart. I thought we would lose. I did not see how you could do it, but you did." He paused. "See how the mighty have fallen," he quoted.

"I don't recall you quoting so much from the Bible," Arden said.

"I don't recall you *recognizing* I was quoting the Bible," Solomon answered him back with a smile.

Solomon let go of Arden's arm, and Arden sat down in a chair next to him. They spoke for a few moments about Solomon's health.

"I don't know what's to be done with the *Jenny Marie*," Arden asked a while later.

"I'm afraid I'm in no shape to help you on the water this season," Solomon replied.

"And I have a lawyer who is telling me I shouldn't be out on the lake this summer, as I need to be ready when we are called to trial."

"Well then, you have three options. The *Jenny Marie* sits. Or you sell her. Or you own it and let someone else sail it."

They sat in silence together as John-Stewart wrote papers at his desk in the front room. Children were playing outside on the street. Arden got up to watch them.

"I have missed seeing children," he told them.

John-Paul invited them to stay for supper. But what nearby café would allow Solomon to sit with them? Solomon could rest for a time in the chair while John-Paul went out for groceries. He would bring the food back to his room where the three of them could share a meal.

"When does Mr. Stewart need you to be here in Chicago for the case?" Solomon asked Arden after John-Paul left.

"It is hard to know for sure, but he thinks it will come up in mid-June."

"That gives you a bit of time to go north for a visit, then, doesn't it?"

"Yes, I suppose it does. But that presumes she would want to see me, and I'm not sure that she does."

Solomon never felt the need to respond quickly. After he was silent for a few minutes, he added, "You have always written good letters. Perhaps you should start there."

"Yes," Arden acknowledged. He nodded. "I *could* do that."

He brought the ottoman over to the chair where Solomon sat, and helped him put up his feet. He threw a blanket over his friend. Solomon closed his eyes and was sleeping in moments.

Arden went to the window and looked out on the street. In between two buildings, far in the distance, he could see just a bit of Lake Michigan. Today it was shining. And blue.

Acknowledgements

I am grateful for the willingness of so many people to help me with this novel. In particular, I want to thank:

Diane Wilson whose class at Write On, Door County, helped me believe that all the disjointed pieces of this book could be put together.

Gary Johnson for his help with historical research.

Krista Johnson for believing as much as I do that my characters are real.

For readers *Amy Phimister*, *Diana Wallace*, *Dan Powers*, *Tom Davis*, *Al DeGenova*, *Marianne Dieckman* and *Anne Emerson*, and, when this novel was fledging, *John Reed*, *Jane Hengse*, and *Janis Falk*. Each one took the time to read my manuscript and give helpful feedback.

For three years while we took walks with our dogs, *Pat Horvath* listened to me talk about plot lines and characters and historical details. In addition, her careful edits of multiple versions were invaluable.

Charity Walton for her careful and expert book formatting skills.